FORGET RUSSIA

L. BORDETSKY-WILLIAMS

TAILWINDS PRESS

Text copyright © 2020 by L. Bordetsky-Williams
All rights reserved. Except as permitted under the U.S. Copyright Act of 1976, no part of this publication may be reproduced, distributed, or transmitted in any form or by any means, or stored in a database or retrieval system, without the written permission of the publisher.

Tailwinds Press
P.O. Box 2283, Radio City Station
New York, NY 10101-2283
www.tailwindspress.com

Published in the United States of America
ISBN: 978-1-7328480-4-7
1st ed. 2020

For the forgotten ancestor, my great-grandmother—

For my grandmother, who journeyed back and forth to unknown lands, who preferred song to speech.

And for my mother

FORGET RUSSIA

Sometimes people enter our lives, even if for a short time, and we never forget them. We continue to love them, long to speak to them, even after they have died.

Long ago, in 1980, I took a journey to Russia, then the Soviet Union. I was searching for a home, so I traveled across the ocean on an Aeroflot plane with other students at twenty-two years old. I went when I barely knew myself—when I was so unsettled into a self that had not formed yet.

I went to the underworld to find dead ancestors, to find a path homeward.

And I did.

It's fascinating to trace the trajectories of people destined to meet.

Lyudmila Ulitskaya, *The Green Tent*

RUSSIAN JOURNEYS

Early morning quiet in the rattling
of heat and blind noises of the noise maker,
a numbing sound to block out sound,
waking in my brown polar fleece jacket,
(always I'm cold) white bathrobe,
I stumble into the kitchen
for English breakfast tea brewed dark,
my husband and son still sleeping.
All night long I'm not really sleeping,
still dreaming of Moscow 1980.
Stalinist skyscrapers, the Hotel Rossiya
overlooked the Moskva river,
glittering in afternoon light by posters
of Misha the Bear plastered everywhere.

"Your problem is you have a Russian soul," I could hear my mother saying as I boarded the Aeroflot plane from Logan airport to Moscow, the night a silver fog, a mist over us all.

The passageway to my seat was narrower than I expected. I understood only fragments of Russian spoken by men with gravelly voices. Their talk blended with the English words from the other American students. We were headed to Moscow to study Russian language at the *Institut Imeni Pushkina*.

"Will we get there in this tin can? What did we expect from a Soviet plane?" The snide remarks had already started. It was the same old stuff I'd been fed all my life. I still didn't believe one word of it. In elementary school my teacher shoved *Animal Farm* down our throats, just so we'd know how evil the Soviet Union was.

"Добрый вечер," the pilot greeted everyone over the PA. *Good Evening.*

"Добрый вечер," the passengers repeated.

I closed my eyes. My legs were shaking. It was my first time out of the country. After a slow glide across cement, we moved up into clouds and then beyond them until only a moonless night surrounded the plane. Next to me, by the aisle, a Russian man sat, his thick bushy mustache quivering. His arms dangled just a bit too close to me.

A large woman in a gray suit, with short-cropped hair,

pushed an aluminum cart through the narrow aisles. "You want something to drink?" she asked in a broken English. When I requested coke, she said, "Only Pepsi," and didn't stop to hear my reply.

"Try to live more in the present." I couldn't get my mother's words out of my head. I wanted to tell her I had already left behind the worn white-columned house off Francis Lewis Boulevard, across from Garden World in Queens, when she married Mort—a short skinny guy who wore a medallion with a shirt unbuttoned just a few notches from the top and a brown leather pocketbook called a man-purse.

We went from barely having an extra dime in the house (my brother had already moved away) to Mort's enormous apartment on Central Park West. They met at a single's weekend at Grossinger's Hotel in the Catskills. In the evenings my beautiful mother sat across from him in the living room, sipping a glass of chardonnay, her hair sprayed into a beehive, while Mort drank martinis. At fifteen, I stayed a lot in my room listening to Joni Mitchell's "Big Yellow Taxi"—paradise paved over with a parking lot.

I read Dostoevsky. First *Notes from the Underground* and then *The Idiot,* imagining the dark and narrow streets of Leningrad, wondering over and over again why someone as good and pure as Prince Myshkin had to be destroyed in the end.

I hated all the stores down Broadway—from Fairway to Zabar's to Thom McAn Shoes. In Russia, I was sure people didn't talk about money but instead spoke of the soul in half-lit, smoke-filled rooms.

On the plane, my belly started grumbling. I was way too nervous to eat before boarding. The flight attendant's black-laced shoes beside the wheels of her cart came closer. When she placed the tray down, the gravy from the mashed potatoes splattered over my arm and dripped on the round pieces of chicken deep-fried in breadcrumbs. After a couple of bites, I knew I couldn't eat that either, so I leaned back against the stiff seat. The man beside me was already snoring.

I remembered how a year ago my mother got pneumonia and borrowed *The Brothers Karamazov* from my bookshelf. She spent the next few days reading it, and by the third night she took a turn for the worse and was hospitalized.

"I guess you have to be strong enough for that book," she said, recovering at home in her bedroom. I rushed back from college to be with her. One night I sat drinking tawny port wine with Mort while she lay upstairs sleeping. Before I knew it, he moved from his black leather chair and was next to me on the white couch, his soggy mustache and wet lips pressed against my own. I pulled away, not believing what was happening. Mort said I shouldn't worry. Just a kiss here and there was all he'd ever do, though he'd been wanting more all these years. I didn't know what to say. I felt like my tongue had been cut out. I went upstairs to my room hating myself. Weeks later, I told my mother about that night. It wasn't easy, but I did it. At first, she was sympathetic, said it must have been terrible for me, but when more weeks went by and I was still upset, my mother said Mort simply had too much drink and didn't mean it, and I should forgive him for it. But even though I did try, I couldn't do it. So I stopped coming back to their home very much.

Six months later, I decided to go to the Soviet Union as a student for a semester abroad. I had to get away. I wanted to return to the country where my great-grandmother died, alone on a boat, raped then murdered in the little town of Gornostaypol. I wanted to understand how her tragic, unspoken life had affected my own.

We arrived in London at three in the morning. Lights glittered off the glass of closed doors—the duty-free shops selling perfumes and jewelry, Chanel and Dior, and bookstores displaying bestsellers from Sheldon and King. In just a few short hours, we'd board a new plane to Moscow. The other American students and I sat in a corner of the airport on chairs connected with metal rods.

Michael, one of our group leaders, skinny with thick glasses, told us he ended up getting a Ph.D. in Russian because once he read *Doctor Zhivago* in English he vowed he'd do what he must to read it in the original, even if it took him almost a decade. This guy must be some romantic to do something like that, I thought. Too bad he wasn't better looking. We were all too tired to say anything back to him, so we just sat there in silence until Miloz, a bit older than all of us, decided to tell us some stuff, too. Miloz said he worked as a Russian teacher at a college in Philly and came originally from Poland. He wore brown khaki pants, a button-down shirt.

"It's always a bitch getting there," he said. "And when you finally arrive, it's even worse."

"So why are you going?" I asked.

"I'm a realist, you know. It will help me make a living

if I'm going to teach Russian." His face was smooth, hairless. He opened up his wallet to find his folded up boarding pass and two pictures fell to the floor. I picked up the small, scissor-cut squares of two very small girls, their arms around each other, smiling.

"Are these your children?" I asked, giving him back the photographs.

"Oh, yeah, sure. They're my bastard children. I have one in every country." Miloz ran his hand through his thinning hair as he laughed into the silence of 3 AM.

It was only five hours from Heathrow to Sheremetyevo. We flew through more than time zones. Outside the clouds obscured the sunrise. It seemed we were descending into a new realm, perhaps to seek advice on how to reach our destination. But before I knew it, the plane started to arrive, to dip down until I saw the trees through the small window—Russian trees, thickets of pine. The plane bumped down noisily onto the runway.

The doors opened and I stepped out of the plane into a dim, flickering passageway. I moved into a gray darkness. Military men in brown uniforms were everywhere in the Sheremetyevo airport, their rifles slung across their chests. The American students nodded wordlessly or else walked very close together, speaking in half-whispers.

The first stop was a glass partition where another man in brown sat and asked for my visa. He looked first at the picture stapled to the document and then at me, his eyes inspecting every aspect of my visa; he stared at my face and then the visa photograph over and over again. Just when I was expecting the military men to escort me somewhere, he nodded and returned the visa to me, so I could proceed with my suitcase to customs. I looked backward and saw the American students standing in a line, one by one, as they approached the glass divider, our first greeting in the Soviet Union.

In the USA, the group leaders had said: The Soviets may search your bags. Don't bring in a Bible. Don't bring in *Time* magazine. Don't write addresses of Russian friends in a book that is easily read. The customs official only opened one of my two suitcases and looked quickly inside before closing it up. But one student, Barry Moskowitz, had all his clothes dumped in a heap for him to refold and squash back inside. I couldn't believe what I was seeing.

I wanted to help Barry repack, but we were kept moving in a line. No one dared speak above a whisper.

The driver of the yellow school bus waited for the American students outside the airport. Two by two we entered. It should be morning, my body told me, but I entered evening and when the bus began to move all I could see was highway and cement pavement.

I had come back to the land where my great-grandmother died, thrown off a boat into the Guilopyat River. Her spirit, it seemed, was in the cracks of cement, in the wide streets and lights rising in the evening, in the thin branches of trees visible before we entered the highway. I wanted somehow to find her.

Darkness was falling on the outskirts of Moscow. I peered across the highway into the center of the city, where Cyrillic letters glittered across the tops of buildings, *Power to the Revolution.* As the bus ambled along, I saw a poster of a man in a dark suit, a torch raised high in his hand, a red hammer and a sickle behind him and the words, *XXVI*

Congress of the Communist Party of the Soviet Union above his arm. Then another one of Brezhnev—his slicked-back hair emphasized his widow's peak, his wide face, and glasses; the circular hammer and sickle with a star hung above him and printed below, *Following Lenin's Course.* There were no advertisements anywhere, no rugged Marlboro man, no Let Your Fingers Do the Talking, no Light My Lady Cigarette, no Coca-Cola Pepsi feuds or Minute Rice. I was relieved to get a break from all the flashy slogans everywhere in the USA, and yet the city looked so stark and austere without them.

I glanced up at the Hotel Rossiya, a rectangular building; its name lit up in all that darkness.

We rode for another thirty minutes, past fields of desolate grass, past posters praising electrical plants and pictures of women in overalls and red kerchiefs covering their heads. Finally, we got to Ulitsa Volgina, dom shest, the address of the dorm. A white circular building spiraled upwards, and beside it, a construction zone with tractors and diggers parked in the soil.

The concierge sat at the desk by the door when we entered. She was a heavy-set woman with red cheeks and black hair cut just below her ears. She spoke Russian quickly, directing us to our rooms. I followed the other students, opened a door after five flights in the elevator and entered the room I'd share with Paula, another American student. Only foreign students lived in this dorm—students from Vietnam, Poland, East Germany, and the United States.

I sat on the bed, unable to move, still landing, arriving, unaware of the time.

"What a trip," Paula sighed as she placed her folded up pants and shirts neatly in her dresser. She had a small, freckled nose and looked like she probably wore a size two. "Aren't you going to unpack?"

"Sure, but just a little later. I need to rest." My flight bag had ripped in London. It looked so shabby next to my nylon suitcase. Everything I owned seemed to have a hole in it. "Are you from New York?" I asked her.

"The Bronx. I work with Russian immigrants. I find them jobs, a place to live. I translate for them. You name it. I do it. At least I'm using the Russian I worked so hard to learn in college."

"So, what made you want to leave that and come here?" Her penny loafer shoes were stored neatly beneath the bed.

"My boyfriend is from Moscow. He was lucky to get out of here. I met him at my agency a couple of years ago. He told me so much about this place, I just had to see it for myself." Paula's reddish-brown hair hung limply above her shoulders. "Well, we have four months here. Let's just hope we survive."

"I'm hoping it doesn't go by so fast."

We sat for a few minutes in silence until I finally said, "You want to get something to eat?"

"Great idea. I'm starved." Paula rushed to put on her coat. I was already wearing a bulky sweater.

By the elevator, we met up with Miloz and Barry, a student from Pennsylvania, the guy who had all his clothes dumped out of his suitcase by the customs official. Barry had come to Moscow with a list of addresses, all friends of his fiancé, Sasha, who had left this country several years before. Though Barry was twenty-one years old, he was beginning to lose his hair and his back was ever so slightly bent.

Outside on the street, clusters of apartment buildings reminded me of the Bronx, of Co-op City: tall identical looking brown buildings everywhere.

"These buildings are cheap. They'll fall apart. They're made like shit," Miloz said.

He has hated this place before he even got here. I breathed in the air that smelled like crisp apples. The boughs of trees leaned down close to my shoulders. Street lamps filtered light into darkness.

"Look," Barry said. "There are places down the block." He started to run and we followed.

At ten o'clock everything was closed except for a bar with two tall doors. Paula turned the knob and found it locked. From inside, we could hear the Beatles singing, *Love Me Do.*

We knocked over and over again until finally an old woman in a long apron, her hair in a bun, peeked her head out and yelled, "Уходите, Уходите." She pushed the door shut.

"Is it because we're Americans?" I asked Miloz.

"No, it's not that. We look like a crowd, I guess, and besides, it's late." Miloz continued to knock until the woman came back. He spoke with her in Russian much too quickly for me to decipher the words. But whatever he said worked because she opened the door for us.

Oh, pleaeeese love . . . filled the bar. Young men and women sat in booths with black vinyl coverings, drinking beer and vodka, their cigarette smoke creating a hazy film we stepped through to get to our table.

"I thought I was getting sent back for a while there in Sheremetyevo," Barry said as he sat down next to me.

"I wanted to help you fold up your stuff." My voice trailed off. I was too tired to say much more.

"It's okay. Sasha, my fiancé, warned me what this place was like before I left Philly. Thank goodness she got out," he said.

"So, why do you want to be here?" I asked.

"I'm trying to understand what her life was like before I was in it."

"That's sweet." I wondered if anyone would ever feel that way about me.

Paula tapped the table with her long fingernails. "My boyfriend was also one of the last ones to get out of here."

"They were the lucky ones." Barry raised his dark plastic glass filled with water. "Because no one's leaving here now."

"That's for sure," Miloz chimed in.

When the food arrived, orders of chicken with thick red gravy, we all ate quickly. Miloz used his fingers to rip into the wings and tear its bones apart on the plate.

After our meal, we walked past brick apartment buildings with thin trees bordering sidewalks. When we entered the dorm, the concierge nodded to us. We slipped past her and stood in an elevator with a long mirror covering one side, so no one could ever forget their reflection in the blaring light, and others too might see and remember them.

My image startled me—long, straggly black hair down my back.

"The mirrors are so typically Soviet," Michael, our group leader, the one in love with *Dr. Zhivago,* said. "We must always be aware of our appearance." He got off on the third floor, while the rest of us continued on to the fifth.

In my room, I put on my flannel nightgown. I wrapped the sheets over me that were too short to cover the whole mattress. But after a few moments, I hopped out of bed, so I could drape my down coat over the blankets that were also too small.

"What are you doing?" Paula asked.

"I'm cold." I liked the weight of the blankets and coat over me.

"But it's only September. What will you do in December if you're wearing your coat to bed now?" In her summer pajamas, Paula nestled into a single sheet falling just over her toes.

"I don't know. We'll see," I said, drifting into a troubled sleep.

Hours before I got on the plane to Moscow, I met my mother in a small train station in Connecticut, not far from my college. It was noon and I had to be at Logan airport at 6 PM, so we had time to sit back and relax on turquoise chairs.

At first, a single tear made its way down her cheek. I asked her why she was crying and she smiled, dabbed the droplet of water from her cheek with a torn-up tissue she pulled out of her pocketbook. "No one goes to Russia in the winter. You're going to freeze there."

"But it's September."

"Yes, I know that. But you won't be back until December." She wiped a strand of hair away from her eyes. "Look at all the people who want to leave that country."

We always seemed to have the same conversation. My

mother wanted to forget the past, and I had become obsessed with it. I longed to understand the family story—how my grandfather came here in 1909 from Minsk and dreamed of returning to his homeland after 1917. He was a carpenter who longed to build the revolution. And finally, in 1931, he brought to Leningrad my mother and aunt, two small girls then, and my grandmother, a young woman of twenty-four, who never wanted to go back to the country where her mother died so violently.

"Anyway, how do you know how cold it is there?"

"Don't you think I had feelings when I was five? I still remember Leningrad even if it was fifty years ago. How for nine months I wanted an orange, or maybe it was a banana. Who knows? But I do know there weren't any.

"I can tell you this. I remember quite clearly that I didn't like it there. My mother made me wait with her in a long line for a tetanus shot, and I wanted to run away. We left that place behind. Why on earth would you want to go there?"

But we didn't leave it all behind, I wanted to say.

I imagined my great-grandmother Zlata lying beneath the Guilopyat River all these years after her murder. I had heard the unburied searched forever for a place to rest. Maybe, and I knew this sounded crazy, if I could in some way find her, I might be able to stop her endless wandering.

My mother didn't want to talk about any of this. So I didn't bother. She wanted to forget that miserable year and the strange journey from Boston that catapulted her as a small child back to Leningrad with her little sister and parents.

"If your grandmother hadn't insisted we get out of that

God-forsaken place after nine months and come back to Boston, we'd all be dead. My mother was the only one with any sense." My mother opened the golden clasp of her black patent leather pocketbook and took out another tissue to dab away the sweat from her forehead. The circles beneath her eyes had deepened since the last time I saw her.

"My parents in all those years afterward never once spoke about our time in Leningrad. There's a reason for that. And they had nothing when they got back here. And I mean nothing."

"Which is why they left Boston in the first place," I said, glancing up at the poster of the Marlboro Man plastered to the train station's walls.

"It was my mother, too. My father hoped being in Russia would lift her mood somehow. I remember her, sometimes in a rocking chair, her fists pounding the sides of her head. Sometimes she stayed in bed a good part of the day, too sad to do anything. And the truth is my father managed to have a little something in the years he had lived in Boston before going back to Russia. We weren't starving here, and we were plenty hungry there, I can tell you that much." My mother brushed a piece of lint off her black cotton skirt.

"You really think your father would have come back from Leningrad just because she wanted to leave? Would he really do that for her?" It just didn't fit in with the way I thought about my grandfather, the mythically strong man who could lift up a house and rest it on his shoulders.

"I don't know. I really don't. My father was a hard person to understand. He worked all the time and when he was around, he didn't speak a lot. I used to think he didn't care that much for any of us. But it wasn't that. I don't think he ever got over leaving Russia. Something must have happened in Leningrad. But I don't know what it was. And I never will. So it's best not to think about it."

"Maybe we should be thinking about it."

"I don't see the point. But I guess you're just complicated while I'm simple." My mother smiled until all the lines on her face disappeared.

Several months ago, her cousin Cookie had shown me the passport picture of my mother taken right before she left Boston for the Soviet Union. My mother's dark hair at five years old fell below her shoulders, her bangs were cropped short; her frightened eyes turned away from the camera.

Now in the heat of early September, my mother's plaid nylon blouse stuck to her skin. I worried she'd grow old while I was away.

Cookie had told me my mother was named Susan in memory of my great-grandmother Zlata, so no one would ever forget her.

"Why do you always have to look backward?" She stroked the strands of my thin hair. "Try and let go of the past. Promise me, okay?"

The train taking me to Boston was about to arrive. I heard it bellowing in the distance. I gathered up my suitcase, flung my blue nylon flight bag over my shoulder. I had never gone so far away from her before. Our arms around each other, we rested in all that remained unsaid between us.

Two weeks before I left for Moscow, I sat with my grandmother. The room smelled of ammonia mixed with urine-soaked bedpans. Her roommate lay on the opposite bed, her back turned away from us. Later on, my Aunt Carol would join us.

"Anushka, why are you going away? You are such a smart girl." She grabbed onto a silver walker and lifted herself out of bed, moving into a wooden chair.

"Would you come with me? I mean, if you could, would you come?" For so long I had visited her in her small doily-filled apartment, before she had fallen and ended up in this horrible place.

"No, I cannot go back there. I wish you luck. You will need it," my grandmother said and stared blankly with her one good eye out the window.

Her roommate, Sophie, woke up from her sleep, her white hair covering most of her face.

"Sophie," my grandmother called. "My Anushka wants to know what it's like in Russia. She's going to be a student there. Would you believe?"

"Why would you want to do that?" Sophie asked.

"She wants to learn the Russian language there."

"Oh. Well, I can tell you what it was like there," Sophie said, her bare legs hairless in the fluorescent light. "It cost twenty-eight dollars to come here, for the ticket, you know. In Russia, we were five children and my mother. My father died. He was in the egg business. Then he took sick. It was terrible. We lost everything." Sophie wore a light blue nightgown. I could see the outline of her sagging breasts.

"There were three sisters left and working. Then my mother died and I still don't know where my sisters are. If they were killed or not killed in Kharkov. I don't know where they are. I was fourteen when I came here all alone.

And my sisters, they are wherever they are. I still don't know."

An aide arrived with two plates of boneless, skinless chicken, cooked peas, some canned peaches and mashed potatoes. "How are you girls today?"

"Pretty good," my grandmother said.

"I can't eat this food," Sophie said. "I have no appetite." She put on a loose-fitting bathrobe, grabbed her cane from the side of the bed and followed the aide out of the room.

Meanwhile, I cut the bland chicken up into small parts. I kept waiting for my grandmother to say something about Sophie's disjointed story, but she didn't. So I gathered up my courage to ask a question I had been wondering about for a while.

"But tell me, will you, what was it like to be in your little village in 1917?"

"In 1917?"

"Yes, during the Revolution."

"You want to know about the Revolution?"

"Yes, the Russian Revolution," I shouted. The thick syrup from the peaches stuck to the one silver hair growing out of her chin.

"It wasn't honey."

"What do you mean by that?"

My grandmother said nothing.

So I asked, "Will you sing for me a little bit?"

"You want me to sing for you?"

"Yes, you know, the one about the guitar." I was trying not to yell.

She straightened her back, placed her hand on the armrest of the chair, and pursed her lips. "Сижу и играю я на гитаре, я сижу и веселюсь . . . Про мое горе никто не знает . . . "

"Did your mother teach you these songs?"

"No, my mother did not sing," she said.

"Then how do you know the songs?"

"I don't know. I just do. All day long the songs come to me." She grabbed onto the walker. "Help me, will you Anushka, get back into bed." I held her hand, guided her out of the chair until first one leg and then the other landed on the mattress.

"Why does everything come in such pain?" she asked.

I had no answer, so I stroked my grandmother's white hair, felt the softness in her curls, touched the brown spots on her arms and legs. With her blind eye, she peered deep inside of me.

"Yes, I know how much you love me," she whispered.

An hour later, she started to call for her mother. She started slowly. "Ma," then silence. "Ma." Her voice blended into the stillness of late afternoon until she fell asleep.

SARAH: 1915-1921

Russian people, awake from your sleep! A short time ago the sun shone and the Russian tsar used to visit Kiev. Now you find Jews everywhere! Let us throw off that yoke, we can no longer bear it! They will destroy the Fatherland. Down with the Jews! Russian people, unite! Bring the tsar back to us.

Razsvet, September 6, 1917

Long after Sarah left the village of Gornostaypol, she continued to believe that if someone died a violent death, his blood must be dug up from beneath the earth and buried with his body, so no further danger could harm his spirit or the land. The body must be kept whole, or else the dead would have to wander, searching for a bit of hair, a droplet splattered onto a blade of grass.

Sarah recalled how the Guilopyat River meandered through Gornostaypol. The town had grown haphazardly around the riverbanks, its thoroughfares radiating outward from the center—a jagged geometry of rough-hewn stone streets that, on more than one occasion, caused wagons to overturn. There butchers and cobblers, bakers and fruit sellers, and those with carts of junk liked to gather by a steel post, black during the winter months and softened into gray when the spring finally arrived and the rain turned the dirt roads to mud. Later in the dry heat of summer, dust would rise like a mist over Gornostaypol. The river ambled by the shacks occupied by the Jewish townspeople; some owned old rowboats, painted in red and blue. For centuries it had been this way, and some days the townspeople were convinced that for hundreds of more years it would remain so, and on other days they believed that at any moment all could be destroyed, their lives changed forever.

In the morning light, the Guilopyat River reflected all

the goings-on in Gornostaypol—the ragged clothes hanging from white rope, often linking one home to another, and the thick and golden grass growing away from squawking chickens.

Gussie, Sarah's neighbor, would take her breads and cakes into the marketplace every Thursday and vie for business with the other merchants selling food and leather, shoes and jackets under cloth canopies. Women in dresses mended and torn and mended once again, baskets in their hands, bought and sold, bargained and haggled, their coins kept in handkerchiefs folded up and stored in pockets sewn inside their dresses.

Sarah lived with her parents, Zlata and Lazar, in a home built of wooden logs piled one on top of another. At the end of the week, when Sarah and her mother set out to buy some meat for the Sabbath, Sarah hated how Moishe, the Shochet, always smelled of blood the moment they entered his store. Sarah kept her eyes on the dirt floor to avoid the red splashes on his nose, droplets smeared all over his hands.

Her father was a tailor who barely scraped by. In the summer months, people didn't need much. Peasants worked in the fields with torn shirts. On Thursdays, Lazar woke up especially early, ate some black bread and an onion and brought the clothes he had so carefully made, the pants and silk caftans for Friday eve, the black silk blouses for the women, to the marketplace. He hung up his goods on a makeshift rack next to a barrel of apples.

Once Sarah overheard her father speaking to her mother just after she had gone to bed. He said he was tired of the learned men of the Torah with their long beards, measuring their words, walking slowly through the town. Those men with their wide foreheads wrinkled from so much study looked down on a tailor who dreamed of making and wearing beautiful clothes.

Another night, when Sarah was lying awake in bed, and the sky was filled with light at ten o'clock, her parents sat talking at the kitchen table.

"No sewing tonight?" she heard her mother say.

"Just a little rest," her father replied.

"Are you sick?"

"No."

"Then what?"

"You know as well as I do that there's no future here for us. There's money to be made in America. It won't take me long to send two tickets for you and Sarochka."

"What are you saying?"

"I've made all my calculations, and I see that soon I can bring you all over," her father said. "Besides, we're not wanted in this place."

"And how are we going to manage, I ask you? You must not be thinking right."

Sarah thought she had to be dreaming their conversation until her father announced that he was taking the ship in two weeks.

"But how did you ever come up with the money for this? Were you saving all this time and not even telling me?" But then her mother's tone softened. "We'll be too lonely here without you. Why can't you wait until we can all go together?"

"I'll send for you both," he said solemnly. "I promise. Soon life will be better for all of us."

Sarah wanted to run out and plead with him too. But she didn't. She wiped away the sweat on her forehead and turned over on her side. She was damp from the heat of early September.

Lazar would sail to Odessa, then pick up another small ship headed for Liverpool, where he'd take the large steamer to New York. Sarah peered at the small boat on this day when clouds promised rain that never did arrive. Her mother wore the dress he had made for her shortly after their marriage. He said we'll soon join him, Sarah sighed; she still felt her father's smooth hands against her cheek. He didn't seem unhappy to be going. It was the way his legs moved in large steps to the dock. He was there now on the wooden passageway to the boat, waving his black hat at them. Sarah's hand swayed back and forth in a frantic good-bye and kept on waving long after Lazar entered the boat and was no longer visible to them.

Two years went by slowly without her father. One afternoon, Sarah snuck into the forest behind the wooden shacks of Gornostaypol. She had finished her morning hours at school and decided to take a little rest before helping her mother with cleaning and cooking. She liked to daydream about her father, trying as hard as possible to imagine him in his new land. But no pictures ever came to her, except for what he looked like on the day he left them. His brown curly hair and green eyes made his skin look pale. Her father was all dressed up, the only man on the boat with a matching jacket and pants.

Sarah sat beneath an oak tree and gathered caterpillars in her hand. Their fuzzy backs rubbed against her fingers before she released them. She stared at the leaves on trees, first green, then yellow in the autumn light. For a while, she had tried to keep track of how many days her father had been away, but last March, when she got to two hundred, she stopped counting.

At first, they received many letters from her father— long ones, telling them of all the work he had found as a tailor. Sarah kept a couple of his letters buried deep in the pockets of her dress. She took one out—the paper had been folded and refolded so many times but the stamps across the top of the envelope still spoke of a faraway land.

November 10, 1915
My dear beloved wife and daughter!
　　I think of you always. Here in America, in New York, I feel like a little flea in a vast ocean compared to our Gornostaypol. How I miss you and our home. So many people are here in this city, you can't even believe it, my dearest ones. And then there are boys on street corners selling newspapers, yelling at the tops of the lungs, Extra, Extra. Can you believe it? And still more unbelievable are the electric trains rattling through the city. They have been built on top of the buildings.
　　Ah, but I miss you. It's difficult to see the sky in this place. And no, I have not found the streets paved with gold, as I was certain they must be. But there is plenty of work for a tailor if a man is willing to work day and night. And I am, so I can scrimp and save for your fare. I pray I can bring you to me soon to this Garden of Eden where a poor man can end up with riches.
　　From me, your husband and father who wishes you life and happiness,

　　Lazar

The day that letter arrived, Zlata recounted for Sarah the story of her marriage; how she was just sixteen and Lazar seventeen when their parents arranged all the details. Zlata came with candlesticks, a white tablecloth, silver tableware and two pillows. "Marriage first; love will follow," both sets of parents told them.

"Your father, so handsome," Zlata said, "the best-looking boy in the village. Who would think a plain girl like me could marry such a good-looking man. But I did. And he could make such things, could fix anything with a hole or a hem. Thanks to him, our poor clothes could last forever."

Then Zlata took out her faded white wedding dress with large black buttons down the center. "The happiest day of my life. You should know such happiness, Sarochka." Still, Sarah noticed how her mother's lip turned slightly downward as she spoke her words.

Her mother told her how the day before the ceremony she went to the baths; and like all brides, the nails from her fingers and toes were cut very short and afterward burned, so at least when she died she would not have to wander about looking for them. Then she entered a pool where an old woman, with two missing front teeth and jowls sagging, pushed Zlata's head beneath the water three times, each time exclaiming that she was now a kosher daughter. Sarah knew, though her mother never said, she had been declared cleansed of all that dreaded monthly bleeding.

Her mother told Sarah that all the villagers gathered at the shul for the wedding; afterwards they danced and drank in the center of the town. The dust beneath their feet rose to form a film on their clothes, smudged their faces; all the while fiddlers played polkas and jigs, and the men lifted Lazar and Zlata up on their shoulders, parading the couple around.

Lazar's letters produced such a response. Usually he

included some money for them, too. But now he was unknown to them, except for his last letter that Sarah kept on her dress as well.

February 3, 1916
Dearest Zlatinka and Sarochka, beloved wife, may she live, and daughter, shining light of her generation!

Not only is this city not paved with gold, but everything costs so much. Much more than you can ever imagine. But I see Jews who have come here with nothing, and now they are wealthy. This, alas, has not happened to me. I live simply in an airless room, just so I can save more. Ah, there are so many possibilities in this land. I may even try my luck in a different city, so I can save even more, and see you both sooner. And best of all, I must tell you, is that there is no dowry in America. As long as a girl is not ugly, she can easily find a groom, so our Sarochka will marry easily here.

Yes, I know it is taking me longer than I thought, but the fare will come. I am working day and night so I can see you.

Your beloved husband and father,
Lazar Bermansky

Sarah stuffed the worn papers back into the deep pockets of her dress and made her way out of the forest, back to her mother. The water would now be receding from the river, leaving a muddy residue. For an entire year after this letter arrived, Sarah and her mother had heard nothing from him. They both wrote, begged him to reply.

"He's got to be dead," Zlata wept. "It's the only explanation."

"Dead. It's not possible, Momichka."

"But maybe it's true."

"How could he die just like that?"

"Ach, men. They're all terrible, if you ask me." Then Zlata spit three times on the ground. "May the evil eye not follow him even in death," she said, and spit some more.

In the marketplace, in 1918, Sarah heard rumors, stories, of the changes sweeping through the land: how the czars' palaces had been seized, how peasants and workers and even Jews were ruling the Ukraine. Every day it was something new. Several months later, the Shochet whispered, as Sarah watched his fat face shrink into his double chins, how the Bolsheviks were fighting to keep control of Kiev from the Ukrainian nationalists, intent on issuing their decrees of independence. He nodded sadly as he handed her the meat.

It was hard for Sarah to follow everything he said. It was all so confusing. She, for the most part, was too busy with the business of survival to pay much heed. Sometimes when Sarah and her mother rubbed their clothes clean in a wash basin, then hung their ragged garments out to dry, Sarah heard her neighbor, Gussie Wiesner, singing folk songs of passionate love, unrequited and unreturned. Sarah heard, "Сижу и играю я на гитаре, я сижу и веселюсь ... "

Sarah went to school for a couple of hours each day and then spent the remainder working with her mother. Every Thursday, since her father left, Sarah helped her mother gather the fruits and vegetables, the apples, carrots, and beets into large baskets. Her mother's brother, her Uncle Shmuel, a tall man with a graying beard, brought the goods by horse and carriage before the sun rose, from the town of Ivankov, where he lived. Zlata added the potatoes she had started growing by the side of the house. Together they all made their way to the marketplace.

Uncle Shmuel insisted they split the profits in half.

"You do too much for us," Zlata said. "You should take most of the money back to Ivankov."

"I have a store to live by. What do I need it for?" he said and gave Sarah a sweet apple to try. Sarah loved the melody of his voice.

That afternoon, Gussie set up her baked goods on a table right near them. Only yesterday, she said, the Shochet told her, "Every few weeks someone new is in power. Sometimes the Reds, other times the Whites. Who can keep track?" Gussie had heard rumors Petliura was advancing towards Kiev with an army to oust the Bolsheviks. "They think all Jews are Reds," Gussie said, so low that Sarah could barely hear her.

Day after day passed, but still no word from Lazar. Then after many more months, in the fall of 1919, just as mother and daughter had gotten used to their life without him, out of nowhere a letter arrived. They both recognized the neat handwriting at once.

"He'll send for us now. Finally, he'll send for us. That's men, for you. They forget us and then when it suits them they remember." Zlata waved the letter back and forth in the air. "What I won't ask is why it took him so long." As she hurriedly opened it, an American five-dollar bill dropped from the envelope to the floor.

"What's this?" She picked up the money before starting to read.

Two or three lines scribbled on a piece of paper granted Zlata a divorce.

"A divorce?" she repeated in disbelief. "Your father wants a divorce after all these years." Her brow creased into a thousand wrinkles. "Your fool of a father must want to take another wife." She pounded the sides of her head with her fists. "I knew all along he'd forget about us, yes, forget about us," she screamed.

Everything happened as if in a dream. Even though Sarah was no longer allowed in the forest ever since the civil war between the Whites and Reds broke out, she went there anyway. She had to get away from her mother, whose cries, she was sure, must be echoing throughout the town.

Today Sarah did not care about her mother's rules. So she ran past the stray chickens and goats, past the Guilopyat River, where brown wooden shacks lined the water, one looking like the next, some connected together by clotheslines—past the center of Gornostaypol, where tailors and cobblers, a general store and a synagogue, filled the main street. Sarah went beyond the noises of the village, beyond the bookseller calling to the girls to buy his love novels by Shomer and Mayer, or the *Brifshteller,* a book of model letters created to fit any mood or occasion.

Sarah entered the dirt path separating rows and rows of trees with branches of delicate green leaves. Why five dollars? The bill had floated to the floor in slow motion, stayed there a while before her mother picked it up. What was a letter of divorce anyway? Could her father have taken another wife? No, it was all too unbelievable. She knew now that he would never return or send for her.

When Sarah thought her father was dead, she believed if she concentrated enough, perhaps he could feel her life in that place wherever the dead might be. But now that she knew her father was actually alive and living across the ocean, it seemed, as she stepped over nettles and dirt, soil and roots, that maybe he could hear her thoughts. She wanted, with all the longing of her fourteen years, to ask her father how he could possibly desert her.

Horses stepped onto dry leaves and made a crackling sound that merged with the voices of soldiers telling jokes.

"The compass says straight ahead. We're going correctly, you idiot," she heard in the distance.

The gruff voices came closer. Soon they would see her. She had to hurry. Sarah managed to hide behind one of the few trees with a wide trunk and bark, then folded her hand and legs together as tightly as possible, her head sunk into her knees, her legs shaking uncontrollably. If the soldiers found her, she would surely be murdered. Or even worse.

"In a few weeks, Petliura will take over and we'll finally be free," one soldier, a boy of no more than eighteen, said.

"Yeah, you can go home and see your wife again. She's been waiting every night for you to return."

"I know it. Well, at least we can have a little fun for now."

"Petliura says leave the Jews alone."

"That's what he says. But he doesn't mean it. Don't tell me you haven't seen the wink in his eye when he speaks to us."

"Don't worry. We'll soon have our chance."

Sarah thought she must have stopped breathing. Maybe she was even dead but didn't know it yet, except her legs were still trembling.

Once the men's voices had disappeared and she could no longer hear the leaves beneath the horses' hooves, Sarah ran past the rows of pine and birch, past the oak trees and out of the forest. But just as Sarah saw the village before her, she tripped on a root. She landed flat on the side of her face, mud everywhere down her legs and arms and in the brown strands of her hair. She lifted herself up, every muscle aching, and made her way back to her home.

"Oh my God, what has happened to you," her mother cried. Zlata stood by the clothesline. The wind created a chill in the October air, buffeted the sheets and pillowcases still hanging to dry. "Where have you been?"

"In the forest," Sarah said quietly. "I saw the soldiers on their horses. And then I fell."

"I've been searching for you everywhere." Her mother's eyes were red and swollen. She took out a handkerchief from the inside of her dress and started to wipe away the dirt from Sarah's cheek. "You can't disappear from me and do this to me, Sarochka. Do you understand what I'm saying?" At first, a single tear crawled down Zlata's face. "Do you understand, I ask you?"

Her mother seemed ancient, older than the oldest woman in the village. Her parched cheekbones sank into the lines forming beneath her mouth. How come, Sarah wondered, she had never before noticed how her mother's hair had turned a silvery gray?

Gussie Wiesner kept Zlata and Sarah informed about the world. Every rumor, fact, or fiction seemed to glide by her. "One day it's Petliura in charge. Another day, it's the White army, and he's out. But they're all united against the Bolsheviks. Not even the newspapers know who's to rule from day to day."

"May they all stay far away from us," Zlata said. Her arms had grown more muscular over the years. She was busy doing both women's and men's work—cooking and hauling, fixing and cleaning.

"No one knows anymore what's to be," Gussie said, as she set up her breads and pastries under a canopy stall. "Tell us what you know, Isak?"

The small and shriveled man dressed in a black coat and long boots traveled from town to town, selling books. Isak had heard the Bolsheviks had seized control of Kiev, finally forcing the Whites, the Cossacks, the Nationalists, and any other bandits out.

"But as they are leaving, they are taking their revenge." His bottom lip quivered as he spoke. "In Gordische, three hundred shot by soldiers. Sore losers. Others buried alive, their toes still moving beneath the sand."

"We have to get out of here," Sarah whispered to her mother.

"You think so. Where are we going to go?"

"Anywhere. Just not here."

"It's the same everywhere, Sarochka."

"What about Kiev? We could go there."

"It's not possible. The two of us will never make it a day there."

"You'll manage here," Gussie said. "You've done well for yourselves without that fool of a husband."

Beneath the jagged stones water had been trapped for many weeks once the snow melted. Its stench made them feel sick. Soon, the townspeople hoped, rain would come and wash it all away.

Ever since her father left, Sarah slept in the same bed with her mother. It seemed to Sarah her mother had the faint smell of birch trees in the morning upon waking, when light nestled into the pockets of clothes, the folded pillowcases in a basket. Sarah and her mother came out into the yard on an early November day to see how the grass curled in the autumn breeze.

Sarah wondered again how old her mother was. If she

asked Zlata, she would get some strange response, like: I was sixteen when I married. I was born a year after my parents' wedding. Numbers and dates were dangerous, her mother said. Easy for spirits to track you down, bring trouble. Don't give them any information, so they keep away. Sarah barely knew her own age. She guessed she must be fifteen because it was 1920, four years since her father went away.

Zlata brought out a bucket and some dirty clothes, a brush, and soap. She knelt into the grass and scrubbed.

"Sarochka, go inside and get a better brush for me," she said.

Sarah hurried into the house. Some days she hardly remembered her father, just his black pants and his matching black jacket as he waved to them from the boat. Why had he left me? A question she had never stopped asking all these years, and so it came as no surprise when, stepping onto the cold wooden floor, the thought appeared once more. She still had no answer.

In the reflection of the window, Sarah noticed that her breasts had become large and her belly plump. Her mother said she ate too much bread, too many pastries with white powdered sugar and cooked apples inside. "You're pretty, Sarochka," her mother would say. "Don't let yourself get fat before your wedding day."

She didn't want to get married, and no one had shown up to ask her, which was fine with her. She had grown used to waking with her mother each morning, the two of them working at their chores and making a meager living together. So many of their potatoes were growing in a patch of land set aside by the side of their house. She only hoped the soldiers would keep far away. Isak's stories interrupted her sleep; she dreamt of the moon, saw a large ship filled with women, their faces turned towards the sea. She had no idea what it all meant.

Sarah looked out once more from the kitchen window. This time a flock of birds swooped down low to the water and then reversed course, rising higher and higher into the sky. Just as she grabbed hold of the brush her mother had requested, she heard the sound of glass shattering everywhere. Glass breaking, falling into tiny pieces from rakes against windows and rocks thrown, a universe of glass echoing across a river and a sky now gray. Chickens squawked, and women and some children screamed, their voices heard throughout the village. Sarah saw from a corner of the kitchen window the men in brown uniforms and red military caps running up to her mother by the clothesline. Others went into Gussie's house; feathers from torn pillows fell like snow out the windows before drifting to the ground.

The soldiers grabbed Zlata's arms. She struggled to take a step forward and fell into the moist ground. The men hoisted her up and three of them ripped her dress off, tearing her undergarments as she shrieked in long staccato sounds, her breath short and gasping.

A sharp blow to her face left her quiet.

"Hurry up now," a soldier said. "Don't let her die on us yet."

The others laughed.

They lifted her mother into the rowboat. The oars, stuck in the muddy earth, gave way easily.

Sarah felt a numb sickness in her stomach. They took her mother, those soldiers with hairy faces. There were no birds anywhere. No words, just sound stuck in her throat.

She wanted to run out to the yard, swim to the boat, cry for help. But she knew no one would come. From far away she heard men arguing and cursing.

What if they came for her next? Sarah pulled out a bunch of her hair and remembered her mother once taught her how to hide. In the closet, beneath the bucket and broom, brushes and basket, was a door leading under the house.

So she went in there, her heart beating so fast, her hands shaking; she opened a latch and slid into the dirt. Weeds were everywhere; when she put her arms around her legs and pushed her chest close to her knees, the bottom of the house rested an inch or two above her head.

What had they done to her mother? Where had they taken her?

Windows were still breaking. Sarah heard tables and chairs smashed against walls, shelves emptied from Gussie's home.

Something, she did not know, made a crackling sound in the wind.

Her body ached, cramped up, nestled into herself. She had to see her mother. She prayed for her mother to be somehow there by the yard in the very last place where she stood before the soldiers came. Time stopped, stood perfectly still. A spider crawled by her foot. She thought about killing it, stomping on it, but let it go into the weeds. So many cobwebs clung to the wood beneath the house.

Then there was an eerie quiet over the town. The soldiers had left, she knew. Sarah crawled over to the trap door, pushed it open and heard the brooms fall onto the kitchen floor as she pulled herself up into the closet, her hands full of splinters. Light returned when she entered the room where she had lived all her life with her mother, had woken and slept beside her; each morning where it seemed her mother had contained all the scents of the town, the grass and water, the soil both of them knew so well.

Coming out into the yard, Sarah saw shards of glass and feathers everywhere, the wheelbarrow knocked over, apples covered by mud. Disheveled and dirty, Sarah walked along the river searching for her mother. But she did not find her anywhere by the weeds and the stones or the tall stalks of yellow grass curled under by the wind.

Some of the townspeople ventured out of their houses and began fixing what had been broken. Later bands of men gathered up the bodies, digging and collecting to make sure they were whole for burial.

Sarah heard Gussie Wiesner calling, "Sarochka, you must come to me now." She sat in the overgrown grass, looking at the place where the rowboat had been.

So Gussie walked over to her.

"We hid in the space above the bread oven, Sarochka. All of us did. It's a miracle they didn't find us."

Sarah didn't want to speak to anyone. She shooed away a fly that buzzed outside of her ear.

"Those bastards must have left her to die in the river," Gussie whispered. It couldn't be true, Sarah thought. She had to be somewhere, unseen by them.

"Raped and killed her," Gussie said even more faintly.

Sarah leaned her head on her knees, felt the grass on her legs, wished she could float far out on the river, her head in the water, a stone in her pocket, pulling her beneath brine and weeds, to a place where she could rest forever.

"Sarochka, you'll be with us until your uncle Shmuel comes for you." Gussie put her arms around Sarah's shoulders.

Gussie had yellow teeth; a single hair grew out of a mole on her left wrist. With her five daughters and a husband who studied all day, one more girl would be no trouble, she told Sarah, who followed, did what she was told; unable to feel anything at all, she dutifully entered Gussie's small and crowded home.

It took several days for word to reach Uncle Shmuel about Zlata's murder. A week later he arrived in Gornostaypol for Sarah, so she could live with him in his general store in Ivankov, a town near Kiev. Uncle Shmuel always smelled of tobacco. His back was slightly stooped over, though he could still climb a ladder easily to get a can for a customer. Ten years ago, he had lost his two sons, boys of ten and fifteen, one afternoon when he went to Kiev to exchange some of his goods. As he bartered over price, outsiders on horses entered Ivankov, men who were angry about the high taxes imposed by Czar Nicholas. It was all the fault of the Jewish merchants, they said, and broke everything they could find.

The smell from the houses burnt to the ground stayed in the air for weeks.

Soon after his sons' murder, his wife took sick and died. Uncle Shmuel spent most of his time in the store, where he sold flour, bread, beans, and other goods. He made as few trips as possible to Kiev; the noise of the city was intolerable to him. So he went only when he had to barter to keep the store going or get goods to help out Zlata and

Sarah at the market in Gornostaypol, but all that was over now, too.

Sarah wanted to be useful to Uncle Shmuel. She liked to count change from customers; she tallied his small profits. She had always been good at arithmetic.

Every day Uncle Shmuel sifted the flour, arranged the rolls on a tin sheet to bake. "Try some of this bread, Sarochka." Uncle Shmuel gave her a roll with a top browned with just a little butter.

"Thank you, but I'm not hungry." She craved little during the day.

"But I need to know if it's good."

"I won't wither away." Still, she ate it. The roll had a sweetness she had never tasted before. For the first time in weeks, she smiled.

A couple of hours after dinner, Sarah went upstairs to a small room with a cot by the window. She looked out on the Prypiat River. As light simmered just before disappearing, she found trees reflected in the water, their majestic branches an arc that wavered as the wind swept through the countryside.

Before Sarah went to sleep, she heard the birds over the Prypiat River, just like in Gornostaypol. Sometimes a branch fell onto the long sloping roof of a house.

What are the sounds, Sarah wondered, that the dead create, to heal the emptiness of their leaving?

In the evenings, Uncle Shmuel sat at a small desk, writing letters to everyone he knew in America. He was intent on locating Sarah's father. Time passed: one year and another. Finally, Uncle Shmuel's efforts paid off.

"Look, Sarochka. Here's a letter from a distant friend,

Gertrude, who knows your father. Listen to this: '*Yes, I have been acquainted with Lazar Bermansky, a tailor in the small town called Roxbury, near the city of Boston. In this town, the houses are built very close together and are connected by yards in the front. So unlike our villages in Russia. Lazar Bermansky is considered the very best tailor for miles around. Just last month, he fixed up an old dress of mine. A very fine tailor, I would call him. That is all I can really tell you, except here, I can give you his address too, so you can write to him yourself.*'"

"I don't remember my father anymore," Sarah said. She had grown used to Uncle Shmuel and their life together. Mornings she learned basic math and reading in Yiddish at school. In the afternoons she and Uncle Shmuel worked together in the store. She knew all the customers, especially liked seeing the women, their hands full of apples and spices.

"He's your father, Sarochka. You can't forget him."

"He was no father to me."

"Still I must write him."

"May he never answer you."

But he did answer. A month later, her father sent money for her journey: a ticket for the ship and a little left over for food.

"You see, your father is making good now," Uncle Shmuel said.

"He has not done good by me."

"You must go to him," he said. "If your father wants you, then you must go."

She wondered if she had been a burden to Uncle Shmuel. Each night she cooked him dinner, remembered recipes from her mother. When business was good, they'd have meat or chicken, which Sarah always made with the crumbs from stale bread, just to make it last longer. Now all this was coming to an end because of her father.

"I won't be any trouble to you."

"You belong to your father, Sarochka."

"I can do more here, I promise."

"You're no longer a child. You're a sixteen-year-old woman now," he said, laughing. "You'll find an American husband. Life will be good for you there."

"Why can't you come, too?" she begged.

"Why can't I come? I'll tell you why. What's a man almost forty going to do in America?"

"But what's here for you?" Sarah couldn't imagine him in his store without her.

"You need to be young for America." Uncle Shmuel leaned back in his favorite rocking chair and sighed. "If I know anything, I know that."

"You can live right near me. I'll watch out for you."

"Ach, Sarochka. You've got your own life. I don't have the money anyway. You need money for America. I'd never even get a passport now."

"Why not?"

"Enough. Your father is sending for you. He's your only parent now. So they let you go there. And you must. America has enough poor Jews from this country. They don't want more." His rocking slowed, the chair coming to a halt. Meanwhile, Sarah gazed outside at the last daylight burnishing the surface of the Prypiat River.

All those years with her mother, waiting for her father to send them the fare, and now it comes, too late, when she doesn't want it at all, Sarah thought. Her mother called him a fool, a nogoodnik, and she was right. But Uncle Shmuel would not let her remain there.

On a brisk November day in 1921, when snow covered town and city alike, they left Ivankov and entered Kiev. Sarah couldn't get over the few trams making their way down the wide streets that had been renamed after the Revolution. On Boulevard Karl Marx, a church stood at the corner with two circular white columns on each side of its grand, oval-shaped doors. Most buildings on Boulevard Marx had three stories to them; on the first floor, Sarah saw stores—markets for meat and bread, another for fruits and vegetables, where a carton of small apples was visible from the window, and then a place to cut hair next to a cobbler and a tailor. The stores were mainly empty; still, the streets bustled with people walking quickly.

"You know I've heard, Sarochka, that the heroes of our revolution live up top on the second and third floors of those buildings in apartments just for them and the good people of our new government." Uncle Shmuel took hold of her hand as they crossed the large boulevard.

Sarah gazed up at the long windows that opened into iron-wrought balconies. "How beautiful they are."

"They say Bolsheviks have repealed all laws banning Jews from the city," Uncle Shmuel said. "We can finally live where we want."

Sarah listened quietly, not quite understanding his words. It was as if she had just awakened from a long sleep and found the world altogether changed. On Boulevard Lenina, they passed more stores with cloth canopies outside.

"Upstairs there the families of Kiev live in one or two

rooms. It's crowded but they manage."

Outside one window, Sarah saw a sign in black letters, Новая Россия, *New Russia.*

Uncle Shmuel pulled her along until they arrived at the station, its wide street covered with snow and ice. Most people came on horses, though there were two lone black automobiles. Sarah and Uncle Shmuel boarded the train, and before they knew it, they were riding over the Dnipo-Slavuta River by way of the Darnitsky Railway Bridge. "It's just opened only a few years ago," Uncle Shmuel said as they sped out of Kiev, passed fields of grass beneath the snow.

They rode for many hours as afternoon turned into evening, then night.

At ten in the morning on the next day, the train pulled into Jonkskis, Lithuania.

"We're near the Belorussian border." Uncle Shmuel tapped her arm.

"How far have we gone?"

"Almost three hundred miles."

Her legs felt heavy; her back ached. Sarah knew the journey still ahead of her was long. They disembarked from the train and entered an official-looking brown brick building. A man with a mustache curling by the edges of his mouth sat behind a desk. Uncle Shmuel opened his wallet and took out some money to pay for the passport.

Before the man handed the document over, he paused, "And tell me," he said, looking intently at Sarah, "Why are you leaving us?"

"I'm going to my father." She didn't like the way the words sounded.

"And your mother?"

"She's dead," Uncle Shmuel intervened.

"I see you're like an orphan here," he said and began to puff on a cigar he took from one of his desk drawers. "And you?" He turned to Uncle Shmuel.

"I'll be returning to Ivankov once she's all set." Uncle Shmuel rummaged through his pockets for another bill. He placed it by the man's large hands.

"Yes, I see. Well . . ." He inhaled his cigar, then exhaled it, until its burnt odor filled the room. "Enough talk." He stamped the passport and dismissed them with a nod of his head.

They hurried to catch another train to Riga, slept overnight again in a pull-out berth, and arrived just a few hours before the *SS Samaria* was scheduled to leave. Her mother had once told her that Lazar had taken a ship from Liverpool to New York. It was hard to believe she would actually transfer in Liverpool to the very same steamer her father had taken to New York years before.

How was she going to say goodbye to Uncle Shmuel? It couldn't be possible she would leave him behind. It was all a terrible mistake caused by her father. She should stay in Ivankov with Uncle Shmuel in his store, cooking for him before they quietly ate their meals together. Sarah looked up at him for what she knew was the last time. His cheekbones seemed to indent inward. Why had he grown so much thinner over the last month?

"It's time." As he spoke, the bells of a church echoed throughout this desolate city.

She threw her arms around his neck, breathed in his tobacco smell. "I'll write you."

"Make your own life, Sarochka."

"You spent all your money coming here with me."

"I'll make more," he said. "Now go." Uncle Shmuel tapped her arm.

Sarah pressed her lips once more against the side of his face; the stubble that had grown over the last couple of days felt like sandpaper against her skin.

"Go," he said.

But she wanted to linger just a little longer with him. "I think—this is a mistake. I don't want to go." Here, she had said it, had blurted out the truth, at least.

"No, Sarochka, you can't do that. You have a father. You must join him now. He's waiting for you. Besides, there's nothing here for you in this country."

"I don't even remember him." There was just a vague picture in her mind of her father in his black jacket and pants, waving to her from far away.

"It doesn't matter." His voice was cold. She had never heard him speak to her like this before.

Sarah had no choice but to obey, to board the *SS Samaria* bound for Liverpool and then New York. She dragged her bag with two dresses, some undergarments and sleeping clothes along the dock and stood behind the others. Sarah sighed, stepping slowly away from Uncle Shmuel. Before she got on the boat, she turned around once more. Uncle Shmuel looked so elegant in his black fur hat. But he didn't seem to see her. She continued to gaze out at the spot where he stood, even as the boat began to sail, until Uncle Shmuel was just a speck against the gray sky.

BEGINNINGS

Lethe

At Sheremetveyo airport
military men
                    ferried us over.
              Power to the revolution,
a large fist clenched,
              Lenin in black clothes
on billboards everywhere.

Two by two
              by windows
rocking back
                    and forth,
learning to forget
what we had never remembered,
until there was only a vague knowing.

The bus driver didn't say much,
just stayed his path by the bow
              along the river
                    to the outskirts
                              of Moscow.

Our two alarms went off at 7 AM the next morning. My clothes were still unpacked, thrown into a blue suitcase, un-zipped on the floor.

From my bed, I saw Paula's pointy thin figure move into the bathroom. She came out three minutes later, fully dressed in navy corduroy pants, loafers, and a button-down shirt.

"You better hurry up. I don't want to be late."

"Okay, okay. I'm coming."

As I showered I felt her outside the door, tapping her foot and waiting for me in our clean but sparse room. There were little towels in there for me to dry myself, but not one of them could be wrapped entirely around any part of me. Just a few more inches would have done the trick. So I took all three large hand towels and tried my best to cover myself up. It didn't really work. Paula just looked downwards and pretended to be busy folding up her clothes in the dresser drawers while I put on my V-neck T-shirt and a black velvet jacket.

"I'm ready. Let's go." I grabbed my belt from the suitcase, glided it through the loops of my pants as we left the room together. "Let's get out of here already."

Outside, more nondescript apartment buildings were being constructed. Black crows flew above me in an oval-shaped sphere of sky.

When the bus came, so many people were squished in

there. It made rush hour in New York look empty. Paula and I pushed our way inside with the others on the line; we poked our elbows, just like everyone else, into the arms of those already on the bus, until we managed to find a place to stand, wedged in between several people and smelling their sweat already.

The bus took us to Kalyshskaya station. I saw in Cyrillic letters the sign, METRO, and then the entrance, two red doors, and once we paid, an escalator took us downwards. Large chandeliers lit up the train station. I had never seen anything like this in my entire life. It was like an underground palace in this place. We walked along a wide entranceway of marble black and white tiled floors; on each side of us were Romanesque-looking archways. Down more stairs, I saw painted tiles on the walls by the tracks that told the story of the revolution, how the czars' palaces had been overrun and given to the people. On another tile, Mayakovsky stood reading his poems to an adoring crowd.

Somehow, we managed to find a seat on the Metro. After several stops, an old woman entered and stood in front of me with a sack of food on her back.

"Here, sit down." I got up but was stopped by her gnarled hand on my shoulder.

"*Devushka,* sit. Sit down," she said sharply. "I'm not tired yet. I haven't yet worked."

We rode the train to station Barricadnaya. "Осторожно, двери закрываются," the conductor's voice boomed. *Be careful of the closing doors.* The people in our car looked exhausted, their bodies bent over. The man beside me smelled like vodka.

As the train entered the station, brown marble walls

came into view. We piled off with the others, crowds of people all going somewhere. I looked up and saw hundreds, no, thousands of tall, slender light bulbs connected to black iron rods zigzagging across the ceiling.

When we left Barricadnaya, a long escalator took us up to the street where a sign, "Lenin Lives," greeted us.

"He seems to live everywhere," Paula said. "I must have already counted five Lenin Lives signs."

"Well, he was important, you know. Did your boyfriend ever mention anything about these subways?"

"Yeah, just in passing," she said and hesitated. "Are you going out with anyone back home?" Her question seemed kind of out of the blue.

"I was, but we broke up. We lasted a whole three months, and that was a while ago. My relationship record has not been great." I still missed Emilio and the month we spent that winter break in his bed, beneath covers most of the day.

"Ah, you'll meet someone else. Just don't get married here. I'm sure you'll get some offers from some Soviet guys desperate to get out of here."

"Don't worry. I won't." I began to like her for the first time. We crossed the wide Moscow streets, filled with identical black cars. On the sidewalks, older women with kerchiefs tied around their heads walked next to younger women wearing short dresses, sheer nylon stockings, and high heels.

Paula and I entered a street bordered by trees on both sides of the road and saw the *Institut Imeni Pushkina,* a brown building with two large doors. In a classroom, Natalia Vladimoravich sat on a folding chair expecting us. She was a plump woman with short blond hair and a nasal voice.

"I will speak to each one of you. Just wait your turn on a chair outside the room," she directed us.

When I finally sat across from Natalia Vladimoravich, whose young face had a double chin, she said, "So tell me about yourself."

I panicked. Such an easy question. I stammered in Russian. "I love the Russian language. My Russian grandmother told me many stories."

"*Raskazala*," she corrected. I got the prefix wrong for the word *told* and said *skazala* instead.

"I want to know this language."

"So, you will try very hard," she said. I could not understand one word, *staratsa,* and would only learn later how to say "try" in Russian. In the meantime, Natalia Vladimoravich noticed the sleepy look in my eyes and put me in the lowest class.

Now that my placement test was finished, I decided to explore the city by myself. On a quiet side street, I entered a *bylochnaya,* or bakery, to buy some sweet rolls. Bread everywhere, dark and white in large bins by women with aprons and loose-fitting dresses falling below their knees. Women filled up their netted bags and gave their money to a plump cashier with one front tooth missing.

Once outside, I walked past shutters of faded yellow buildings. Two old women, walking arm linked through arm, passed by me. I let myself be guided, by what I did not know, along these streets until I was led to the center of the city—Red Square with its gray pavement cobblestones and military men outside everywhere, guarding the city's treasures; the Kremlin, bordered by the Moscow

River, the star of the revolution shining atop its pinnacle on this cloudy fall day. I wanted, right then and there, to tell my father how beautiful the streets were in Moscow. "If you're going to study the language, then do something different from the others. Go there for God's sake," he had said.

So I did. Besides, I had to get away. My father also believed I should forgive Mort after I told him what happened. He does, after all, pay a lot of your expenses, he said. I thought he'd be really mad, but he wasn't. Remembering Mort's wet, soggy lips, I didn't feel very forgiving at all.

I stared at the bold Cyrillic letters, GUM, the largest department store in the Soviet Union, where there was hardly anything to buy, and the historical museum, a stately red brick building across from Lenin's Mausoleum. The military men lifted their legs in unison, their arms rose at the same time, the guns shifted from right to left as they marched silently past the whispering crowds that stood by in a long line. My brother David had all of Lenin's works on his bookshelf. *What Is to Be Done?* A question looming over me. Hey, I wanted to tell him. I dropped out of the fancy, hard-to-get-into college with just a few women, or co-eds, as some of them called us. All the guys had a rod up their ass at that place. I was sick of all these weirdos from Choate and Exeter, skinny, hairless boys ready to take over the world. That was except for Emilio. But it didn't work out with him either.

I was still a lot better off once I got out of there after a couple of years and transferred to UConn. The people were a lot more down to earth—that was for sure.

I entered the dimly lit corridor of the Mausoleum. I

saw Lenin there behind a glass case, lying down in a black suit, black vest and tie, his skin sallow, his eyes closed, a mummy not wrapped up in a closed tomb, but right here on view. It was dark and cold where all the viewers were, like an ancient cave, but light was everywhere in Lenin's makeshift room. He looked so uncomfortable.

This small man lying there, looking like a figure in a wax museum, had somehow determined so much of my grandparents' lives. They had returned in 1931 to the Soviet Union, to the city named for him, with two small children, my mother and aunt, to build a revolution he had led. The sight of his unburied body, pumped up with chemicals, made me stagger out of there. I almost tripped over the cobblestones leading to Ploschad Revolyutsii Metro Station.

Arches and bronze statues of workers and sailors, humble men and women, many of them soldiers and all heroes of the Revolution, decorated the station. I wanted to keep looking everywhere around me. When the train pulled into the station, I didn't notice how large the gap was between the platform and the train, and before I knew it, as I boarded, my right foot fell straight into that hole. I tried and tried to pull my leg out, but there was no way, and in that split second, I imagined the train leaving with my leg; or the train would take me with it, across the platform. I was half in and half out of the train car. I kept trying to lift my leg out, but it was no use. I was sinking into a glove I couldn't get out of.

Soon the train would take off. I looked up at the mosaics, the tiles, the statues of revolutionary heroes and the chandeliers glittering down where I would be dragged. Just as I imagined the doors starting to close, I felt a man grab hold of my arms and lift me out of the dead space between the platform and the train car. For a few seconds, I dangled in mid-air.

Before I could even thank him, he placed me down inside the train and blended in with the hundreds of others inside, so I barely got a glimpse of him, just saw some military men as I grabbed on to a pole, squished my hand there among the sweat of many others and tried to stop shaking.

In the dorm, the concierge at her desk looked up at me as I entered.

I had to face that mirror in the elevator reminding me of my short self, my overweight legs. It didn't seem possible I had almost lost one of them. Just keep going, don't think about it, I told myself. I practically walked into the elevator door as it opened.

"How'd it go today?" Miloz asked. I didn't expect to see him coming out from his room the minute I got off the elevator. He took long strides up to me.

"I'm stuck in the lowest class. As usual. You must have done well?"

"Like I told you, we were forced into learning Russian from when we were little," he said.

"I wish I had started then."

"Not if you had no choice. We all hated it. Anyway, listen, I have some food I bought when we were at Heathrow. I somehow managed to get it in here. Just some pastries."

He was surprisingly clean-shaven. He was large but not fat, with broad shoulders and legs. I figured he was at least ten years older than me.

"Let me make you some tea. You're looking really tired. And we could talk some more." He hesitated for a moment. "Just as a friend, you know."

I didn't find him attractive, but I was still drawn to him. It was already 8 PM, the day had somehow slid into evening, and it was only twenty-four hours ago that the Aeroflot plane had landed here.

"So what do you think?"

His words jarred me out of my trance. I took another look at Miloz. He wore a plaid button-down shirt, brown leather shoes. I was so hungry. I couldn't even remember the last time I had eaten anything. His voice seemed kind, so I said, Yeah, sure, and followed him.

Inside his room there were two single beds, one across from the other. I sat on the one with no sheets on it, just a worn blue mattress; he took the bed with a white sheet thrown over it.

Miloz rummaged through his canvas bag, unstrapped the buckles carefully and took out a paper bag. Two pieces of coffee cake were wrapped in plastic, folded up in paper plates and napkins. His trunk served as a table. In the corner on the windowsill, he boiled water for tea on an electric metal contraption.

"You're certainly prepared."

"In this place, you have to be." Miloz poured the water for tea in styrofoam cups that also came out of his off-white dirty canvas bag, and placed it all beside the two pieces of sweet coffee cake.

I walked over to the trunk, took the tea and cake and returned to the bed opposite him. The cake remained in my lap; the tea rested in my right hand. I sipped it slowly.

"You wear nice clothes," he said, and I glanced down

at my black velvet jacket, white T-shirt and jeans. I figured by now I must look like shit.

"In Poland, everything is, you know, repressed. It's the church. It's Catholicism, and it makes you feel so guilty all the time."

"I'm the opposite from you. I've been wanting to come here for years."

"Why would you want to do that?" He took a large bite of the sugary pastry. "The Soviets have always treated my people like crap."

"My family was from this place. I guess I'm trying to figure something out here, though I'm not sure what."

"Maybe I can help you."

"How?"

"I don't know," he paused. "I'll tell you what," he said, patting the mattress with his hand. "Why don't you come here and sit next to me. I won't even touch you, believe me. We can just sit here and talk, just like this."

"That's okay. I'm fine where I am." I finished the tea and placed the cup on the floor in front of me, moving so the cake in my lap wouldn't fall. Then with the plastic fork Miloz had given me, I started on the pastry. Its sweetness made me dizzy.

I looked at him once more and came to the same conclusion I had reached thirty minutes earlier. He was definitely not good-looking. But I was still drawn to him.

"I hope you find what you're looking for in Moscow," he said.

"I hope so too. It has to do with an ending to a song." I wiped the crumbs off my face with a brown napkin.

"What do you mean?"

"A song my grandmother remembered from her

girlhood. Сижу и играю я на гитаре, я сижу и веселюсь
. . . Про мое горе никто не знает . . . *I sit and play the guitar. I sit happily . . . No one knows my grief.*"

"It's a beautiful song. But why is the singer happy and then full of grief?"

"In all the songs my grandmother sang to me, the singer loves someone who doesn't love him back."

"I see. Come and sit next to me. You can sit right next to me, and I won't even touch you. Come on. What are you afraid of?"

"I'm not afraid of anything." I felt the skin near my mouth twitch and wondered if he noticed it.

"Then come here, Anna. You could sleep right next to me in this bed, and all I'll do is hug you. Believe me, I'm your friend."

I thought of my mother at the train station and wished I had hugged her one more time before I left. I longed for someone to hold me, so I went over to him, plopped down on the bed right next to him.

"You're safe here," he said, his fingers on my back. He kissed me a little, his breath sweet from the pastry.

It had been a while since I had kissed anyone, and it felt pretty good. But then it seemed like I had just gotten up from some strange and awful dream, and I wanted to return to my little narrow bed across the hall.

"I better go."

"How 'bout in five minutes?"

I kissed him once more. He wasn't a bad kisser. I hesitated a moment. But then I knew I had to get out of there. "I'll see you tomorrow. I feel like I haven't slept in days."

"You should stay for just a little bit."

"No, it's late. I really need to sleep." I took my cup and plate, careful not to get any crumbs on the floor. I threw it all in a brown wastepaper basket by the door.

"I'll clean this stuff up."

"It's okay," I said. "I got it."

"It's not even nine o'clock."

"Feels like 3 AM to me." I didn't even know anymore what I was saying. I moved right up to the door and turned the knob. It was locked. "It won't open. Come on. Please get this open for me."

"It must be stuck. That's all. Don't worry, I'll fix it. You need to turn it just right," Miloz said and got up from his bed. But instead of opening the door, he shoved me down with him onto his sheet. "Come on, I know you want to be here."

"What are you doing?" I tried to shout, but my voice ended up as a throaty whisper. He grabbed my wrist, shoved my pants down to my knees. "You want this. I know you do."

"No, I don't," I said. "I don't." Once more I wanted to scream, "What are you doing? You have to stop." But my words sounded faint as his hands pressed against my shoulders. He climbed on top of me, entered, thrusting back and forth, back and forth. He came quickly as I pushed, pushed, tried to push him out of me until he jumped out of the bed.

"Why'd you do that?"

"Do what?"

"You know what I mean."

"I didn't do anything you didn't want. And you know it."

"That's not true."

"You're nothing but a tease."

I was starting to get even more scared. "Listen, you have to get me out of here." I sat, my legs nestled up to my chest, holding myself. I wanted to disappear, to fade into the darkness outside.

"I know, I know." He pulled his pants up, sauntered over to the door, and on the side of the knob, pressed a very small button. I couldn't believe I hadn't seen it. I felt like such a jerk.

Slowly I put on my blue jeans. From the corner of my eye, I saw him by the bathroom sink. I wished I could scrub him off of me. I turned the knob, started back to my own room. From the off-white hallway, settling into the emptiness of just past nine o'clock, I heard him mutter, "Cunt."

When I got to my room, Paula was sitting up in her bed, her head propped against a pillow, reading Lermontov's *A Hero of Our Time.*

"Are you okay?" She put the book down on a sheet too small to cover the entire mattress.

"I'm fine. Just beat. I have to get some sleep." Her eyes glanced down at my suitcase, still unpacked. "I promise. I'll get to this tomorrow."

"Sure. Don't worry about it. You don't look right."

"I really need to sleep." I smoothed my hair back with my fingers. It was sweat-filled, oily. "But first I'm going to shower." I had to clean him off of me.

"Now?"

"I'll be out in a minute." The warm water soothed me as it ran over my breasts and legs. I took the small piece of soap and washed inside of me, but still I felt disgusting.

I hated his smell on me.

I couldn't bear the small towel not quite large enough to wrap around me. I did my best to dry myself off and put on my blue flannel pajamas.

"Since you're ready now, I'll turn out the light," Paula said.

If only she would stop talking. I slipped beneath my blanket. The hard mattress beneath me rubbed against the base of my back.

"There's one more thing I need to tell you. I'm sorry but it's important."

"What?" I groaned.

"Let's be careful what we say when we're in this room. I'm sure it's bugged."

"Okay," I said and turned onto my side. I tried to sleep, but all night long my grandmother visited me in my dreams.

1921-1922

If you could by magic instantly transport a person from your shtetl and set him down in one of the bustling streets of New York, I am sure that he would go crazy. He would under no circumstances be able to understand what was going on around him.

Yitskhok Dov Ayzenshtayn

Sarah sailed for a long while on the River Daugava, and then the sea, before getting to England. The wind bit into her face. She grew sick of the ocean; the choppy currents made her stomach curdle, her head spin.

She could still smell the tobacco on Uncle Shmuel's clothes. Dear Uncle Shmuel. She would never again hear his low-toned voice or watch him move slowly in his small home above his store. Now she was on her way to her father, the one person she wanted to forget.

Would there ever be a day when she woke without this grief, without wishing her mother could appear somehow, some apparition from the ocean, a mist of spray that she longed for? If only she could speak to her once more. And what would she even say? How the heart grows weary from waiting, for what she did not know, only sometimes she wanted to stay cramped up in her little berth, in darkness, rocking to and fro with the movement of the boat.

In Liverpool fog covered the water, the city with its squat, gray factories barely visible in the damp gloom. The air had a chill that never went away. Sarah stayed on the *SS Samaria* while many got off and others boarded; she was one of the few young women who traveled alone. One day became another; she never knew what time it was as she huddled up into herself, her arms wrapped around her knees for warmth.

There were so many sick and pregnant women on the

boat. Would she ever become a mother, have a child in her arms? Such a question made her large breasts feel full, her nipples hardened beneath her soiled shirt. At sixteen, no man had ever touched her, though some had looked, their eyes searching beneath her clothes. Other times she wanted to fade into the ocean, to throw herself overboard (if only it weren't so cold) and find her mother in the water lapping against the ship.

Often at two in the morning she woke and vomited up everything she had eaten that day. Sarah tried to keep to herself, but it wasn't possible. She was surrounded by the smells of illness and nausea.

A young woman, a few years older than Sarah, sought her out to talk to in Yiddish even though Sarah only wished for silence.

"I'm going to my brother. He tells me he lives in a neighborhood with a million couples? How about you?"

"I'm going to my father," Sarah said, noticing the girl's large brown eyes and bushy eyebrows.

"You're lucky. My father died when I was two days old. He left my mother with a bunch of children. She had to go to work. So, the neighbors, they gave me something to eat. I was so sick, just like a dog in the street. I hear they have an orphan home in America for babies and they can adopt you. I was just hard luck, you know."

Why is she telling me all this? Sarah thought. I don't want to tell her one word about my own life.

"My mother had sixteen children. Two sets of twins, and no water, no food, nothing. She used to paint the walls. She used to do that with such swollen feet, for a piece of bread, not even money. But here I am rattling on and on. Tell me, what is your name?"

"Sarah." What if Uncle Shmuel was right and there wasn't anything left for her anymore in Russia, except more hard luck stories like these? The truth was that the moment she got to his store, he was trying to find her father and arrange for her passage to America. Was there something he knew that she did not?

"Well, I'm Ida." Ida rested her face in the palms of her hands. "Ah, Sarochka, my mother was a good woman. She used to come home from a day's work, going around washing walls and different things. When she heard somebody was sick, miles away, she'd go to them and say, 'I'll stay with this sick person and you go to sleep for the night.' In the morning she went to work. Stupid. And your mother, Sarochka, where is she?"

"She died." Would this girl ever stop speaking?

"Ach, my mother too. She worked herself to death and then got herself sick, too." Ida placed one arm around Sarah's shoulders.

Sarah shrank from the woman's touch.

"Tell me, do you have a trade, you know, something you can do here in America?"

She knew how to use the cash register and count money. But that wouldn't really count as a trade. "I don't think so." But then Sarah remembered she could grow potatoes and bring them to a market, and she told Ida about that.

"Well, I don't know about that," Ida laughed. "With a trade, you can make money in America."

"Oh," was all Sarah could muster up to say. She had never given it a second thought, this subject of money, and just figured her father would take care of her. But Ida knew so much more about how the world worked.

"You see, when I was little, my mother sent me to learn a trade. They should teach me to sew, my mother said. But they made a maid out of me. The woman had a baby. I was the nurse.

"So anyway, when I was old enough, I decided I didn't want to be a maid. My mother knew a woman who was a dressmaker. She said, 'Come, do you want to teach her not to be a maid?' The woman said it would be eight dollars, so my mother had to take her shawl. It was a Spanish shawl. It was so pretty. My mother gave it to her. She pawned that shawl for five rubles so the woman could teach me.

"I went to work. I got two rubles a week. You know, eventually, you catch on. They pay you better and better. Then I went and got six rubles a week. And over a long time, I saved to come here."

Sarah only had some coins left from the money her father had sent her. They remained in the pocket sewn into her skirt, a small weight rubbing against her leg.

"I'm so scared. I'm scared of Ellis Island. What if we don't make it through? Every night I pray, Dear God, let me go through. Otherwise, I'll kill myself," Ida said.

"What do you mean, get through?" Sarah asked.

"You haven't heard? They inspect every part of you to make sure you're healthy enough. If they find something wrong with you, you can't stay in America. You don't know that?"

"No, I didn't. Are you sure about this?"

"Look, will you at my left eye. Is it red?"

"Only a little."

"I'm so scared I won't make it through."

The thought had never occurred to Sarah that she

might be sent back to Russia. From behind her the men were chanting, praying. One man called out, *And they went in unto Noah into the ark, two and two of all flesh, wherein is the breath of life.*

"Why that part of the bible?" Ida asked, wrinkling up her face.

"I don't know. I guess he thinks we're being saved."

"Oh."

Now that she saw Ellis Island in the distance, so many majestic buildings connected, and then the main one with all those steeples and the statue of the green lady with a crown, she felt they had to let her stay. She had no words to describe the thrill, the rush of emotions. It was as if she had landed on another planet where boats with windows, someone called them ferries, went back and forth along the harbor, and she saw neatly trimmed bushes, a garden of flowers by the long row of buildings, and behind was the Manhattan skyline, triangular and square, glass and steel all mixed together in a fog that made them seem distant and dream-like.

"Oh, my God," Ida said. "Look at that, will you. It's so beautiful. We're here. Can you believe it? Can you believe it?"

Sarah noticed a mangy dog by the dock. Ah, they have dogs here, too, she said to herself, even if this one looks hungry.

"May luck be with you, Sarochka. Ach, how we both need it," Ida said and went to gather up her bag. But first, she threw her arms around Sarah, kissed her on the cheek. They were surrounded by hundreds of others, it seemed like thousands, all dressed in torn clothes.

"Good-bye," Sarah called to her, but Ida was already

way ahead and did not hear.

Uncle Shmuel, she wanted to call to him, but Uncle Shmuel was nowhere. He was far away in Ivankov, in another land, worlds away. How she wished she could see him even one more time. And her father? How would she ever even recognize him, she wondered and felt herself a stranger in this new land.

Sarah entered a large waiting room with a ceiling so high it made her neck ache to look up. She sat on a bench with others speaking in languages she could not understand. She was scared of the men in blue uniforms barking orders and the doctors who would soon inspect her. The smell of all these unwashed bodies was unbearable. In front of her, Sarah saw the same man from the ship, his long-bearded face huddled over, shaking back and forth as he chanted softly in Hebrew but loud enough for her to hear, "*While the earth remaineth, seedtime and harvest, and cold and heat, and summer and winter, and day and night shall not cease.*"

Sarah proceeded on to a doctor. He looked inside her ear with a sharp-edged light, then pulled her lower eyelids down to peer into her pupils. Her eyes felt so stretched in all sorts of directions that she wanted to cry, but bit her lower lip instead. She felt him noticing her torn skirt, and his gaze made her want to look down at the floor. Strand by strand, he started to inspect every piece of her hair, pulling it, as he made his way from left to right, his hands so rough and calloused.

"What is this?" he muttered to himself when some white powder stuck to his fingers, all sticky and moist. It must have come from her head.

He's going to send me back, Sarah panicked, this man,

the doctor with large veins sticking out of his neck. Then he took out a strange instrument and put the rubber into his ears and listened to her chest. She knew her heart must sound unnatural to him. He squeezed her arms, stared her up and down, stopping for a moment at her breasts until Sarah once more looked away from him.

"You can proceed," he said gruffly and gave her a push at the rim of her neck.

And day and night shall not cease. She repeated to herself the words the old man from the ship had been chanting as she went where she was told, with hundreds of others.

"Your name?" shouted a woman in a white blouse. "Your name, I said." She switched to a broken Russian.

"Obermansky." Sarah wasn't sure at first what the woman wanted from her.

"You're Berman now," the woman said stiffly. There were all sorts of questions about her father, points of departure and entry, her head got so dizzy until the woman stamped Sarah's passport and dismissed her with a nod.

Now she had to find her father. She hated him again as she came out to some holding pen with people shouting. Her eyes squinted from so much light because the fog from several hours before had lifted. *He was no father to me, this man who left and did not turn back, even once.* But where could he be? Sarah looked into the bearded faces of men with dark eyes, grime and dirt all over their arms. She gazed at each one of them. Many held up signs. She only recognized some—Minsk, Bialystok, she knew. She saw no Gornostaypol or Ivankov.

Then she heard someone call, "Sarochka," and other voices shouted names, all blending together. Sarah wondered what happened to Ida but didn't see her anywhere.

"Sarochka." A clean-shaven man elbowed his way through the crowds to her. He wore a round black hat with a rim instead of the caps so many wore in Russia. He was more distinguished-looking and beautiful than she could ever remember.

He had a wide forehead and small mouth, and when his hand took hers, she breathed in a flowery scent. They both just stood there for several moments as the others swarmed by them, knocking against their legs and backs.

"Sarochka," he repeated. He pushed strands of her hair away from her face.

What clothes my father has, with his blue shirt and cufflinks in his sleeves, Sarah marveled as he buttoned up his long wool coat. Her thin black jacket, with a hood kept in place by a black scarf tied around her neck, was stained with sweat. She wanted to hug her father, to wrap her arms around him. But no, she would not.

Together they boarded a small ferry, huddled inside with hundreds of others; he carried her bag. Her legs, her arms were so tired, she could barely move; still, she gasped when she got closer to the view of lower Manhattan. She had never seen such a bridge, her father said it was called Brooklyn Bridge, and so many tall, skinny buildings.

"You didn't get sick on the boat?" He spoke to her in Yiddish.

She shook her head. She wanted to call him Papa, but couldn't.

"Here, you must drink." He handed her a small jug of water. She hadn't before realized how thirsty she was, her throat dry and parched. She wondered once more about Ida. Had she made it through?

"We'll get you something to eat, too. You must be

hungry."

"No." She felt a vague nausea in the pit of her belly and then a bunch of emotions she had no words to describe. She followed where he led.

It didn't take long to arrive at the port in lower Manhattan. The others leaving the ferry pushed and pulled them along. Her father held her hand even more tightly. Hundreds, maybe thousands of people were out on the streets, selling their fruits and vegetables, pots and pans, pillows, sheets, fish and meat—all of them shouting they had the best prices.

She saw a large park bordering the harbor where men stood in booths exchanging foreign currency for dollars, and more merchants brought their wares. "Hey green one," someone called to her.

"Just ignore him," her father said.

The city was a huge marketplace with peddlers every-where. Sarah stepped off the curb with her father. They were surrounded by men with carts of towels and medi-cines in tubes and small bottles. Her father bought a chunk of coarse rye bread from another man on the corner. It was so dry it burned her throat. Sarah felt the hunger in her belly for the first time since her arrival, so she ate it.

For what seemed like an hour, Sarah and her father waded through crowds just to get to Broadway, one block away. Cloth canopies hung over red and brown buildings, and more men lined the streets with their carts, yelling at everyone walking by to come over and inspect their goods. Trains on railroad tracks above the ground made a roaring noise passing by them.

How could a city be so loud, filled with more people than it was possible to count? Her head pounded; everything began to swirl around her. She became dizzy, faint, clinging on to her father as he guided her. It was hard to keep moving. So much to buy, anything you could possibly want, here in New York. But dirt everywhere, paper strewn along the sides of streets. Why didn't people throw their garbage away? And why did that shop have a candy cane design enclosed in glass right in front of it? Next to it, a man with an organ and a monkey on his shoulders stood making music. She wished she could stop for just a moment to listen.

"I'm not Lazar anymore," her father shouted above the voices. "I'm Louis now. You have to take an American name here. So that's what everyone calls me."

She didn't want a new name. She wanted to remain always the same person her mother had called to in the mornings. Besides, this Louis was strange to her in his pressed pants and shined-up shoes.

"We still have to get to Boston," he said.

"Boston?" Could she possibly go any farther?

"I had to get the ticket for you coming into New York. But the trains in America are wonderful."

Sarah glanced up again at the railroad tracks for as long as she could see above all the stores.

"Those are the local trains making stops in the city. But we're going to another state, so we'll ride on something much larger." Her father's smooth hands pointed to the sky.

Sarah was sure she had been awake for more than a day and a night. Her father lifted her into a trolley that glided to their next destination. She had never seen so many people everywhere, moving quickly.

Curled up in a corner by the window, Sarah slept fitfully

on the train. Her head bumped into the glass, and she'd wake up for a few seconds, wonder where she was; her head, arms, and legs were heavier than ever before. Her father sat awkwardly beside her, but thank goodness, Sarah thought, this sleep would fill the silence between us.

"Your Uncle Shmuel—" her father began to say, after about an hour on the train.

Sarah opened her eyes to face her father. So elegant he was in his fine clothes. She hated to admit he was the most handsome man on the train.

"How is he, you know, Uncle Shmuel? I've been wondering."

The strange part was that she had no memory of her father and Uncle Shmuel ever together. In her mind, they were separate, belonging to different and faraway worlds.

"But you never even knew him." Her father must be trying to trick her, she felt.

"Of course, I did." Louis coughed to clear his throat. "Well, how was he before you left Russia? From time to time he came to Gornostaypol from Ivankov for a short visit. But you don't remember, I see."

"Uncle Shmuel did everything for me after my mother—" She hesitated and said no more.

"I thank God his letter found me. We'll always be together now." Her father leaned back on the seat. He ran his finger over the fold in his pants to make sure the crease had taken firm hold. His fine clothes were unruffled by the wind.

Was he saying this to make himself feel better? Could he possibly mean these words? Or was he just lying again? From the window of the train, she saw a cemetery that went on for many miles.

"There is something I need to tell you, Sarochka."

Sarah stared out at all those dead beneath the stones and wondered if they were at rest beneath the earth. Or did they, too, long for water?

"You'll find a wonderful brother and baby sister in your new home."

She had never considered there were children. Never. How could she be so stupid, so foolish, the dead whispered to her as the train whizzed by them.

"Some years ago, I took another wife." Sarah's left eye hurt. So her mother had been right when she had screamed *Your father must want a new wife,* and Sarah hadn't believed her, had thought it could not be true. What an idiot she had been.

"Nothing, Sarochka, you must understand, happened the way I once planned."

Sarah turned further away from her father. She didn't want to look at his well-shaven face or his finely cut nails. Did Uncle Shmuel know? Yes, of course, he did and never told her. But how could he have known and not warned her?

"You have a new family now," her father said gently. She would not say one word back to him. From the window, she saw black smoke coming out of factories.

"But for now, we have to get you some American clothes," he said. "You look like a greenhorn just off the boat." Those were the last words she heard before she fell asleep, her head leaning into the glass pane.

Her father woke her when they got to Boston. From there they took a local train to Roxbury, where rows and rows of wooden houses built close together, with long rectangular front doors, lined the streets. Sarah looked but did not see any chickens or goats, no Guilopyat or Prypiat Rivers, no store with Uncle Shmuel loading up his shelves with flour and bread. Instead, she clung onto her father's arm, too weak to take another step. So he pulled her along. How many days had she worn this awful skirt, this soiled blouse, she wondered, and breathed in her own sour smell. She wrapped her black scarf round her neck and face. Sarah was used to cold, but still every part of her was shaking as she approached her father's home on a December day in 1921, her fingers chapped and almost frozen.

A round woman, with dark hair pulled back in a bun, opened the door. She had an unusually large chest, Sarah thought, and a face like a dog. Before Sarah could even say hello, she vomited all over the brown wooden floor.

"Oh, my God, will you look at this mess," the woman gasped.

Sarah wanted more than anything to disappear. The stink was unbearable.

"Sadie, you'll clean this up, while I get Sarah settled?" Sarah thought his question sounded more like a command. Her father led her to a small room off of the kitchen, where a baby girl with dark curly hair lay sleeping in a crib and a boy, she figured he was about six, rolled a bunch of marbles on the floor. Two single beds lined up against the wall, one after the other.

"Who is this, Papa?" The boy wrinkled up his brow and spoke, like his parents, in Yiddish.

"This is your new sister, Sarah. And this, Sarochka, is your brother, Ben."

"How long will she be staying?" Ben, a skinny child with freckles on his nose and cheeks, looked Sarah up and down.

"For forever. But now she needs to rest, so you must take your toys and yourself out of here," he said to his son.

"Why?" The boy stomped his foot and folded his arms across his chest.

"You must listen to me now. Come on . . . out of here. Your sister has come here from very far away."

"I don't see why I have to," he said, gathering up his marbles and starting for the door.

Sarah didn't have the energy to say one word to him. She closed her eyes and fell asleep. When she woke, she figured many hours had gone by. Outside the window, it was only darkness. Sweat covered Sarah's arms and legs; even her hands were wet.

By the door, Sarah saw the same severe-looking woman; clearly her father's wife, with the baby girl in her arms whimpering for something, then stopping for a second or two, before crying.

"Maybe she's hungry," Sarah said weakly.

"No, that's not it," the woman replied. "It's time for her to sleep." She stroked the baby's back and placed her gently in the crib. "This is Elena. See how she's quieted down now."

"She's pretty," Sarah said.

"Yes, she is. I hope you'll be some help in taking care of her."

"Sarochka." Her father appeared in the doorway. "I see you've met Sadie, your new mother."

His words brought back the queasy feeling in the pit of her belly. Sarah forced herself to sit up in the bed, her arms still shivering. When the tips of Sadie's bony fingers extended rather formally, touched Sarah's hand, she knew she would never be welcome there.

In the morning, Sarah woke to Ben's face just a few inches away, peering intently at her.

"Hello," she said. He must have just gotten up, too, Sarah thought. His breath smelled like unwashed sheets mixed with stale urine.

"How come you're here?" he asked.

"You're quite a big boy," she replied and took his hand. He quickly pulled away from her.

"Is it true that you'll be here forever?" His question made her wonder how long she could remain in this cramped little room with that awful woman in charge of the house.

"No, I don't think so. Actually, I'm sure I won't be. I come from a faraway . . . "

"Good, that's all I wanted to know," he said and skipped away.

When she opened her door and entered the kitchen, she found an egg and a piece of toast on a plate for her. Sadie bustled around in a tight-fitting apron, washing up the dishes, drying them and then putting them away. Sarah couldn't believe the water magically rushing out of two spouts into a large sink.

"Good morning." Sadie turned for a moment to face her.

"Good morning," Sarah replied timidly.

"This is what we have for breakfast in America." Her father guided her into a chair. "Eat up. We have to make you strong."

Sarah had not realized how hungry she was until she ate every bit of food offered to her. Her belly still felt empty, but she didn't dare ask for anything else.

But her father seemed to notice everything. "Here, more bread for you." He stood up and took out a loaf of bread wrapped up in paper decorated with red, yellow, and green balloons. He sliced a couple of pieces for her. Sarah wondered what the festive-looking English print covering the bread said.

"Look at her, will you. After her first sleep in America, she's regained her beauty already."

"Yes, I see." Sadie wiped up the crumbs with an old cloth. Beneath Sadie's apron, Sarah admired her loose dress that tightened around her waist and fell mid-way down her calves. If only her face wasn't so terrible to look at, Sarah thought, as she finished up her food.

"Are you done now?" Sadie reached for Sarah's plate.

"It looks like you've licked it clean," her father smiled.

"Yes, the girl can certainly eat," Sadie said, dropping the plate into the sink.

At night during the next several weeks, after the baby had gone to sleep and the house was quiet, Sarah usually remained in her room to watch over her little half-sister and brother. Just a few hours earlier, her father had returned home from his tailor shop. He knocked two times on the door before opening it, poked his head inside, and said, "Sarochka, how are you?" His greeting eased some of her loneliness away.

"Fine, Papa." She had even started to address him as her father. Her anger had been replaced by fear. She knew no one in this country. The streets were large with such skinny sidewalks. If she walked alone, she might get lost. And Sadie—well, Sarah did her best to stay away from her.

Baby Elena slept peacefully, her little hand clung on to her teddy bear. Sarah loved to hear her soft little snores. But Ben did not want to speak to her.

"She's a beautiful girl. She should marry," Sarah heard Sadie say from behind her closed door after all the dinner dishes had been washed. Her father and Sadie sat in the kitchen drinking tea.

"Yes, she is. But why the rush? She's only just here."

"Okay, but what's she going to do with herself here? Another mouth to feed is hard on us."

"She doesn't eat much," her father said.

"That's not the point. Look here, will you. Every month we're just a little short. Don't you see how hard this is on the others? Ben will have to wear his shoes with the hole in them this winter."

Sarah heard the clanking sound of her father placing his teacup down into its matching plate.

"Besides, I didn't know you had a wife and child still in Russia when I met you. You were just a few months off the boat. You told me, I thought, everything there was to know about you."

So that dog of a woman had taken her father away from them, convinced him to send her mother a notice of divorce, Sarah now understood. She bit down hard on her lip until the blood dripped out onto her chin.

"Okay, but at least I did right by you," her father said as Sarah leaned closer to the door to hear him.

A few days later Sadie announced to Sarah, "Next week there'll be a big dance at the community center. It's good for you to go."

Sarah spent her days inside her mind as morning moved languidly into afternoon, then evening. She liked to sit on the rocking chair in the living room, staring out the window at the other small houses across the street.

"Did you hear what I said? About the dance?"

"Yes." Sarah stopped swaying back and forth in the chair and looked up at Sadie. "I did." She wished that woman would not raise her voice so much.

"So, you're going?"

"Yes, I'll go." Sarah noticed how the left side of Sadie's mouth curled downward.

"It will be good for you, Sarah. You're a young woman. You shouldn't be inside all day doing nothing." Sadie pulled her housedress down until it clung closer to her round body. "Yes, you need to get out a bit. I know what I'm talking about. I was once young too, you know."

That was hard for Sarah to imagine.

On the afternoon of the dance, Sadie washed and primped and perfumed Sarah. Sadie even lent her one of her green, low-cut dresses, something she used to wear. "So you can show off your figure a bit."

Sarah peered at herself in the long, narrow mirror attached to the closet door and didn't like the way Sadie's dress fit her snugly around her chest and waist.

"You look beautiful, Sarochka. Like a real American girl," her father said, entering the room.

She didn't believe him. Her nose was long and narrow, her brown eyes too large for her face.

"You don't look like you're some green one off the boat anymore with my nice dress on you."

Sadie's high-pitched voice made the gray December

day even duller. Sarah didn't want to go to this dance, but she had no choice. She had to go, to do what she was told.

The truth was Sadie scared her. Sarah knew she had better do what Sadie wanted. She didn't want to find out what would happen if she refused. Besides, Sadie seemed everywhere at once— cleaning and dusting, sorting papers, making notations of expenses, Sarah figured, in a black book that Sadie called her ledger book.

"Come, I'll walk you over," her father said. Outside they stepped silently.

From far away Sarah heard the sounds of a dog barking as she moved with her father along the darkening streets.

He left her at the door of the Roxbury Hebrew Center. At first, Sarah stood on the sidelines of the hall with the other young women, who were dressed, for the most part, in cheap lace dresses. On the whole, the men were an unattractive bunch. They wore black pants and white shirts that fit awkwardly on their lanky bodies. Sarah noticed the dirt beneath their fingernails, the way they smelled of the ocean even after they were washed and scrubbed.

The first dance Sarah sat out on a folding chair. From behind her, Sarah heard someone say the name of the song filling the room was *I Ain't Got Nobody*. She understood none of the lyrics but liked the lively beat of it. Other girls here seemed to know each other. None of them spoke to her. Besides, she hated her dress, cut so low and in such a loud green color. She folded her arms above her chest so no one could see too much of her.

When the waltz was about to start, Sarah saw a man, just a bit younger than her father, dressed in orange pants and a green shirt that oddly matched her dress. He had large, muscular arms and walked right up to her. She felt his eyes on her neck and face; his gaze rested for a moment on her breasts, then moved to her small waist. What a good-looking man he is, she thought, and laughed when she saw he wore a gray sock on his left foot and a brown one on the other.

He smelled of a sweet cologne and said his name was Leon Vitsky. It all happened so quickly. When Leon placed his arm around her waist for the waltz, his other hand on her shoulder, Sarah felt her legs tremble. His breath had a nice, minty scent. In all of her seventeen years, she had never experienced anything like this before. His fingers were gentle, did not press into her skin. Sarah wanted nothing more than to follow anywhere he led.

She imagined the way his body must look beneath his clothes, chiseled and hardened from work. Such thoughts made her blush.

"Do you come dancing much here?" Sarah tried to think of something to ask him.

"Sometimes." He trailed his finger up her arm. She wanted to drop her head into his chest and rest there.

"I'm here two months." One word would lead to another, Sarah thought, and keep him by her.

"Ah, you're still a green one," he smiled. "You need someone to show you the ways here."

Yes, you are right, she thought. But she didn't say anything.

"Thirteen years here—from near Minsk, I came." Leon pushed a strand of his dwindling hair away from his forehead.

"Oh, you're here such a very long time."

"Yes, I am what is called an expert on America."

"I'm from Gornostyapol." Sarah admired once more his broad shoulders. She even liked how at the back of his head a slight bald spot had started to form.

"Well, now you've found a new home," Leon said, as he pulled her closer into his arms.

Six weeks later, Sarah was engaged to be Leon Vitsky's wife.

As for Leon, most who knew him were shocked at his sudden marriage.

"What about your girl, Rezha? Two years you go with her and she's sick one night. So, you go to the dance without her, then drop her like that?" Leon's sister, Rose said.

"I never felt this for Rezha."

"You're old enough to be Sarah's father, Lenya."

"I'm old enough to know what I want."

"But what do you need with such a young girl? And right off the boat? Why don't you get an American girl?"

"I can't afford an American girl," he said. "Besides, I want this girl."

"Okay, okay. I wish you many long years of happiness," Rose said.

Baby Elena marked the occasion of Sarah and Leon's marriage by taking her first steps, while Ben wore a suit that Louis made especially for the wedding.

Maybe, just maybe, Sarah told herself, life might begin anew for her.

MOSCOW, 1980

Once

there was no time
a journey to the dead,
a dimly lit airport at night
guards with their guns
to one side
fingers on a glass

there was no future
only what had become before
        its terror

I wanted to speak
after arriving
words in a place
beyond words
so silent
shipwrecked
        beyond time

Rosh Hashanah the Jewish New Year, Rosh Hashanah the beginning of my own new year, coming home to myself on the dark wide streets of Moscow.

On Rosh Hashanah, in the late afternoon, Barry and I gathered in front of the bus stop, across the street from the dormitory for foreign students, surrounded by diggers in the soil and clusters of brown apartment buildings that were all similar in tone and style. He had already found Volodya, a Russian guy, a friend, he said, to take us to the one synagogue in Moscow on Rosh Hashanah eve. Volodya had a scruffy beard, barely formed. Stray pieces of hair grew out of his face. He wore a denim jacket that matched his denim pants. Volodya took large steps, jumped off the mound of grass where we met and landed on the sidewalk.

"*Poshli,*" Volodya said and led us onto the crowded bus. Just like yesterday, we poked and pushed to find a space, my face shoved into a man's armpits covered up by a light black jacket. At Kalyshskaya Station we took the Metro to the center of Moscow, not far from the Kremlin.

Volodya found us a place to eat—a stand-up café with several tables where we could order a *buterbrod* or sandwich and coffee that always came with sugar and milk. A round Russian woman gave me a piece of white fish on a bite-size piece of bread. I also bought a small, sweet apple.

"Hey Volodya," I called to him once we were outside. "Can you tell me why everyone is staring at my boots?"

"They figure you must be a rich foreigner to wear such leather boots," Volodya said and paused for a moment. "Anna, can you help me, please? I have a favor to ask you." He spoke just loud enough for me to hear, slowing down so Barry would naturally walk in front of him.

"You know, we can't get books here. Good books, I mean literature. It's all banned, forbidden, unavailable to us. But you can buy them with your dollars in a special store where only foreigners are allowed to shop. I'll pay you everything back in rubles."

"If I can help you, I will . . . but I'm not doing anything illegal."

"Of course not. This is legal. You are simply buying me books, giving me a present. You will help me . . . Yes?"

"Okay, okay." I didn't even realize what I was saying. I just wanted to get him away from me. He was so pushy, and I was worried. The group leaders had warned us that using dollars and exchanging them for stuff for Soviet friends could be against the law, even though everyone was probably doing it.

"We'll talk about this another time," Volodya said, catching up to Barry. We soon reached a corner where hundreds of people had gathered outside the only synagogue in Moscow.

"I have to go. I have an appointment to keep," Volodya said. "We'll see each other again." Soon he was nowhere and everywhere in the crowd of men with large black hats, black pants, and women with dresses just below their knees.

"What was that about?" Barry asked.

"He wants me to buy him some books."

"At the Beriozka?"

"Yes, if that's the store that only takes foreign money."

"That's it. It's really pathetic. All the great writers have simply disappeared from the shelves of regular bookstores. Just be careful."

Barry took off to meet several friends of Sasha, his fiancé, by the white steps of the synagogue. I had someone to see, too. Before I left for Moscow, Professor Jay Cohen, my Russian teacher from my university in Connecticut, asked me to deliver a book to a friend of his, Maxim Belonsky, a children's writer he had met in Moscow two years before. Professor Cohen said that no books, not even a letter could get through to Moscow, so he gave me a thin book for kids that could slip easily into my suitcase and a number to call Belonsky.

Yesterday I dropped my coins into a phone booth across the street from the dorm. The coins came out of the phone booth slot, so I just pushed them back in. With the glass doors shut behind me, I barely managed to breathe in there.

"Ето не работает," a man outside shouted to me. *It doesn't work.*

A few blocks away, there was another booth. More coins slid into a silver phone. A voice on the other side brusquely answered, "Да."

In Russian I managed to tell Maxim about my teacher, how I had something, and Maxim interrupted me before I could say anything more. We bantered back and forth about how and when we would meet, and then he asked me about Friday. I said I'd be at—I didn't want to say the word synagogue, so I stumbled over the name of the street,

Bolshoy Spasogolinischevsky, and he said, "Perfect."

"My son Iosif will be there. Stand by the doors at 7 PM and he'll find you."

"How will he know who I am?"

"Don't worry. He'll know."

I still had thirty minutes before I would meet Iosif. I didn't see how he would find me. I tied the scarf I brought with me from New York around my face—pink on calico cloth. There were crowds I needed to wade through, stairs to climb. I entered the Choralnaya Synagogue and went up the stairs where the women were. No empty seats anywhere. Even the aisles were filled with women standing. Downstairs, I saw all the men. The rabbi stood several feet from the cantor, both of them singing Hebrew melodies I could not decipher.

After ten minutes, I wanted to leave the hordes of people and be outside once more. I slipped through the spaces in between women, down a whole lot of stairs and out the door. I looked for Barry, but I didn't see him, so I meandered through the crowd and looked into faces. A few men stared at me and refused to glance away.

At nearly 7 PM I went to the synagogue steps once more. Men and women came in and out of the two wide doors. I knew Maxim Belonsky was right when a young guy came right up to me and said, "You must be Anna?" I glanced down at my brown leather boots and woolen red skirt. All the women around me wore high heels or simple pumps.

He was tall and thin with dark, large eyes, black hair—quite beautiful. I couldn't believe my Russian teacher had brought him to me.

Iosif spoke to me in an English marked by round o's and flattened r's. When I told him I had something for his father, he said, "You do? But wait. Let's walk." We moved down the white steps onto the cobblestoned street filled with hundreds of people, and there in the midst of the crowd, I handed him a book called *The Enormous Crocodile.*

"What a gift. My father could never find this here. Really, you can't imagine how happy he will be." Iosif placed the book in his fake leather bag strung over his shoulder.

As we walked, the noise of the crowd seemed to disappear. Even though there were hundreds of people jammed into the street, it seemed as if we were quite alone. Our meeting felt like a reunion from a time I could no longer remember.

"I'm glad I saw my father yesterday, and he told me to find you here. You see, I live with my mother, and we don't have a telephone. The area has not been wired yet for service."

"How can that be? Your country can land a man on the moon but not everyone here has a telephone?" I asked.

"Nothing much works in this place. Have you noticed?"

"I've only been here three days."

"Everything is broken. Nothing, absolutely nothing works," he said. "You'll see for yourself soon. But let's talk of something different. Tell me," and he switched from English to Russian. "Where are you studying in Moscow?"

"*Institut Imeni Pushkina* for foreign students." I looked up at his tall and graceful body. I wanted to keep walking with him for as long as possible.

"How long have you studied the language?"

"Four years before I came here." It was the usual conversation opener. I had practically memorized my responses.

"You speak so well."

"Not really. This is all I know how to say. But tell me, what do you do in Moscow?" I didn't want to run out of Russian words, to have our conversation ended.

"Mainly I give English lessons. I started studying English when I was eight years old in school. But I have so little practice speaking."

All of a sudden, the crowd parted. Someone was driving a black car full speed down the street. The Jews rebounded from the curb and chased after the car, forcing it to slow down. A few threw stones at the fender, then climbed onto the trunk, hurling whatever objects they could find. Even windshield wipers became a weapon as hands grabbed hold of them and tried to separate the metal from the car window.

"Welcome, welcome to the Soviet Union," Iosif laughed. Slowly the car made its way down the street and disappeared.

"Weren't you frightened?"

"Yes, of course, I was. But we're used to it. You see how many people fill this street. Yet the government refuses to close it."

In a few moments, everyone gathered in groups as before.

"Now they close the street. But it always comes too late," Iosif said.

We walked back to the six white columns of the synagogue, to its majestic silver dome, where Barry stood with his newly found friends.

"Привет," Iosif smiled. All the bitterness in his face disappeared, replaced by some joy and wish to celebrate.

"You know them?" I asked.

"Yes, we're a small group in Moscow. Young religious Jews . . . not many of us here. Let me introduce you to Nadezhda. Hopefully, she won't become our next very favorite Refusenik. You know what that is, don't you?"

I didn't say anything.

"Well, let me explain it to you this way. Nadezhda's parents filed their papers to leave this country. Next thing that happens is they both lose their jobs, and so they are forced to sell what they can just to survive. Hopefully, it will all turn out for them and the letter will arrive granting them permission to leave. But if not, and they are denied an exit visa, they officially join the Refusenik ranks."

"So, then what can they do?"

"File again. What else can they do? But come, you must meet her."

Nadezhda had thick black hair down to her shoulders and a skirt that fell just below her knees.

Once Iosif introduced us, she threw her arms around me, as if she had known me forever. "But wait," Iosif said and pulled me in another direction, introducing me to a woman with short-cropped brown hair. "There's someone else I want you to meet. This is my cousin Tanya. We've grown up almost like brother and sister." Before I could say more than hello to Tanya, Nadezhda announced we were all going to a friend's house and led us down the cobblestoned street, away from the synagogue.

Barry and I followed down dimly lit streets that narrowed and forced us to step two by two on the sidewalk until we came to a gray building. Upstairs we entered an apartment filled with smoke and flowered trays of bread, cheese, potatoes, and cakes. Iosif disappeared into a misty part of the room. But all night long I kept my eyes on him.

In the corner of the apartment, an elfish-looking young man played the guitar. His fingers strummed and plucked his instrument. I didn't understand the words, could only follow the sounds winding into a continuous thread of melodies that spoke to me of wandering for many years in search of a home.

A tiny old woman, her white hair tied in a bun, offered the guests dark chocolate cake cut into thin layers. "Ешь, девушка," she said and handed me a piece. "Where are you from?" she asked in Russian.

"New York."

"Ah, New York," she sighed.

"But my grandfather was from Minsk."

"And your grandmother?" she asked.

"From a small town outside of Kiev."

"We wait each day for the permission or refusal to leave this country. My husband and children . . . we all wait. Your grandparents were smart to leave when they did," she said and moved with her cakes away from me.

A man with black greasy hair all awry, his glasses down his nose, sat in the center of the room. "You must understand," he said and turned to Barry and me. "We are afraid in this country. It gets tighter and tighter. You must understand because we believe life is going to get even worse for us here."

He seemed to speak to document the moment here in Moscow, wanting us to understand the loss of hope that forms deep lines on many faces.

His words continued to repeat in my mind as Barry and I made our way back to the Metro taking us to Kalyshskaya Station, and then boarded a bus to Ulitsa Volgina, dom shest. Street lamps bordered an occasional car on the road before all went dark on the path leading us to the dorm.

GET READY, WE'RE GOING BACK TO THE USSR: 1925-1931

And now it was as if the light had been extinguished in that night window, and reality had turned into memory.

Andrey Platonovich Platonov, *The Third Son*

For a short time, they were happy, but it did not last. While Leon worked at the docks as a carpenter, Sarah liked to sit on the bench outside Moishe's Delicatessen and watch the people go by. Sophie Goldman, dressed in a red kerchief wrapped around her head and tied beneath her chin, came in every day. Cookie, her neighbor, had a slight limp, a stooped back, and always ordered white fish; while Boris Cooperman, a large man with a sagging belly known as the sage of the neighborhood, would brag about his days in the Czar's prison when he was arrested for revolutionary activity in Russia. Only a big fat bribe got him released so he could flee the country, as long as he promised not to ever return. He longed to see the worker's state. But an accident at the docks had left him lame; now he could never go back.

Sometimes Boris sat on the bench next to Sarah with a cigar, the smells of his smoking blending with the odors of fish and meat.

A mother scolded her child for running too close to the street. The sun collided with pavement, reminded Sarah of the light on windows, and the quiet that precedes sound when glass is forced suddenly to shatter. She knew they had thrown her mother's body deep beneath the water.

She should go home and clean her house. The clothes from yesterday were lying on chairs, the breakfast dishes with thick layers of syrup, crusts of French toast, tossed into the sink.

The melodies always arrived in the morning when she sat in front of the Delicatessen, next door to Ida's Bakery on one side and Grossman's Butcher Shop on the other. Sarah just had to listen and wait until she could see her mother rise up, it seemed, out of the hot pavement, singing songs of love that would never be returned. She remembered the five dollars in an envelope for her mother. Five dollars from America, from her father—five dollars and a letter of divorce.

"Cookie, don't forget you owe me for the fish from last week, too," Moishe told the old, stooped woman.

The morning went by quickly when Sarah sat outside the delicatessen, humming her mother's songs. Still, she must go home. First, there was the marketing, then getting dinner ready for the two of them. She would make meatballs stuffed with some breadcrumbs and spaghetti. Uncle Shmuel always loved that dish. Dear Uncle Shmuel. She had written to him about her marriage. He sent a small, ceramic statue of a girl holding roses; it once belonged to her mother. Today Sarah knew she would see all afternoon the torn letter from her father, the envelope ripped open, and her mother in a gray dress crouching on the wooden floor.

At twenty, Sarah was going to have a child. Everywhere she looked, whether it was a clothing store, or the canopy rafters hanging over Bernie's Dry Goods, and especially it seemed in the still air hanging over this Roxbury street in August, Sarah saw her own mother. It was lonely in America. She missed Uncle Shmuel, his strong tobacco smell in his clothes and on his skin when he kissed her cheek to say goodbye to her.

She better go home and start her cooking. He always came back from work so hungry. A whole loaf of bread her husband could eat.

At first, most nights, they were busy finding one another beneath woolen blankets.

But now it seemed they had little to say to each other at the dinner table. Sarah noticed how Leon would look askance at the clothes strewn throughout rooms, wondering what she must be doing all day. He did not, and could not, understand such sadness.

Five years later, he still did not understand how when their first daughter was born, Sarah stayed in bed all day long, unable to do anything. Even when Leon's mother died from such a strange illness, and his father was robbed and murdered near Minsk, even then no one ever took to their beds. His sister Rose saved him. He didn't know how to care for a newborn baby and a wife who couldn't even lift her head off her pillow. So Rose stayed with them until Sarah was better. At least with their second daughter, Sarah didn't fall apart like that again.

There were times she'd seem a little better. Leon might even hear her singing to the girls. The house would be neater, no clothes all over the floors and dishes unwashed in the sink. Just when Leon was convinced Sarah was finally happier, he'd come home from work and find her on a rocking chair, her head down, her fists hitting the side of her face.

"Lenya, we have to get Sarochka to a doctor. Something is very wrong. They have doctors in this country for everything, even sadness," Rose said. His sister said to go, and they did. What did he know of such things? You do what you have to do to survive. This had been his way of thinking ever since his father disappeared in the woods by Kolpenitsa, killed by roaming thieves many years ago. When he came to this country in 1909, they wanted to make him a boxer, so impressed they were with his strength. But he wanted no part of it. He didn't spend all those years apprenticing to be a master cabinetmaker to spend his time in a ring taking punches.

Rose sat with him in the waiting room, knitting a blanket for his daughters, while Dr. Myerson examined Sarah behind his closed doors. The clicking of Rose's needles made him think of a grandfather clock with wings, taking him back so briefly to their small town of Baronovich. He and Rose had always been close. Even after they all had become orphans, as the eldest brother and a newly anointed thirteen-year-old man, Leon kept a careful eye on her, made sure no one got fresh, especially in their family tavern.

Leon crossed and uncrossed his legs, folded and unfolded his arms, unused to so much sitting in a room of black leather seats and a round clock on the wall. For so long he had saved and scrimped to just get a little ahead. But then 1929 came, and what little anyone had disappeared. And he was one of the lucky ones scraping together a meager living as a carpenter. To make matters worse, now his wife had taken to her bed again. If he asked her what was the matter, she said nothing.

It's the corruption of capitalism that's made her feel so miserable, Leon concluded. Who wouldn't be sad in such a country where the rich own everything? These days everybody was going somewhere else looking for work. The papers said it was twenty-five percent unemployment, but it had to be more. So Rose and her family got all the way to California. They scraped up their last cent for the journey. But there was nothing there either. They arrived at the edge of the country, and six months later they turned right around and came back to Roxbury. Thank goodness for that. He didn't know what he would do without her living near him.

Often, he got up at dawn and walked past mothers and fathers already out on the streets, their children begging. They held out a tin cup and pleaded for some change, their faces dirty, their eyes large with hunger.

There were muffled voices, doors closed and opened, and then Dr. Myerson, dressed in an elegant gray suit, called them both into his office. Sarah stayed outside in the waiting room. Leon noticed his medical degree, an all-white piece of paper in a frame, from a place called Cornell. Some big shot he must be.

For a few moments, no one said a word. Then Dr. Myerson cleared his throat and spoke so softly, Leon strained to hear what he was saying.

"Your wife suffers from melancholia."

Leon wanted to know why this Dr. Myerson had to use such a big word.

"Melancholia comes from the Latin, you see, and refers to a pathological state of despondency," Dr. Myerson said. Leon glanced over at his sister, both of their brows wrinkled up at the same moment.

"This means a state when someone is severely depressed," Dr. Myerson continued.

Yes, I know all that about my wife, Leon thought. "But

what can we do, Dr. Myerson?"

"Nothing." Dr. Myerson said, running his fingers through his receding hair.

"Nothing can be done?" Rose repeated his words.

"Just be nice to her." Dr. Myerson scratched his finely shaven goatee.

Leon wondered why the doctor appeared to be looking directly at him. He saw the dirt beneath his fingernails and hid his hands in his lap.

"You see, we have no medicines to cure what she has seen, all she has lost. Just kindness."

The fancy doctor cannot help us, Leon knew. It was no use.

"She needs to rest, eat regularly, of course. Balance is crucial," Dr. Myerson said. "But consideration is most important."

Dr. Myerson coughed a few times, straightened his handkerchief in his suit jacket pocket, a signal that made Leon and Rose understand their consultation was now formally over.

Later that day, Leon and Rose met to take a short walk together. They passed so many houses, dilapidated from disrepair, and groups of men just milling around with nothing to do. They both agreed that Dr. Myerson was a disappointment.

"What did he mean, just be kind to her? Tell me, Rose. That's all the doctor could come up with for Sarah?"

Leon imagined that Dr. Myerson must eat his breakfast of a single egg and toast at 7 AM each morning, and then take a sandwich for lunch promptly at 12:30, so he could begin his evening meal by 7 PM. No doubt he went to bed at the same time each night as well, so the good doctor could keep his life regular and balanced, as he said.

"I don't know what to say. He's a big shot, after all, with all those degrees. If you ask me, he wears too much starch in his shirt."

"Does he think I'm actually not nice to her?" With his nail, Leon picked away a soft piece of bread that had lodged in his side tooth.

"Of course not. You're doing your best with a wife in constant mourning."

Leon Vitsky decided after his meeting with Dr. Myerson that he had to get his family out of Roxbury, Massachusetts and back to the Soviet Union. This was the solution to Sarah's melancholia and the larger problem of capitalism's disintegration, he told himself. It was more than Sarah's mood. Only last week, thousands and thousands of people marched on City Hall in New York City demanding "Work or Wages," chanting their words until the police came on mounted horses, trampled so many men, women, even children, beating the demonstrators' heads with their clubs. Leon read the newspapers over and over again, couldn't believe the blood running down faces, the bodies crumpled up on the ground, all because the people demanded work. And if there's no work, then let them get some kind of money until they can find work, so they can eat, feed their family, live their lives with a bit of dignity.

The first socialist revolution had occurred in his beloved homeland, one of the poorest, most backward countries in the world. Just imagine. A worker's state, a place of freedom, equality for all citizens. Leon felt dizzy when he thought of it. Not just Sarah, but all of them, needed to be in a place where there was hope for the future.

In the evenings, after a day's work hauling and lifting, pounding and sanding, Leon often sat in a cigar-filled room with the other men and discussed their situation. Circumstances were clearly getting worse. They were lucky to get a few days' work a week, to scrape together a little food, lucky even to get used to never having enough. The Yiddish papers, the socialist dailies, and the *Daily Worker* all said life was different in the Soviet Union. The five-year plan was underway. And there were jobs for all, plenty to eat for everyone.

The Communists were the only ones doing anything for them, the men agreed. They organized the demonstration demanding wages or work, created unemployment councils throughout the country. Nobody else demanded the government step up and help them out. After all, they were men, not dogs.

Now he had to convince Sarah of his plan. It would be no easy task. He knew, was absolutely sure, she had to feel better there.

Leon came to her one evening after dinner when the girls were already asleep and Sarah sat in her rocking chair, swaying to and fro, rhythmically moving to some melody in her head. Where did she go, Leon wondered, in those moments when she seemed so far away, so remote in her chair, by the window, her eyes closed; drops of water ran down the pane of glass.

"Sarochka," he said, making extra sure his voice had none of the gruffness he often carried in from a day's work. "Look at what the *Daily Worker* says about life in our homeland."

"*Daily Worker*. I wouldn't believe a word they said."

"Just listen to this. At least listen. That's all I ask." He tried to speak gently. "I'll read you what it says about life in the Soviet Union. '*Textile workers have six- or seven-hour days, a month's vacation with pay, and their houses— compared to the houses of workers in the South—are like palaces.*' And that's an American southerner telling all this to the newspaper. It's got to be true." Leon remembered all the way back to 1912, just a few years after he arrived in this country, how the textile workers in Lawrence, all 25,000 of them, ground the industry down to a halt when they went on strike. He had never seen anything like that before. All they wanted was a measly wage increase. And they got it all right.

"You can't truly believe this," she said so softly he strained to hear her.

He didn't want to get angry; he really didn't. He tried to keep his voice from rising. "Surely you must see what's going on in this country. You can't be blind to it. You have eyes. Look at all the people out of work, all those practically starving. And we're just scraping by here."

"At least we're scraping. Thank God for that."

She never spoke about God before. He had stopped believing a long time ago. He saw her grief. He was not stupid or uncaring. But he had lost a lot, too. Everyone had. It was the way under the czars, until the revolution broke out, outlawing all this hatred. But you do what you have to do to survive. You move on. You leave what hurts you behind. It's the only way. And a revolution had occurred in his beloved homeland. It would spread throughout the world.

"Nothing is the same there anymore. The czars are dead and gone. Imagine, it's a crime now to hate a Jew. Imagine that! We can finally return to our home. There are jobs for all, a place to live for everyone." Every day for the past thirteen years, Leon had longed to go back there.

But his wife closed her eyes, moving, he knew, into a place far away from him. He had never before noticed how at twenty-six, she had a few gray strands of hair. The rocker creaked as she moved back and forth. Tomorrow he would oil it. If only he could go to her, take her hand, so small, without a line or blemish on it. But he couldn't. Something prevented him. He didn't know what.

"It's all lies. Nothing but lies." She opened her eyes, stopped her swaying for a moment.

"Sarochka, I can barely hear you." If only he could tell her he wanted to protect her. She looked so frail, so delicate in her chair. "My brother said he would lend me the money to go."

She said nothing. He knew she didn't have the strength to defy him. But he didn't want to feel he was forcing her to go either.

"This country is falling apart." He took a sip of water and moved his wooden chair closer to the rocker. The dim light from the window made her look more beautiful. Still, her eyes were always so sad.

"I'll have plenty of work there. A man needs to work, you know. Everything here is so piecemeal. I can't depend on it." He placed his coarse hand on her arm. "Our Russia, now the Soviet Union, will be a model for the rest of the world to follow. You'll see that it's true."

"None of it is." She turned to him, stopped her rocking back and forth.

"What do you mean? Speak up, will you." He took a deep breath to stop the gruffness rising in his voice. "How do you know this?"

"I just do."

Did she think she was some kind of prophet, some seer the way she spoke? Her confidence unnerved him for just a short second.

"This is stupidity. Lots of people like us are going back there. And look, the *Freihoft* wouldn't lie about the better life they have found there. You know if we don't do it now, we never will."

Life in the Soviet Union would give her a sense of purpose, would cure her of this illness. America was a decadent place. The rich controlled the land here, snuffed out everybody else.

She must miss their great country as well. Why else would she sing those songs to herself in the evening after the girls were asleep? Every night he heard her humming Russian love songs, as she sat on her chair by the window.

"I don't want to go," she said.

"You'll feel better there. I know this." He breathed in the faint scent of lilacs from her hair. "We all will."

"Where would we even stay?" Her voice so faint that he strained to hear her. Such a question made him think that perhaps she didn't mind so much, after all, to return to their homeland. His mind raced forward, figured within a couple of months he could make all the arrangements.

"My friend Victor, from Baronovich, all those years ago, is in Leningrad. He will help us with everything if I write him and tell him we're coming. What a beautiful city Leningrad is, Sarochka." He walked into the kitchen to pour her a glass of water.

Just imagine, a poor Jew like himself settling in Leningrad with his family. If only she could see it his way.

"It's craziness to leave this country. And our girls, our little girls, how could you drag them all the way over there?"

"Our girls will have a future we can only dream of for them. You must, please, believe me on this." He gave her the water, a small offering of peace. Then he took a sip from his glass to quench the thirst from so much talking.

"One thing you must promise me. I can't go there if you won't promise me."

"I'll promise you whatever you want. Just tell me." He placed his large, sinuous hand over her smaller, smoother hand resting on the rocking chair.

"And if I hate it there, will you promise me we'll come back here to Roxbury? Or if the girls are too unhappy, we will leave. You have to promise me, Lenya. Do you understand that?" Her eyes looked more sorrowful than he had ever seen before, glassy, filled with tears that had not yet fallen down her face.

"Okay, okay. You think I'd force you to stay there. Anyway, I know you'll be happy there. Food, work, and a good place to live for everyone, the papers tell us." He was waiting for her to relent, and now, thank goodness, it had happened.

"I'm afraid it's all a bunch of rot." Her voice, just above a whisper. Sarah turned away from him, towards the window and the darkness outside there. He understood she was too weak in spirit to oppose him. In the Soviet Union, she would grow stronger and heal from all this sadness.

So Leon went back to his newspapers. She had agreed

to his plan in the end. But there she was in her chair, so remote; he didn't even know how to be with her in whatever place she went to without him in the evenings, her eyes closed, humming some song from her girlhood.

Leon resumed his reading. The *Daily Worker* reported on the workers bullied and beaten in Union Square, the hungry in lines for some morsels of food, the millions out of work, and the dream of the Soviet Union, how everyone there had a job and enough to eat. Imagine textile workers living in palaces compared to our own American South. Finally, the workers had a voice and a country of their own. And he would soon return there.

That night in his dreams, Leon traveled back to Baron- ovich by holding onto the fins of a blue fish soaring in a cloudless sky. This was especially strange because Leon did not share in the townspeople's beliefs in the supernat- ural, how the dead might possess an animal's soul or how inanimate objects might contain spirits, even ancestors from long ago.

The dirt on the roads in Baronovich once swirled into sawdust, baked dry from the summer sun. On Marinski Street, where his family lived, all the wooden shacks had sloping roofs and front doors that creaked. Leon's father Abraham owned the only tavern in Baronovich. The tall and lanky man with a brown beard loved to stand by the door in the early evening and greet each one of his customers, the merchants and peasants from the neighbor- ing towns. He'd often sit down at a round table with them and take a shot of vodka, though Abraham was careful not to neglect his cash register.

Leon liked to help his father in the tavern so he could

overhear stories, rumors. Some whispered revolution would spread throughout the country. The Czar's palaces would one day belong to the cobblers and butchers, to the poor peasants working the land, to the men toiling away in factories in large cities like Moscow and St. Petersburg. Leon only hoped it might be true.

Despite life's difficulties, Leon remembered his childhood with his six siblings fondly. That was until his mother became sick. Not yet thirty, she lay beneath blankets for two weeks with a high fever, shaking and perspiring. The local doctor came, spoke grave words to his father that Leon could not understand, though he certainly tried to listen outside her room. Leon sat by her bed, held his mother's pale and beautiful hands. She tried to whisper something to him; he couldn't make out her meaning, so he stroked her thin hair, stared at her unwrinkled skin as she faded away from him. For many years after he left Baronovich, Leon could recall the exact moment of his mother's death, how her white cheeks blended into the cover of her pillow, how her small hands folded above her chest.

These mysterious deaths were not uncommon. One winter it seemed half the village was wiped out by this illness.

Leon was ten years old when his mother died, two years before the beginning of the twentieth century. Six months later, his father married Koyna, a kindly round woman of twenty-three. Koyna cooked meals, cleaned and did her best to care for a motley group of children who did not want to be looked after. Koyna's father was terribly worried she'd be an old maid; he reasoned a man with six children was better than no man at all. But a year later, Koyna also took sick with this strange illness. Within two weeks, she was gone from them as well.

The children learned to fend for themselves. His sister Rose, along with the younger sisters, became the house cooks. Abraham reacted to his wives' deaths by becoming quick-tempered; he worried someone would steal money from the tavern, and so he always carried his earnings sewed into the pockets of his trousers. If someone broke a glass, he fretted that more bad luck might come to them. Perhaps Leon's father was a bit of a fortune-teller.

One day Abraham was returning home through woods near Kolpenitsa with some supplies for the tavern when a group of young men from another town surrounded him. They ripped the wad of money from his pants and called him a cheap dirty Jew. He tried to fight them, kicking and struggling, until a knife through his heart left him dead.

The town magistrate of Kolpenitsa conducted an investigation, but nothing ever came of it.

With their father gone, none of the children knew how to proceed. Abraham had been patriarch, head of the large family, almost king. The younger children consoled themselves by believing that even though he was dead, their father would surely find a way to punish those thieves. His spirit would inhabit those woods, waiting patiently for his killers to return.

But they had no time to wallow in their feelings. Food had to be bought, money made. So, they ran the tavern by themselves, all six of them. The girls delivered liquor to customers sitting at round tables while the boys tended bar. As the eldest, Leon counted the money at the end of the day, figured out how much to spend on food, how much on alcohol and other materials. All of them pitched in to clean up the place late at night after their last customers, a bunch of toothless drunken men, staggered back out onto the Baronovich roads.

Life was proceeding as smoothly as it could when one day their mother's older sister, Aunt Fanny, showed up unexpectedly from the town of Volakhava Bolshaya. They had last seen her at their mother's funeral, two years earlier. Aunt Fanny was a woman with a large chest who liked to wear unflatteringly low-cut dresses. Once, the story goes, she had been married to a well-to-do butcher. They tried, but she could produce no children. Perhaps it's the smell of blood on his fingers that is scaring away any new life, women liked to gossip behind Fanny's back.

After six years, her husband requested a divorce from the rabbi. It was granted. Fanny withdrew from the village and kept mainly to herself, so ashamed she was of her barrenness. When word reached her that her nieces and nephews were running the tavern, she got on a train to see what was going on there.

Aunt Fanny wore a green kerchief tied in a knot beneath her chin. She walked with a limp that made her body tilt from side to side. She shifted her weight first to the left leg and then over to the right as she made her way along the dirt road to the Vitsky home.

"This is no life for children," she repeated over and over again, using her cane to lift herself up the wide steps into the tavern. She hobbled over to a seat at a round table and wiped the sweat off her face with a clean rag stored in the pocket of her dress.

The Vitsky siblings sensed no good would come from her visit. They reassured her all was well with them, but it was no use.

"No children, no. I'm sorry it has taken me so long to

get here. My health has been bad. But never should I have let this happen to you."

Leon ran to get a shot of vodka to calm her nerves. His friend Victor was there, helping them out. As Aunt Fanny addressed them, Victor continued to deliver drinks to the customers from behind the bar; he did his best to console an old man lamenting his two horses that had taken sick and died over the winter.

"We're doing fine, Aunt Fanny," Leon said. As eldest, he spoke for them all.

"You need a manager for the tavern. This is no life for children. And all of you orphans, too." And with her words, she began to weep and blow her nose into her crumpled up rag. "I will get you a manager myself."

"Aunt Fanny, this is craziness. I'm taking care of the tavern, making sure the little ones are even going to school half of each day," Leon said.

"No, no," and she hobbled out of the tavern, refusing to listen to any protests.

An hour later she returned with Simon, a man with just one front tooth and a lisp that resulted from the problems in his mouth. As a cobbler, Simon was doing so badly that he made his bed upon all his broken shoes and slept there each night. He, of course, jumped at the opportunity to manage the tavern. Anything that could bring some extra income for him seemed like a miracle.

"This is the best you can get for us?" Leon was angry now. "Absolutely not, Aunt Fanny. I speak for all of us. He won't last in the tavern more than one night."

"Okay, I understand you're right, Lenya." But despite her attempts when she ventured through the town once more with her cane, swaying from side to side, even she had to admit that no one trustworthy enough could be found.

So Aunt Fanny made her way back to the train station in Baronovich alone, her legs swollen, her cheeks flushed, muttering incomprehensible words that annoyed her fellow passengers all the way back to Volakhava Bolshaya.

Still, life changed after her visit. The children worried that some distant relative might show up one day and take over the tavern. Then where would they be? A month later, at the age of fifteen, Leon started as an apprentice with a master-cabinet maker. Boris and Dmitri were learning to become tailors, and the girls met daily with a seamstress. The tavern was only open in the evenings. There Leon's friend Victor and other young men gathered at round tables as before and spoke of revolution. They predicted how one day machines would free them all from their backwardness.

Victor helped out in the tavern when he could. He had joined the Marxist Russian Social Democratic Labor Party, aimed at overthrowing the czarist regime, and had little time for them now. Leon worried Victor could be thrown in jail, or even worse, shot in the head by a firing squad.

Sometimes Victor managed to squeeze out an hour late at night. He'd show up at the tavern as it was closing and help Leon wash the floors. The thick soapsuds and the swishing sound of the mop being drained of excess water created enough noise to cover up their conversation even though they were the only ones in the tavern.

"A resolution has actually been passed by the Moscow City Duma calling for freedom of the press, freedom of religion, and even an elected legislature. Can you believe it, Lenya? Can you?"

Leon had been so busy keeping the tavern going, making sure his brothers and sisters were fed and schooled, it was hard to know what was really going on out there in the world beyond Baronovich.

"Right now, we're demanding, but in time it will happen. Protests are happening in all the big cities," Victor said in a hushed voice.

"But Vitya, what if you're caught? Everyone knows Nicholas is one mean bastard."

"I'm not afraid, Lenya. And in the end, we'll win. You'll see."

Not his mother dying, or his step-mother soon afterward, or even the murder of his father caused Leon to weep. But in 1905, when Victor was arrested for revolutionary activity and thrown into solitary confinement, Leon's tears were uncontrollable. Leon stayed up most nights, imagining Victor in a dark cell with a toilet, sleeping on the floor, freezing; never any light in solitary, that was for sure. Victor must have kept sane by humming revolutionary songs, Leon figured. But then, he didn't know how Victor did it; he somehow got out of the prison, disappeared, it seemed, into thin air. He must have fled the country. Later, when Leon ended up in Roxbury, Massachusetts, he wrote to his old neighbors in Baronovich for word of Victor, some address or location for him.

Finally, months after the October Revolution of 1917, after the czars were all dead and Lenin was securely in power, Victor wrote to Leon in that faraway town called Roxbury.

Dearest and oldest friend and Comrade!

I am finally free to write you. The tyrants are gone and I don't have to be afraid anymore. The Bolsheviks have seized power in our beloved homeland. Workers are part of collective soviets. The world is on the brink of change. If only you were here with me, Lenya. Now I can tell you what happened to your oldest friend. How I did my vanishing act. It was simple, really. My father, the poor man, paid a big fat bribe to the Baronovich Police Chief, and before I knew it, I was free so long as I promised to leave the country and never return. So I ran, Lenya. I ran for my life, all the way to Egypt, would you believe. I lived like a nomad there and settled for a while in Germany, started writing for the Communist paper there, then waited for the right moment to sneak back into Russia. It came for me in 1913, four long years ago. Thank goodness I went to Baronovich even for just a little while. Would you believe old Simon the cobbler, he's so ancient now, he's more dead than alive? Well, he gave me the letter you sent to Baronovich years before. I don't even know how he got it. Maybe he found it floating somewhere on one of our dirt roads and picked it up and put it with his piles of stinking shoes. Who can say?

Well, Lenya, Leningrad is like a dream compared to Baronovich. A Jew can live in any city he wants now. The Revolution is sure to spread even to America! But that's enough for now. I'll write more when I can.

Yours forever in solidarity,
Vitya

Fourteen years later, in 1931, Leon's hand shook as it did when he first read the letter on a winter day in Roxbury. From that moment on, he longed every day of his life to return to Russia, now the Soviet Union.

The men exchanged letters once every year or two. Victor had not only survived, he had risen up the ranks of the Communist Party. He had even become a writer for *Izvestia*. It was all too wonderful to be true.

A month after his talk with Sarah, after he had made all the arrangements, Leon rummaged through the drawers of his desk for Victor's address and wrote him once more to tell him of his arrival with his wife and two children on the tenth of September, sometime in the afternoon. Would he, Leon asked, meet them all then?

Victor wrote back immediately, even though it took two weeks for the letter to arrive.

> *My dearest Lenya!*
>
> *I don't have enough words to describe my joy. The white nights of this grand city keep me awake, and now since I got your letter all I can do is await your arrival. Do not worry about anything. I will arrange a place for all of you to stay. We may be poor in Leningrad, but we are happy.*
>
> *Look for me in the crowd. I am very much changed.*
>
> *Your dear comrade,*
> *Vitya*

Leon, Sarah, and their girls boarded the ship with just a trunk filled with very green bananas and some old shoes, skirts, working pants, shirts and worn woolen coats. They were all cramped together in a small berth downstairs; the girls shared one single bed, Sarah and Leon had the other.

When the girls didn't need her, Sarah spent her time looking out of an oval window onto oceans of water against an indifferent sky. She didn't want to go back. He kept saying life would be better for all of them there—jobs for all, a good place to live. She knew it was nothing but lies. How could Lenya believe it—not in that country? Nothing good for her there. Never in that country, where her mother still lay unburied. And Uncle Shmuel no longer. A month before they left, a letter came in an ink-stained envelope covered with stamps of Lenin and

Marx. It announced in two lines that Uncle Shmuel had died of dysentery. She didn't even know the name of the person who signed the letter.

Dear Uncle Shmuel. She had no home anymore. This was no land to return to, not ever, and yet here she was on a boat. Only ten years had passed since she arrived in Boston, alone and motherless. Only ten years ago her father, Louis now he called himself, had appeared out of nowhere for her—he took her to his house that was no home for her. After the girls were born, he'd often come by on a Sunday to see them, all spiffed up in a fancy suit. But it was all out of guilt, Sarah figured. Worst of all was when he showed up with that witch of a woman, his wife.

No one had told her, had prepared her, for how much she would miss her own mother when she gave birth. Her arms and legs so heavy she couldn't get out of bed after Susan was born. At least she was a little better with the second one. She did not, with every ounce of her being, want to return to the land where her mother was raped and murdered, left unburied in the Guilopyat River. Sometimes Sarah imagined silver algae surrounded her, made a tomb for her mother. But other days her mother was simply gone forever without a trace of her anywhere.

There was something terrible still waiting for Sarah there. She knew it. The past did not go away. It stayed in the country, in the soil and the wind. But Leon did not understand.

In Liverpool the one-day layover seemed like forever. Amidst the fog and the factories, her girls skipped along the streets, relieved to be off the boat for a little while. But all Sarah saw was a gray that covered the buildings and wharves; gray spread over the sea. "Carol, don't get too far ahead," she called out to that little one. She was always so mischievous and not afraid of anything.

"Girls, don't get lost now," Sarah shouted. She even surprised herself and laughed just a little bit. From up the block, she saw Leon smiling. His expression bothered her. How could he be so sure of himself and this crazy idea of a journey back to a country she only wanted to forget.

Later that night, after the ship had set sail again, Leon left her and the girls to go out on the deck upstairs. The girls snored, a soft sound against the slightly rocking ship. Sarah worried she'd soon be sick so she left the berth to get some fresh air. From outside, she overheard a couple of crew members talking.

"At least in the Soviet Union, everything's getting better and better, even if it's happening slowly," one man said.

"Yeah, now that the depression has hit the capitalist countries, it's getting worse fast over there."

"With socialism as our goal, life for us will only improve."

"Yeah, the workers in the imperialist countries are in big trouble."

"They'll just have to learn to survive on less."

She knew Leon was up there with them, listening to their every word, enjoying their talk. If only they were right and maybe life might start to improve for them all.

She returned to her bed to face her already sleeping girls and whispered beneath her breath, "But that's nonsense."

A HARD DAY'S NIGHT

Because

I could not woo the gods with song
they didn't guide me there slowly.
Instead I had to take a plane, Soviet style Aeroflot
into the underworld,
this invisible layer where the dead go.
Their songs can still be heard by this earthly world,
especially in Moscow,
        1980.
Dead ancestors returned from their migrations and settled
        there permanently.
They refused
                however
to attend Lenin's mausoleum, where he
lay pumped up with chemicals behind glass for all to see.

I hoped they wouldn't be too mad at me for standing
on line and catching a glimpse of him.

They were the grandchildren of the Bolsheviks. They were disappointed, betrayed, religious, and rebellious. They were outsiders, their ancestors were revolutionaries who had been murdered or sent to Siberia. So they studied Hebrew, came to the only synagogue for holidays, tried to leave the country if they could, and welcomed the American students to their homes.

In a kitchen in Moscow, women gathered, peeling carrots into a large bowl—onions were chopped one by one, and the smell of potatoes baking filled the room. Nadezhda wore a long-flowered apron covering her dress. She kneaded the dough before dropping it into a pan to sizzle and cook, oil popping all over.

Nadezhda let the water run out of the tap until it splashed everywhere. She scrubbed the remaining carrots. She cleaned and prepared, her dinner a welcoming party for the Americans this Sabbath evening. Only two days had passed since we met them at the synagogue on Rosh Hashanah.

The hair on Nadezhda's legs was fuzzy, friendly hair—roots breaking open beneath her beige nylon stockings. Her movements spoke of longing humming far into the night.

Women filled this kitchen. Some washed; others peeled or scraped, sliced or chopped the vegetables.

"How can I help?" I asked, looking for an extra knife on the counter.

"No, you must sit. You are our guest," Nadezhda said. She wore a dark skirt and pumps. "Tell me about your life. I want to know of your life."

I wanted to tell her of my journey, started long ago, wandering after Russian sounds—this maze where I slowly found edges of order.

"So, Anna, what do you think of Moscow?" another woman, who said her name was Adelanda, asked.

"I've seen so little, and yet it is a beautiful city with wide streets and then passageways to explore," I struggled to say in Russian.

"Yes, of course, but this city is a prison," she said and continued chopping her vegetables.

On a very small TV in the kitchen a woman sang in Russian, *I am sorry, I am sorry, over and over again.* She wore a long gown and held a microphone to her mouth.

"I hope to return to America with you in four months. My parents filed our papers sixteen months ago and lost their jobs. We should be getting permission any day now." Nadezhda leaned her back against the TV table.

"But how do you live?" I asked.

"Piece by piece we sell our furniture." Nadezhda laughed, pushed her hair away from her face. "Tell me, how much do apartments cost in America?"

"It depends where."

"How much in New York?"

"It depends on what part of New York."

"You mean there is no set price?"

"If you come, you will manage."

The front door bell rang and interrupted her questions.

"Excuse me," she whispered, then ran to open the door. "Заходите, Заходите," she giggled.

"Anna, remember, of course, Iosif and his cousin Tanya?"

Finally, he had arrived. I had been waiting, hoping I would see him here.

"I met him even before you." I told Nadezhda how my Russian teacher had a small present for his father.

Iosif smiled, thanked me once more and joined the men in the other room; Tanya stayed with us. Men in the living room discussed politics while women in the kitchen made dinner.

"он замечательный," Nadezhda said, glancing over at him.

"Замечательный?" I didn't understand the Russian word.

"It means he's wonderful," Nadezhda said, with a tinge of impatience. I wanted to tell her yes, I too have noticed him.

Lev, Nadezhda's boyfriend and official resident of the apartment, appeared in the doorway of the kitchen. His Russian words sounded like pieces of gravel turned over quickly.

"Is it almost ready? Will the food be served soon?" he asked and once she nodded, he disappeared into the only other room where the men had gathered.

Then the food was ready: fried potato pancakes, raisins mixed with carrots adorned with slices of tomatoes on top, and potatoes crusted with a dark brown skin.

Surrounded by these women, I felt I could rest from my long journey to Moscow.

Nadezhda placed two thin candles on the table and lit them. Once Lev nodded, she began. She recited the first prayer in Hebrew over the flickering lights and then another one for the bread. The white loaves passed around the table crumbled into many pieces.

"Barry, it's your turn. You say the prayer over the wine." Iosif handed him a book filled with Hebrew and Cyrillic letters.

Barry stood up, chanted over a wineglass filled with vodka, a ritual that got everyone drinking; women passed the dishes around.

Tanya sat by me. "I teach English to the workers in hotels," she said shyly. Her eyes were somber. "I teach them enough so they have some words to say to the foreigners."

"Let me hear your English," I prodded, since we had been talking in Russian.

"No, I cannot speak. I know too few words."

"Try a little. I'll help you."

"No, I cannot." I noticed the beginning of a smile forming on her face.

"But you must tell me about your grandparents. Where were they from in Russia?" she asked.

So I recited my story, how my grandfather lived in Minsk and came to the U.S. in 1909, while my grandmother was from a small village outside of Kiev and left after the revolution, around 1921, after her mother was killed in a pogrom. But then I told them how they returned to the Soviet Union because my grandfather wanted to build the revolution.

"What year was this? What year did they come?" Nadezhda interrupted.

"In 1931 they arrived in Leningrad. The story goes that after nine months my grandmother wanted to leave. If they stayed any longer, they would have lost their U.S. citizenship. So they left this place once again, my grandparents with my mother and aunt, girls five and three years old."

"Ah, Anichka, you are practically one of us." Iosif tapped my shoulder gently. His words made me blush.

"Your grandparents were lucky to get out of here," Tanya said. "So many Jews who were once from here and came back were murdered by Stalin."

I imagined my grandmother in some small room in Leningrad fifty years earlier, pleading with my grandfather, at first, and then insisting with all the strength she could muster that they must get back to Boston before they lost their U.S. citizenship and had to remain here forever. Her leaving, a gift she gave to me.

After dinner the women cleared away the dishes and piled them in rows by the sink. When they were finished, Lev got out his Beatles album and played "A Hard Day's Night."

We danced until our arms and legs were weary, until we could no longer move. Barry drank a few shots of vodka, took his flannel shirt off, twirled it around for Nadezhda to catch, and then it ripped, and they stood in the center of the room laughing.

Once more the men gathered into groups while the women made their way into the kitchen.

Nadezhda's hands dripped into the soapy water. "You must understand. My life is broken. I must get out of here." She circled the wet cloth round the dishes. "And last night, I met you in a dream and you stepped towards me and said, yes, we will grow very close."

I was sure I would know her forever, had been waiting all my life to meet her, here in this kitchen, in Moscow.

I didn't want to leave her or any of the women I had met. But it was past ten o'clock. The concierge at the dormitory kept track of everyone's comings and goings. So Barry and I gathered up our belongings and began to say good-bye.

"You must come back next week," Nadezhda said. She held Barry's hand and leaned ever so slightly backwards. Barry nodded and smiled.

"Wait, I'll walk with you." Iosif jumped up to get a jacket he seemed to have overgrown a while ago.

I kissed first Nadezhda, then Tanya good-bye, and left with the image of women and men standing in a smoky room by a glass bookcase, filled with books of Chekhov, Dostoevsky, Goncharov, Gorky, and Tolstoy.

Outside the darkness blended with the street lamps. There was only the occasional swishing sound of buses stopping at a street corner or cars on the road.

"Let me try on your rucksack and vest for a moment. I want to see what it feels like to be an American," Iosif said.

I unstrapped the knapsack from my shoulders and gave him my down vest. My stuff fit awkwardly on him since it was way too small for him. Iosif looked almost clownish next to the posters on each street corner of Misha the bear—Misha, mascot of the Olympics. Misha had a brown furry face, moist nostrils; above his head were the words, *Moskva 1980*.

Out of nowhere, Iosif raised up one leg to kick,

karate-style, the picture of the bear plastered to the lamppost.

"I'm sick of seeing him everywhere."

I looked around. What if someone saw him deface the Olympic mascot? Thank goodness, the street was empty, and we quickly arrived at the bus stop.

"We'll see each other soon. As you know, I have no phone. So you can reach me through Tanya," Iosif said, unzipping my vest to return it and my knapsack to me.

He shook Barry's hand, bent down low to hug me through my thick vest. I wished I knew when I would meet him again.

Around us the night was a mist drizzling downwards. We passed signs and posters put up by the Communist Party: *Power to the Revolution, The Workers of the World Will Win.*

"Nadezhda came to the airport when Sasha, my fiancé, left. But it's so much harder to get the permission to leave now," Barry said.

"Do you think she'll get out?"

"No, I don't. But I'm not going to tell her that."

I imagined Nadezhda at Sheremetyevo airport, a deep flowered scarf around her head, and the military men everywhere, their rifles in a sling hanging to their sides.

The cranes that seemed to bite the dirt around the white oval dormitory on Ulitsa Volgina made the picture in my mind disappear. The woman at the desk nodded when we entered. We rode up five flights and separated to find our rooms. I slipped inside my bed, already longing for morning.

WELCOME TO
THE SOVIET UNION:
1931

"Light," she says, "makes life seem horribly, shabby. Why," she says, "shine light on our poverty? The bedbugs will die of laughter."

Mikhail Mikhailovich Zoschenko, *Electrification*

The ship approached the city on an autumn night in late September. The lights from the boat shimmered on the water. Leningrad, so beautiful in the distance; Sarah had never seen anything like it before. There were large cobblestoned squares and faded yellow buildings, symmetrical in form and appearance. On the ship she had overheard that the czars' palaces had become museums. Others said she would find statues everywhere of Lenin, Stalin, Pushkin, Dzerzhinsky. She started to weep, not knowing why or where her tears came from, only that she had returned to her homeland and was not prepared for the feelings welling up within her.

Once the boat entered the harbor, Sarah thought she heard her mother calling to her in the rain that fell softly, creating a mist over the city.

On the ship, no one spoke; they just peered at the city in front of them. The pier widened in places where few people walked. From across the dock, Sarah saw a poster of Stalin in a long black coat and white button-down shirt and boots, marching alongside a line of Soviet soldiers, and then the words, *The Realization of Our Plan.*

Her girls clutched her hands, their small fingers entwined in hers. "Are we almost there?" they whined.

"Yes, can't you see the city in front of us?"

"No, there are too many people," Susan said. "And the smell is terrible." Sarah shot a look at Susan, the firstborn, named for her mother. But she could never stay angry at her for very long.

"Can't you lift me up?" Carol stood on her tiptoes. "I can't see a thing, and it's not fair."

"You've gotten too big for me. But your father can." But where was he? Sarah didn't remember when or why Leon had walked away from them.

"I don't see him." Carol began to cry.

"Look, he's coming. Thank goodness."

Leon emerged from the lower level of the ship with a man in a torn shirt.

"Come, we're here, here in Leningrad," Leon said excitedly. "Kolya here is going to help us get the trunk off the boat."

"But Papa, will you pick me up." Carol tugged at her father's pants.

"No. I have to get the trunk out of here."

"But I can't see anything. I want to see." Carol said. "It's not fair."

"Okay, okay, come with me." In his left arm, Leon whisked Carol up and folded her into the side of his upper body. His right hand took hold of the trunk. Kolya grabbed the trunk's other handle and led them off the boat.

"She always gets her way," Susan pouted and leaned against her mother.

"Come now. Don't be like that." Sarah reached for her older daughter's hand.

"I'm hungry." Susan's words pierced right through her. Her belly was empty too. She rummaged through her pocketbook for a piece of stale bread from yesterday— anything to eat would be better than nothing.

"Here, take this." The bread was crumbling in her fingers.

"But it's rotten."

"It's all I have now." Was this some sign of what would be in store for them here, Sarah worried. Would there be little food in this city?

"Come, let's go find the others." Sarah pulled Susan along. She hurried to catch up to Leon and Carol. They walked by the other passengers until they exited the boat and came out of a narrow passageway into a chilly room with customs agents ready to inspect their documents. They joined the long line of people, their hair unwashed, their shoes ragged with holes, seams ripped easily on blouses stitched together with cheap material. The passengers walked with backs stooped from lifting and dragging luggage.

"We're over here," Leon waved them over to him from the line. Military men, their faces expressionless, stood in corners of the custom's area.

"When are we going to eat?" Carol asked. Leon had put her down on the wooden floor. She looked especially small to Sarah today. Her blond hair all wind-blown, while Susan, the darker one, with bangs and black hair cut just below her ears, started to whimper.

"Girls, shh . . . please." Leon turned around. "We'll eat soon enough. I promise you. Just a little longer, that's all. We're here finally in Leningrad, the greatest city in the world. We're so lucky to have made it here. So please stop your crying now."

Sarah stroked their hair. No wonder everyone felt starved. Their last meal, millet and onions, was hours ago.

"Girls, we'll be out of here sooner if you're quiet," Leon

said. Sarah knew he was trying to make his voice as gentle as possible, just like he did with her when he was irritated. Carol and Susan sucked on the black cotton material of their mother's skirt, as Sarah pulled their small bodies closer to her.

She heard all sorts of languages from the line. Bits of English were interspersed with other words she could not understand. And there were two American youth, so exceptionally clean-cut looking, standing behind her. One said to the other that he hadn't worked in a year since Iowa had absolutely no jobs.

"Well, Virginia's no better. At least there'll be some work for us in this place," his new friend in paint-stained pants replied.

Everyone was here for the same reason, Sarah thought, the promise of a job. Would the Soviet Union deliver one to all of them? After what seemed like an hour, though it was probably half that time, they finally got to the customs official. Dressed in the same brown uniform as the military men, he took all of their passports and began to inspect them.

"So, you're Americans now?" He turned from his desk to address Leon. Sarah noticed a large wart on the side of his face. She sat beside Leon in a folding chair, the two girls on each one of her knees. Their eyes were closing. Thank goodness, the children were close to sleep.

"Yes, but we're Russians first. This is our homeland, of course."

"You mean, Soviets now. Right?" The official chewed on the tip of his pen. He had a double chin and a balding head that was covered by his military cap. He wore khaki breeches and high leather boots. When he placed his hand down on the table, it shook slightly.

"Yes, of course. That's what I meant." Leon crossed his left leg over his right.

"So, tell me, what has brought you to the Soviet Union?"

"I'm here to build this great revolution." Leon jumped up from the seat, straightened out his shirt and overalls, and saluted the man with this thick, muscular arm. Sarah wondered if she were seeing things. Why was he acting so strangely?

"That's quite all right." He directed Leon back to his chair. "Another American Jew has come to construct socialism. I've seen a lot of this lately. But we need good men like you," he said and smiled. Sarah tried not to look at the stray hair growing out of his left nostril.

"Yes, but I'm a Russian Jew. I mean a Soviet Jew, ready to serve my homeland. I'll do anything. My friend here in Leningrad, from my boyhood, will help me find work. Whatever the city needs, I will do. I will make the five-year plan a reality."

Sarah had never seen Leon so animated before. He looked like a boy and not a forty-two-year-old man with a wife and two children.

"Baronovich. So that's where you're originally from." The official paused, took out a notepad from his desk filled with piles of papers and wrote something down. "And who is this friend of yours?"

"Victor Shasky. He's outside waiting for us, I'm sure. He fought bravely to liberate our country from the czars' stranglehold."

"Ah, it's good to have such a friend like that," the official said and scribbled some more. That man gave Sarah a bad feeling. She could not make out what he was writing, even when she strained her neck to look.

"Well, Comrade Stalin said, 'We're marching full steam ahead on the road to industrialization, to socialism.'" With those words, he stamped the passports of Leon and Sarah and their two little girls and said, "Welcome to the Soviet Union."

The girls cried when she had to wake them to leave the stuffy customs room. "Soon, just a bit more, and we'll be settled," she said, not believing her words. The skin below Susan's eyes was red and puffy; Carol's hair, tangled and knotted. She grabbed hold of their hands. All the people exiting the pier made her dizzy. How would they survive in this place, Sarah wondered, as she peered across the street at the worn-looking citizens of Leningrad in their old, fraying clothes.

"If I could bend down right now and kiss this patch of cement, I would do it. But I guess I'd look a bit like a fool," Leon said, lugging the trunk into a safe corner outside.

"So, why don't you?" Sarah was sick of all of his grand talk.

"I want to go home," Carol stomped her foot, folded up her hands on her small chest and then leaned into her mother's skirt once more.

"Me too," Susan whispered. "My head hurts."

"Girls, soon, soon, we'll get something to eat. I promise you. Once I find Victor, we'll be on our way."

Sarah searched through her bag again. There were some dirty clothes, medicines, all sorts of junk in there. She found two more pieces of old bread, thank God, just stuffed in there. Her girls gobbled up the stale food.

"He's out there, somewhere, I know it." Leon squinted,

put one hand over his forehead.

"But how will you recognize him after all these years?"

"I'll know him. And he'll see me first, probably."

"What if we're stranded here with no one to help us? Then what will we do?" Sarah pulled the girls closer to her.

"That's craziness. Just wait. We'll find him."

But then Carol, her blond knotted hair bouncing up and down, let go of Sarah's hand and started to scamper through the crowd. "I'll find him, Papa," she shouted, already far in front of them.

"Carooooool," Sarah screamed. "Get back here right now."

"I'll go get her." Susan wriggled out from her mother's grasp.

"Oh, no, you won't." Sarah clutched Susan's hand even tighter. Sarah could see Carol's small chubby legs. *She'll get herself trampled.* "Carol," Sarah yelled. "Carroool." Then Carol disappeared. Sarah didn't see her anywhere. She looked everywhere into that crowd. But Carol was nowhere. Where could she be? She was so small, so easily lost, and she knew coming back to this country would only bring trouble and here it was, her little one already lost. This place was nothing but bad luck.

"Come on, let's find her," Susan insisted.

"No, wait here. Stay with the trunk," Leon yelled. He had already taken off after Carol. With long strides, he pushed his way through hundreds of people. "Carol, stop right now," he called to her. But she didn't hear him, so Leon had to redouble his speed. He almost knocked over an old man, who hissed at him, until the man realized what was going on and then calmed down. Leon came right up to Carol, caught her small hand and pulled her gruffly towards him.

"I just wanted to help you find your friend, Papa. That's all," she cried. Just as Leon scooped her up in his large hands, a man waving frantically, with round spectacles, black wavy hair and a mustache, inched his way towards them.

"There he is," Leon shouted. "He's here. I see him."

"Come, let's get to Papa and Carol," Sarah said. Her legs felt heavy, unable to move. The ship, the dock, the nameless faces swirled around her. But at least Carol was found. Thank goodness for that.

"No, Mama. The trunk. We have to stay here," Susan said.

"Yes, of course. You have more sense than anyone." All of their belongings were in that trunk. Its golden clasp glistened in the fading afternoon light.

"Lenya," Victor called. "Lenya." And then once more, "Lenya."

In the distance, Sarah saw them embracing. The men kissed one another first on the left side of the face and then the right; all the time Carol bobbed up and down in Leon's arms. "Yes, this is my littlest one," Leon said, as Carol's head brushed against Victor's cheek.

So this was Leon's childhood friend, the fellow who had convinced him to spend his last penny and borrow the rest to come to Leningrad. Sarah already didn't like him.

She heard Victor say something about wanting to hold her Carol. She didn't want her littlest one getting used to strangers. Besides, Carol had only just met this Victor.

But Carol squealed with delight as Victor lifted her up

high, so she could see the grand city, the canals and walking bridges. Victor carried Carol close to his shoulder, placed his other arm round Leon.

Meanwhile, Sarah and Susan remained by the black trunk on the pier until Victor put Carol down in front of Sarah, and both girls, at the same moment, huddled into the folds of their mother's long skirt, their faces hidden in the soft black material.

"I found him. Just like I said I would," Leon said proudly.

"I've got a room for you all in a communal apartment." Victor stepped closer to Sarah. His lips were moist on her chapped, wind-burnt face. "You'll live like regular Soviet citizens, not like some of the other foreigners here put up in hotels."

"Ah, that's good, Vitya. You've done well for us," Leon said.

"Our life here is not easy. But still we are happy."

Sarah wiped away the remnants of Victor's kiss from her cheek; his saliva smelled tart, a little like onions. She could only ask herself over and over again how she ever ended up here again. She dragged the girls, one in each of her hands, behind Victor and Leon. Victor led them down darkening streets. Parts of the city widened into large cobblestoned squares, bordered by yellow and white buildings with oval archways built beneath, so it was possible to pass through by foot or even horse. This evening there were mainly young people in the square, gathered in groups, speaking with great animation.

"It's like a dream, an absolute dream to be here once again. And look at you, Vitya. What a boy you still are."

"Not you. You're already losing your hair," Victor

laughed.

"All my life, I wanted to see this city. Not one day has passed since the Revolution that I haven't longed to be here."

"Lenya, the Bolsheviks have eradicated all anti-Semitism! Even made it illegal."

"Incredible."

Leon would believe it all, Sarah knew, listening from behind to their conversation.

Sarah looked out on the barefoot children with dirt-smudged faces. They stood on corners with their ragged looking parents. The few with shoes had one or more toes sticking out of a hole. What would become of her girls here? This was not the land of plenty Leon had bragged about from their Roxbury home.

"They're peasants from the countryside," Victor said. "They've come to Leningrad to find food. Right now, food is scarce, but we're working so soon there will be enough for all of our citizens."

Sarah felt droplets of sweat on her forehead even though the evening was cool.

"I can't walk anymore," Carol whined.

"Me too." Susan stopped, her hand clenched tightly round her mother's fingers.

"Give them to us. We'll carry them," Leon said. Gently he took hold of Susan, hoisted her up by his shoulder, and Victor did the same with Carol. The girls fell immediately asleep. With their free arms, each man grasped the handles of the trunk.

"What do you have in here?" Victor asked.

"Just some old clothes and bananas. The girls love bananas, so we brought them from Liverpool. Crazy, but it was Sarah's idea, so I said okay."

The bananas, Sarah remembered. She could have given the girls some bananas. She hadn't even thought of it. The bananas were all green when she packed them in England. But getting that trunk opened and closed up again out on the street would have been impossible.

"We better stop to eat. Lenya, if you have some dollars, we can get a good meal at *The People's* Restaurant. It's for foreigners."

The word, Народ, was carved into the restaurant's front window in yellow and orange letters. Once inside, Sarah couldn't believe the English in American and British accents she heard everywhere.

She and the girls sat on a wooden bench with a long, picnic-style table, while Leon and Victor waited in line for a dinner bought with Leon's dollars. The girls' heads leaned into the fleshy part of her upper arms; they snored softly. When the food came, she'd have to wake them up to feed them. "For now, sleep," she whispered and stroked their hair.

Listening to the other American and British people, Sarah found out a great deal at the table. Something about a baseball team. In a million years, she had never expected to find baseball here. Some young men were discussing a game between the Foreign Workers Club and the Stalin Auto Plant later in the week. Leon wasn't much of a sports fan, Sarah thought, but he'd want to go. She didn't even know any of the rules.

"We're bringing the best of America here," Sarah overhead someone say from another table.

The restaurant was dirty—food stained the floor, cigarette butts too. Her head pounded with hunger. In about twenty minutes, Victor and Leon returned with trays of cabbage soup, black bread, and a small piece of meat for each of them. Leon kept repeating, "This is fantastic!" She was so sick of those words already.

"Do you speak English?" Sarah turned to Victor.

"I understand most of it," Victor stumbled in English to reply.

Leon shook hands with the person next to him and those seated on the bench behind him as well, and suddenly the room buzzed with conversation. Sarah was shocked to find so many American men in their early twenties in Leningrad. A fellow who introduced himself as John from Minnesota came over to them. "There's no future, nothing to look forward to back home. I couldn't take it anymore and heard there was work for everyone here," John said. He had a small pug nose and freckles on his face.

"The Soviet Union has been good to us," John said, a forkful of cabbage in his hand. "This country needs workers for their industries. Steel, aluminum, factories are on the rise. We're bringing in our American muscle to build this Soviet state." In between bites of food, he smiled just enough so Sarah could see his yellowing teeth.

"The truth is we're like honored guests here," his friend Mike said. "Sure, we're sleeping in a room the factory provided for us, filled with single cots and a lot of guys. But we don't mind. One day we'll be able to tell our kids how we created a new future, not just for the Soviet Union but for the entire world."

"You have to come to the Foreign Workers Club." John took a spoonful of the deep purple soup made from beets. "We've actually formed a choir. We meet a few evenings a week and perform workers' songs. Other nights we take excursions around the city together. There was even a party at the Club a couple of weeks before and Comrade Bukharin came to address us."

"Bukharin came to see you?" Victor asked excitedly.

"So fantastic. Absolutely fantastic." Sarah cringed at Leon's words.

"Comrade Bukharin said, 'To build up a new world is the highest joy for man.' And that pretty much sums up what we're doing here," Mike said. He had short, buzz-cut hair. "Nothing like this is happening in North Carolina. I can tell you that much."

"Please tell me, what is life like in America for someone born there? Not like my friend, Lenya who came from a little Russian village and then went to America at eighteen years old," Victor asked.

"People wait in lines to get a small handout of bread, some milk maybe. At least here in the Soviet Union, we have problems but we know life is going to get better." John spoke slowly so Victor could understand him.

Mike stood up and raised his glass full of vodka. "To the Soviet Union, to its prosperity. To the five-year plan, and to the workers of the world," he shouted. Most people in the Народ restaurant echoed his very words back to him. They tilted their glasses back and swallowed the vodka in one big gulp.

"To our homeland," Leon lifted his glass once more. "Here, Sarochka, take just a little bit, won't you," he whispered, giving his glass to her for a sip or two.

"And Comrade Stalin and his vision for us all."

Sarah ignored him and woke the girls so they could at least eat something. They moaned they were no longer hungry, but they nibbled on the cabbage and bread anyway. She wanted to get out of there, to rest, along with her girls, after their long journey. She looked over at Leon; he was grinning. So happy he is, she thought. But Sarah knew he saw her glance, saw Carol and Susan curling back up in her lap when he announced to Victor they had all better go.

"Да, Пошли," Victor said.

"Come to the baseball game at Yelagin Island," Mike called out to them. He hugged first Victor, then Leon. "It's the Americans versus the Soviets every Friday evening. We're teaching them how to play. And they're pretty good."

"But we're still better," John said.

"We'll find you there," Leon said, as he and Victor grabbed on to the handles of the black trunk and each cradled a sleeping girl into their arms.

"This trunk is good luck, Vitya. It's been following me around from Baronovitch all these years."

"And now you finally made it home."

Sarah and the girls trudged behind the men for several more blocks until Victor announced, "We're here," and stopped before a worn brown building. "We all live together, share together, instead of being so concerned with our own individual units of family."

The communal apartment was laid out in railroad fashion. One, sometimes two rooms for a family, a common kitchen in the center of the floor, and at the end of the hall, a toilet and a sink; downstairs, a tub for bathing. A small, old woman sat in a chair by the entranceway of the building. She recognized Victor and greeted him, "Добрый вечер товарищ." *Good Evening*

Comrade. He entered first with a trunk handle and child, followed by Leon right behind him. Sarah felt the woman look at her. Was she envious, Sarah wondered, of her black coat. The woman's sagging face turned into a frown, and that made Sarah lean her body forward in shame as she stepped into a narrow hallway.

A single bare bulb lit their new room. There were two double beds with torn mattresses. We'll cover them up immediately with sheets, Sarah thought, but the task at hand seemed to require more strength than she had. Still she would do it. She had to push herself. She wanted to weep when she saw how dirty the walls were, piles of dust gathered in corners where Leon and Victor put the black trunk, the sleeping girls still in their arms. Once the beds were made, the men placed the girls down, and Sarah kissed their foreheads, felt their soft skin on the edges of her mouth.

"I know we don't live well here," Victor said. "But these difficulties are temporary."

"I'm not afraid of struggling, Vitya."

"I know. I know this. Tomorrow you'll register for your ration cards for food. Don't lose them or you'll starve," Victor said. "But for now, I have a little something for you—some bread, a cabbage, two potatoes." He lifted the food out of a canvas bag hanging from his shoulder.

"I can't accept this. Please, eat them yourself." Leon pushed Victor's arm away from him.

"You have to. It's for your wife, your children. It's nothing, but at least when you wake up tomorrow, there'll be something for you to eat." Victor placed the food on the black trunk.

"But the bananas. We almost forgot them. Sarochka,

come see how our bananas have turned out." Leon lifted the trunk open. "Ah, they're perfect, aren't they? What a good idea you had after all," Leon said and handed Sarah a ripe, yellow banana.

The taste was sweeter than she had remembered bananas tasting.

"Take some yourself, Vitya. And give a few to the old woman at the desk. Maybe that will make her a bit friendlier. Don't you think?" Leon shoved a bunch into his hands.

"It's too much. I don't need all this."

"Just take it. You see we're rich in bananas at least."

Sarah sat on her bed and watched the men. She was used to being the silent one; she listened without commenting much, and, as usual, the people around her seemed to forget she was even there.

Victor didn't stay long. He said he had a meeting, but he'd be back the next day. He hugged his childhood friend and then bent down to kiss Sarah's cheek. This time his lips were dry on her skin.

Their dirty white walls seemed even dingier after Victor left them. She took the piece of black bread Leon offered her. It stuck in her throat, but she was still hungry, so she continued eating with Leon, a chunk of the bread in his hand. Sarah knew he was taking very little, trying to save some for tomorrow, for when the girls got up, their bellies would be empty from a night's sleep. At least she could give them some bananas then. The yellowed fruit should last a few days more.

They didn't speak. There wasn't much to say. He had insisted they all come here, and she had relented, too tired or weak to oppose him. Nothing seemed real. This bare room, surrounded by seven families in their own single rooms, all of them crammed in together. For this they had traveled two long weeks by boat. Had everyone around her gone mad, Sarah wondered. In Roxbury, though they were considered poor, they at least lived in a house, even if the paint peeled off the front door and the floors were cold to their feet.

"Let's sleep now, Sarochka." He still called her by the affectionate form of her name. It didn't mean anything to her. He said it, she knew, to make himself feel better.

When she slipped beneath the sheets, he kissed her on the cheek and then turned away from her. She lay awake for a long time. In the room next door, a couple was intent on arguing about something. Sarah could not make out the words, only the anger in their voices. Once she finally fell asleep, from beneath the surface of her dreams, she saw her mother as a young woman, with a cow beside her and red, mournful eyes, by the Guilopyat River.

Sarah awoke in the middle of the night, not sure where she was. She felt a new rash itching down her arms and legs. It must be bedbugs. She groaned and got out of bed to put on a long-sleeved shirt over her nightgown, a pair of loose-fitting pants—the only ones she owned—so at least her skin would be covered up when she returned.

In the morning the girls scratched the new welts on their skin until they bled. Sarah and Leon did their best to scrub the mattresses with the scraps of soap they could find in the kitchen. "You need kerosene to fight the bedbugs," one woman told Sarah as she poured a cup of tea for her. She said her name was Katya.

"It's my turn to make the tea. How is it?"

"Yes, good, thank you." Sarah stared at the floating tea leaves that had settled on top of her glass. She guessed Katya was around her age, maybe a year or two older. She had dark circles under her eyes that were a stark contrast to her rosy red cheeks.

"What place have you come from?"

"A small town outside of Boston." Sarah sat down across from Katya on a small, square table in the kitchen; she looked out at the pots and pans strewn everywhere on counters and walls.

"Ah, so far you've come. All the way from America. And you're Russian, too. We love the Russian Americans who have returned to us."

"You do?"

"Oh, yes. You're the purest of revolutionaries," Katya said and handed Sarah a basin to fill with boiling water for the sheets. "Well, here, I'll give you some kerosene too, but you must be careful. You can try and plug up any holes in the room. But you won't win this battle, I'm afraid."

After her attempts at extermination, Sarah waited in line for the bathroom. It was Sunday, so there was no usual schedule. When her turn came up, she couldn't believe the filth encrusted on the toilet—no top seat. How was she going to sit down on this dirt? Just newspapers instead of toilet paper. Sarah draped a newspaper, squatted as best as she could, and found a sliver of soap to wash her hands; her skirt would have to suffice for a towel. Above the sink, Sarah was surprised to see a note, "Comrades, please, we must try and keep this cleaner. For our health, Comrades." It wasn't quite in correct Russian.

From the hallway, she heard Victor's voice. "Don't argue with me. You'll need this, but that's not why I came."

More bread, beets, and three potatoes from Victor. Thanks to him, the girls were busy eating, Sarah thought and entered the room.

"I have great news. I found a position for you in the aluminum plant that's being built, the first one in the Soviet Union. Can you imagine, Lenya? You'll be part of this grand undertaking. What's more, you can even start right away," Victor said.

"What's luminum, Papa?" Susan looked up from her breakfast of bread and bananas.

"Yeah, what's that?" Carol asked.

"It's a metal found in the earth. All sorts of wonderful things can be built with it."

"Yes, and it will make our country rich one day. And then we'll share this new wealth with all of our Soviet citizens." Victor sat cross-legged on the floor by the trunk.

"Really? You will?" Susan wiped the crumbs of bread from her face with her fingers.

'You see, girls," Leon said, "This country has been so poor, dirt poor for hundreds of years, but now it's starting to change."

"And you, Lenya, will help make the five-year plan a success. Comrade Stalin says we must transform our country by building our industries. This plant will change the entire country. It will bring the Soviet Union into the world. And your papa, girls, will be a part of it."

"Fantastic, Vitya. How fantastic."

Sarah left for the kitchen. She didn't want to listen anymore. She hoped she could find another glass of the watery tea on some counter or table there.

"Everything is happening more quickly than I could have ever wished for," Leon said, his voice booming across the hall to the kitchen. "More proof, Vitya, that we all belong here." She heard every word they said. It was always so predictable, the same excuses, how we were all sacrificing for the sake of the future, how these hardships were just temporary. She hoped somehow it might be true and this miserable life here might get better.

"And my poor Aunt Fanny. You know, that fat lady who wobbled from leg to leg and tried to get us to shut that tavern down. Do you know what happened to her?" Leon asked.

"Old Simon the cobbler, that old buffoon, told me, and I don't know how he knew. He said she just fell over one day and died. That's what he said when I re-entered the country and went back to Baronovich before coming to Leningrad."

Sarah came back with two glasses of tea for the men. In the corner of the room, the girls rolled marbles to each other; above them, the plaster from the ceiling hung, about to fall.

TALES OF SILENCE

I went there looking for a home
        (oldest story there is)
except it's still true
                how the self sees the past
in mid-November moonlight.

I grew up in my room
        with the door shut, of course.
It's what girls do when they're miserable.
        It's safe there on a winter morning.
There's a kind of solace in a room.

Several days after our Sabbath celebration, I saw Iosif as I left the *Institut Imeni Pushkina* and turned onto Prospect Tolstova, where large oak trees bordered each side of the street. He was standing there at the end of the corner, waiting close enough for me to see him, and yet far enough from the school.

"Hello . . . Привет, I mean," I said, switching to Russian.

"Привет, Anna. I figured I'd find you here. Today I want to show you the streets of Moscow."

This easy rapport, our fragments of greeting, still seemed as if we were continuing some conversation interrupted long ago. We walked past the Metro station Barricadnaya; an old woman stood on a corner selling мороженое, ice cream covered by a thin layer of chocolate wrapped in a silver foil. The man beside her, his hair greased back behind his ears, had znachki for sale—pins with brightly painted pictures of Moscow, the Lenin Library, the Pushkin Museum, the Kremlin, and ancient churches.

"In America, do you always know what will be tomorrow? Here nothing changes. Each day is the same."

He stepped more quickly as he spoke, and I too increased my pace to keep up with him. "There's no future for any of us in this place," he said.

"But Iosif, you went to the University in Moscow. I've

heard it's almost impossible for Jews to get in there."

"Yes, I did go. I'm not sure myself how it happened."

We passed the Moscow zoo; giraffes nibbled the leaves from trees growing just above the bars.

"But what about the Jews? How do they manage in this place?"

"I can say nothing except that you'll see for yourself."

Iosif turned down a block and led me into a small café with not much to eat in there. After waiting in line for twenty minutes, we sat down at a table. In another ten minutes, the waitress brought us braided bread with raisins. Butter melted easily into the soft doughy layers.

"This is Russian bread, real Russian bread. You can't find bread like this anywhere else," Iosif said.

It was true. The bread had a sweetness I had never before tasted.

"We've spoken enough Russian for today. Let's switch to English. I have so little practice. Most of the time, I just create imaginary conversations in my head. "

That's enough to make anyone a little crazy, I thought.

"So where is your university located?" His English was definitely a bit stiff.

"In Connecticut. You know, my teacher knew your . . . "

Iosif cut me off. His brow wrinkled and then just as quickly all creases disappeared and he was smiling again.

"So, tell me, Anichka, how long have you studied Russian?"

"This will be my fourth year." He had already asked me these questions when I first met him at the synagogue. I figured maybe he had forgotten.

"Good, let's walk more." So we finished up our tea and bread, left the many men and women still waiting in line for a table.

"In public places, we don't talk much. Someone could be listening," he whispered.

I nodded. It was hard to believe anyone could care about our conversation.

The architecture changed from medieval churches with cupolas glittering in the afternoon sun to Stalinist steel structures of skyscrapers—from a little *bylochnaya* to a tall glass building mirroring the people passing hurriedly by.

Soon we arrived at the Arbat, an older section of Moscow. A silence settled on these streets, on the soft green or yellow painted buildings with stucco shutters. A woman, her back bent low with the weight of her netted bag—some heads of cabbage, cheese, a few loaves of bread—walked in the center of the road, swaying to and fro as she moved, her hair tied up in a bun. Vendors were scattered along the sides of streets selling znachki, Russian scarves, and fur hats.

"The women here wait two to three hours a day in a line for food. You've seen how little food is in these stores at one time. So they have to go every day. First the bread store, the meat store, then the grocery store that only has canned goods. You must understand this about our life here. The women are all growing old."

"They do all this after work?"

"Yes, of course. When else?"

No wonder they look exhausted. I remembered how once my mother told me that her own mother had always seemed old to her. My grandmother's hair fully gray in her thirties, her large body carried her grief.

As we walked, the afternoon light seemed to disfigure the leaves falling onto cement.

A few more days passed and it was Yom Kippur eve. I returned to the Choralnaya Synagogue with Barry, but we soon dispersed into separate paths, and I was left looking into the crowd, hoping somehow to find Iosif there. The mood was not somber or repentant, the way I remembered this holiday back home. Instead, men and women marched down the street almost defiantly in twos and threes, their heads covered but not bowed; they blended into the larger stream of people in front of the synagogue.

I felt someone tapping my shoulder. At first, I was frightened, but when I turned around I saw Iosif, his dark eyes, dark hair, his face smiling.

"Привет!"

"Привет, Аничка. Как дела?" Iosif bent down just a little when he spoke to me, just close enough, so if I reached upwards a bit, I could pull him towards me. But I didn't.

Together we moved through the crowd, past the white synagogue steps.

"Let's go and drink tea in my home. We can speak there," Iosif said. So we walked beyond the people gathered in groups, their conversations buzzing into the evening air. I noticed a store where pounds of creamy cheese were stacked up high in the window just before the cobblestones ended, and we proceeded onto another wide street smoothly paved with cars and traffic, then downstairs to the Metro at Station Proletarskaya.

We held onto the train's silver pole. I liked being near him, my arms brushed up against his shoulder.

"We're almost there," he smiled. "You must be tired."

"No, not much." I knew the rules—only small talk.

After several stops on the train, we got off and ran to a bus that took us to the outskirts of Moscow. From the window, I could see tall apartment buildings painted in greens, yellows, blues and reds—clusters of buildings separated by a playground or piles of dirt with tractors in the soil. We got to Iosif's place soon, his building one of many, its top edges decorated in blue and white. Not far from the entrance, we passed by huge plastic barrels of garbage grouped together.

"This is how we live. With garbage piled up high," Iosif said. "But at least it's our own home. And we don't have to share it with ten other families."

"What do you mean?"

"That's the way it used to be right after the revolution. And now, at least, it's gotten so much better. I can live in an entire apartment with just me and my mother. It's a big change. A big improvement."

How do you find your home, I wanted to ask him, when everything looks alike. The elevator moved through my stomach until it stopped abruptly on the twentieth floor.

First Iosif knocked before he slipped the key inside, then turned the knob. As we entered, a door off the hallway opened, and an old man peeked his head out. White hair fell haphazardly, almost covered the tips of his glasses.

"This is my grandfather. Come, you must meet him."

I stepped out from behind Iosif. The old man took my hand; his grip felt like a soft feather against my palm.

"Очень приятно." I proudly recalled the greeting I had learned to use at school when meeting someone for the first time.

Iosif laughed at my effort to speak properly. He kissed his grandfather on the cheek and whispered, "It's late. He needs to go to sleep."

"So Marina has come to see me from Leningrad," he said, bending closer to me.

"No, *dedulya*. This is not Marina. Get some rest, will you?"

"Then wake me when she comes. You won't forget to get me up now?"

"Yes, of course."

"She looks a bit like her you know. Are you sure this is not Marina?"

"Very sure."

"Приятно познакомиться," his grandfather nodded at me before disappearing behind the door he had only just opened.

"Sometimes he gets so confused. Marina is my great-aunt, an old woman he hasn't seen in more than twenty years." Iosif handed me a pair of red, felt slippers. "*Tapochki*. Here, take some."

The walls of the apartment were faded yellow; the main area had a wooden table and chairs, and then there was Iosif's room. We sat down on a small couch that I assumed was also his bed. On the opposite wall, I saw a large, framed photograph of Tolstoy. His long white beard and somber eyes filled the entire room. Beside it, rows and rows of Tolstoy's books were tucked into wooden shelves, and in a corner Iosif's desk stood with many papers strewn everywhere.

"Let me bring you some tea and biscuits." Iosif left for the kitchen while I sat on the couch gazing at Tolstoy. A few minutes later, he returned with a samovar on a flowered tray. He poured two cups of hot, steaming tea into small ceramic, oval-shaped cups.

"I really must look like a foreigner," I told him. "You spotted me immediately the first day at the synagogue."

"Yes, you stuck out a bit. But that's a good thing, Anichka. Already you're starting to blend in more."

I liked the way my name sounded with the ending he had now added.

As I placed my cup down on his table by the couch, I noticed several issues of *Time* and *Newsweek*.

"Iosif, how did you get these?"

"A friend of mine is able to give them to me. I can't tell you anything more."

There were always so many secrets here, secrets to protect people, secrets beneath conversations, secrets between people. No one could be entirely trusted. Not even me. To make matters worse, I had to look at the smiling face of Ronald Reagan on the cover of *Time*.

Iosif seemed to read my thoughts. "This country needs a tough American president. The Soviets only listen when they're scared," he said.

"You don't understand. If Reagan is elected, relations between our countries will only get worse."

"No, that won't be true. The Soviets bend under pressure. They respect and only listen to power."

"You are very conservative, you know."

"Conservatif, conservatif. But what does that mean? These words make no sense to me."

"What I mean to say is that if you lived in my country and held your views, you would be considered a politically conservative person."

"You must understand. This government is a nightmare. Nothing, absolutely nothing at all works," Iosif said. "And Brezhnev is old. He will die soon and then what will be? We fear every time someone new comes to power. For everything is getting tighter and tighter here."

"In the U.S. so many people are also suffering."

"Yes, I'm sure. Everywhere there are problems." He smiled for a moment. "But still you don't understand." He got up and walked over to the window.

"Surely you must know what happened here in the thirties?"

I nodded.

"My great uncle was a Bolshevik. In the thirties, he was mayor of a town. And then out of nowhere, Stalin had him arrested and shot. Stalin was cleaning out the party, so he had my uncle lined up against a wall with the others. For nothing. For absolutely nothing."

Iosif looked very gaunt by the window. I wanted him to come back to the couch, to sit once more next to me.

"My great-grandmother too was murdered. She was raped and drowned in a river by Cossacks." For so long I had been wondering what my grandmother had seen when she looked out of the window and the soldiers dragged her mother away.

"Oh, no," Iosif said. I could feel my words slice through him. His face grew pale again. Then he said, "I'll get more tea and crackers," and ran out of the room.

When he returned a few moments later, he was smiling. "We'll eat and drink more." He placed the chaynik in front of me.

"Iosif, if you could leave Moscow and come to the U.S., would you want to?"

"But I can't. My mother has a secret job. So it's

impossible for either one of us to ever leave the country."

More secrets, now a job. Must be defense, I figured.

"But if you could come, would you want to?"

"No." He paused. "I suppose not. I would miss the streets of this city."

Iosif poured more tea into our cups; the steam warmed my face.

I started to feel scared. I remembered Miloz and tried to push him out of my mind.

"Is anything the matter? Tell me, Anichka. I feel something's wrong."

I glanced at the huge stacks of papers on Iosif's desk, at the multiple images of Reagan from the American magazines. We sat very close together on his couch, across from Tolstoy's photograph, his white hair and beard in a splendid state of disarray.

"I'm afraid," I said.

"I want to give you this chaynik to keep inside you." He leaned closer to me.

"Why?"

"The chaynik can take all fears away." I imagined this old teakettle full of golden flowers against a dark background inside me, healing me.

We sat without speaking, just drinking the Russian black tea. He was the most beautiful man I had ever known.

"It's late. I have to get back soon." I remembered the round dimpled woman behind the concierge desk. I better not stay any longer.

"Okay, I'll ride with you. You seem a little happier now that you are leaving."

"No, it's not true. I'm just worried they'll be looking

for me." I followed Iosif out of his room into the kitchen. Maybe I did feel relieved now that I was going, yet once I was away from him, I only thought of when I might see him again.

On the way out, we saw Iosif's mother, a woman with reddish, almost orange-like hair, cut just below her ears. She stood by the kitchen table, rummaging through her bag for six large ripened tomatoes.

"Mamochka." Iosif kissed her on the cheek. "This is Anna."

Her lips brushed against my face. I felt the solitude of her life.

"Анна Американка," Iosif said. "Она студентка в москве."

With a spoon, Iosif's mother crushed several tomatoes into a glass bowl on the counter.

"Пожалуйста ешь девушка." She poured some tomatoes into another plate for me, the over-ripe seeds glistening in the dim light.

"Only in Russia can you taste tomatoes like these," Iosif said.

The taste was of the earth, sweetly brewed in soil.

Iosif's mother didn't speak a word of English. She just kept refilling my plate with more crushed tomatoes. She wore a brown dress just below her knees and beige stockings.

"How long are you here for?" she asked me in Russian.

"Just four months."

"Ah, Америка," she sighed. "A place so far away."

"She grew up in New York," Iosif added.

"New York," she repeated. "So why do you come to Moscow?"

"To study Russian language."

"Mamochka, she has to get back to Ulitsa Volgina, her dorm."

"Да." She took away my plate. "You must go with her now."

She placed a soft kiss on my cheek. When she hugged me good-bye, I felt her broad shoulders as her arms wrapped around me.

In the hallway, I returned the slippers to their narrow shelf by the door, pushed my feet back into my clunky leather shoes.

"My mother's not well. She's sick so much of the time." Iosif spoke so she would not hear. His words a pronounce-ment, a declaration—the women of the Soviet Union sentenced to premature old age.

Outside droplets of moisture had gathered into a fog over the outskirts of Moscow, partially obscuring the red and blue tops of apartment buildings and the fenced-in construction sites of soil and stones.

When the bus arrived, we were surprised to find we were the only passengers. The driver waited for a long time at the stop for some more people, his arms folded around the steering wheel of the bus. But still, he didn't start the engine.

"Что с тобой не так?" *What's wrong with you?* Iosif's sharp voice startled the driver out of his sleep. He pressed his foot on the gas, pushed his greasy hair back behind his ears and began to proceed along the Moscow streets. I could see the massive cookie-cutter clusters of apartment buildings and billboards, Коммунизм Победит, hung near stores with signs, гастроном, фрукты и овощи.

Finally, we arrived at Ulitsa Volgina, dom shest, the

round white dormitory spiraling upwards, surrounded by overturned dirt and diggers. I didn't want to leave him, but I knew I couldn't say that. We had to put on our public selves. Suddenly there was a formality between us; it surrounded the darkness on the dirt path to the dorm, where a single street lamp made a path to the entrance.

"I have to go now. I don't want to be seen," Iosif whispered. This was a dorm for foreign students only. "We'll see each other soon," he said. His mouth grazed my cheek.

I took a few steps to the dorm, turned back once, wanting to say something more to Iosif. I saw only the street forming just beyond the soil. I looked and looked, but he had already disappeared.

1931

Listen,
        comrades of posterity,
to the agitator
            the rabble-rouser.

Vladimir Mayakovsky, "At the Top of My Voice"

There was a hunger in Sarah's belly, a longing the cabbage and potatoes did not satisfy. As she lay awake her fifth night in Leningrad, Sarah could feel the fitful sleep of her girls. She knew they needed something more to eat. Even the bananas were gone. Beside her, Leon slept, his noisy breathing disturbing any quiet the night might offer her in between those moments when the bugs didn't bite her skin.

Ten days on a ship had humbled them. From the moment Sarah entered Russia, she could feel her mother there in the lapping of water against the dock, in the narrow streets where pock-marked children stood beside women carrying the burden of their belongings wrapped up on their backs. Sarah's mother haunted the empty store windows where there was little to sell.

Uncle Shmuel dead, too. His face, gravelly sand against her cheek, as he kissed her good-bye. There was nothing for her here anymore.

Victor told them where to wait in line to exchange their ration cards for the little bit of food available. The girls would at least get their milk. Sometimes Sarah even managed to get a bit extra for them from the peasants who were fleeing the countryside. They were all starving there. Katya told her they came to Leningrad and exchanged milk for grains to feed their dying animals.

The Yiddish papers, *The Daily Worker,* Sarah knew

now had lied to them. How could Leon have been so easily duped? There certainly wasn't food for all here. And what about the conditions of these apartments? Who could have believed it? Yes, everyone did have a place to live. She had to admit that. But the newspapers never reported about entire families living together in one room, never said anything about twenty people sharing one filthy bathroom.

A week after they arrived, Victor told her about an opening in a shoe factory.

"But who will look after my girls?" she asked.

"We have free daycare centers for all children provided by the state. Women have been freed up to work. They don't have to be tied anymore to the home," Victor said.

"And what's more, the daycare will be good for them. They won't be pampered with the eyes of one parent always on them. Instead, they'll be with other children and learn the ways of this new world we are building," Leon chimed in. It irritated Sarah, how he always agreed with everything Victor said.

"But what if I don't want to work at the shoe factory?" She glanced over at her sleeping girls sharing one double bed. "What if I want to be home with my girls?"

"You don't want to be considered some parasite who doesn't work or contribute to this society," Leon said. "Besides, we need the extra money. I'm sure I'll advance as time goes on, but for now ... "

"I'm tired of your fine talk," she mustered up the strength to say. "Look at all the promises you made to me. And none of it true. Look at this dirty room. We had a house, Lenya, a house. And now you tell me I have to work in a factory." She sat down on the wooden chair.

"What will become of our girls? That's what I want to know."

"Our girls will inherit a world we've been dreaming about for years."

Sarah was tired of him always having a saying for everything.

"Here, let's drink. I was able to get some vodka for us. Can you get us a few glasses, Sarochka?" Victor took out a bottle from a bag filled with notebooks.

"I don't drink much myself," Leon said.

"You're in the Soviet Union now. You've got to drink some," Victor laughed. Besides, you owned a tavern. How could that be?"

Sarah sauntered into the kitchen. She knew it was no use to fight against them. She couldn't win. But it was impossible to find anything there. Pots, pans, and knives left lying around. Nothing put back. Finally, she saw the little glasses behind a pile of plates.

When she returned, the men were already taking swigs from the bottle. "To the future, Sarochka." Leon began to pour the vodka.

"You know I don't like to drink."

"Just a little sip. Try it. It will be good for you." Victor urged.

Sarah took a taste of it. The alcohol burned her throat, made her head ache for just a moment. So she pushed the glass away from her.

A few days later Sarah started working at the factory. She hated descending into the dark caverns of machines where she stitched the soles of shoes together. She returned to the communal apartment with her fingers pricked and bleeding. The girls did stay in a daycare center, crowded together with what seemed like hundreds of children. They clung to her blouse when Sarah dropped them off, and they wouldn't let go of her legs when she picked them up. After getting off work at 3 PM, she waited in line for two to three hours. First, there was the bread store, then the fruit store, and a vegetable store that only sold cabbage and maybe a few carrots.

In the factory she was the newcomer, the outsider, a stranger who had left the country and then returned. So Sarah kept to herself. It was what she had always been used to anyway. After queuing up for some food for dinner—if only there was enough in the stores to last them more than a day—Sarah took a bus over to the daycare center. She had to rush to get there on time. She ran up the long staircase to a massive room filled with children and a smaller room for babies. The woman in charge clapped her hands three times and blew a whistle, which meant it was time to put all toys away in cupboards. The children did as she ordered. Their noses were runny, their clothes torn. Once Carol and Susan saw their mother, they ran over to her, buried their heads in her skirt to wipe their noses.

"What took you so long?" Carol wrapped her arms around Sarah's knees.

"We thought you'd never come." Susan leaned her head on Sarah's thigh. "It's so cold here. I'm freezing."

"Yeah," Carol squeezed her mother's leg even tighter.

Sarah had to admit it was very drafty. The cardigan sweaters she put on them weren't heavy enough for such cold. She'd give them an extra shirt tomorrow.

"Let's go now. And hurry." She got their woolen coats

thrown into a pile by the entranceway. They had already lost a button from each of their coats. Oh, well, we'll just have to make do, Sarah reasoned. She worried how they'd manage once the winter came in just another month or so.

"Here girls, take some bread." Sarah tore off a huge chunk for both of them from her blue-netted bag once they were outside. She had waited over an hour in line for it.

"I'm sick of bread," Carol said. "That's all we eat here."

"Bread and more bread," Susan said. "Bread for breakfast, bread and soup for lunch."

"It will fill up your bellies until I can make our dinner." Sarah took a piece of the bread as well. How she wished she had something more to offer them.

The bus back to the communal apartment had to wind around streets filled with hordes of people. They passed by a poster that Sarah could not help but notice. A large open eye looked out on a work camp and the words above: *GPU—The Unblinking Eye of the Proletarian Dictatorship.* She grabbed the shoulders of her girls closer to her as the bus ambled through the city. There were plenty of posters and slogans written everywhere. In ten more minutes, they got off the bus and her tired girls slipped over the cobblestones jutting out of the street. They walked just a couple of blocks until they arrived at their apartment, 110 Izmaylovsky Prospekt.

They entered the vestibule where the old woman sat with her red kerchief tied around her head. Why is she always staring at us, Sarah wondered, as she ever so slightly hung her head down and pushed the girls in front of her. She wanted them to get to their room, away from that woman with her eyes roaming over everyone.

She'd better start the cooking. Katya told her some of

the families in the communal apartment building hired a peasant girl to wait in line for them at the store and do their food shopping.

"These young peasant girls are like slaves," Katya had whispered to her several days ago as they chopped up cabbage and potatoes. "At night they sleep on the kitchen floor or on the communal table. And our large black bugs crawl over them there." Sarah decided right then and there that she would do the waiting and the working, the cooking and the cleaning after work, even if it took her last morsel of energy.

By the end of dinner, her legs were so heavy it was difficult to move one in front of the other, so she collapsed into a deep sleep once the girls were in bed. She couldn't get used to the hunger in her belly, the girls crying out for more food, and the seven families sharing seven rooms, a single toilet, tub, and sink.

"Socialism won't be built in a day," Leon said as she wept to him one evening. "We all have to make sacrifices to build this country. Sarochka, it will get better."

Even when she mustered up the strength to clean, the room remained dirty. Paint peeled off of walls. In the corners, clumps of dust mixed with brown who-knows-what. Small bugs made a home there.

"I'm glad there's no room to eat in that kitchen," Sarah announced, putting a little sheet over the trunk. "I prefer anyway having dinner in our room."

"We should try and mix with the people here," Leon insisted. "You'll never be part of this community if you always stay by yourself." He was muscular and short, and his face, no matter how little he slept, or how badly he ate, always maintained a ruddy glow.

"I don't need to be mixing." Sarah put a glass over a tear in the sheet.

"But you don't understand. This is a communal apartment. The whole point is to get out of our little rigid boxes of family and expand our connections to people."

"That's for you to do."

"I hate sitting on the floor by that trunk to eat," Susan pouted.

Sarah looked askance at her older one, the dark-eyed one. Susan was named for Zlata, her mother. Both of them had the same beautiful black hair.

"Yeah." Carol imitated her older sister and then stuck her pinky through a hole in the thin, white material.

"Girls, you must listen now," Sarah said sharply without raising her voice.

"Okay." Susan hung her head down, slumped her shoulders forward until she could easily touch her toes with her fingers. This child somehow steadies me, Sarah thought, giving Susan some plates to put on the trunk.

"Yes, you can also have one." Susan handed a plate to Carol.

"Here, put the bread down in the middle of the table," Sarah said.

"It's a trunk, Mama, not a table."

"Well, whatever it is. Please watch your little sister while I finish up in the kitchen." Sarah looked over in Leon's direction before leaving; his face was already behind a newspaper, engrossed in the day's happenings.

"Look, she's stuck her finger in the cheese. Just a minute please, I'll cut you a piece." Susan put the dull knife through the creamy, soft wedge. "Here, take some bread, too, before you start crying." Susan tugged at the black bread and gave a piece to her sister.

"Girls, settle down now. Your mother will be back soon from the kitchen with our dinner," Leon said as he turned the pages of *Izvestia*.

The smells of cabbage, sometimes meat, if anyone was lucky enough to find some, made Sarah dizzy. The women in the kitchen dipped everything in oil until the room hissed with the sizzling sounds. You have to be a genius to understand the whole system of who gets what in this country, Sarah thought. There seemed to be seventeen categories of rationing, depending on who you were. And they would have all been at the bottom if Victor hadn't arranged, even before they got to Leningrad, for them to shop at the Insnab Shop, which was mainly for foreigners. But for the last few weeks, even there, she had seen less of the produce she needed and hardly any milk for the girls.

In the kitchen, Sarah heard the murmurs of women's voices by the stove. It was a large, chaotic room with lots of small tables filled with the residents' pots and pans.

Katya, her long and already graying hair tied back, stood by the stove talking to her friend Nadya, a short woman with a spoon in her hand. Nadya stirred the white potatoes, the water in the pot almost boiling. Sarah didn't want to interrupt their conversation, so she just listened from the table where she sat peeling the two carrots she had managed to find. Neither of them noticed her.

"Kolya was in Kharkov a week ago." Katya's voice was so faint that Sarah could hardly hear her, but still she tried to listen. "My God, Nadya, so many people are starving there. There's hardly a scrap to eat. You can't imagine.

On one road, he saw an old man just lying there, his eyes closed."

"It's all the fault of the Kulaks." Nadya scooped the potatoes out from the boiling water with a large ladle. "Comrade Stalin says they're the enemies of our Revolution."

That afternoon on the bus with her girls, Sarah noticed Stalin's new poster throughout the city; the leader in a military uniform took off his brown hat, saluting the people. "*Life is better,*" its slogan read. "*Life is getting happier.*"

Well, Stalin could afford those thoughts. Stalin didn't have to work from break of dawn to sunset, only to return to two hungry girls and a filthy, small room. His opinion about life might change if he did, Sarah reasoned. She could only wonder how their lives had been reduced to this poverty in a mere few weeks.

"Sarochka." Katya turned around with the potatoes drained and cut on a plate. "You've been quite the stranger." Her smile softened the effect of her words.

Sarah leaned her shoulders forward. Katya, with her rosy cheeks, looked like she belonged in a field with some rivers and chickens near her—not in some cramped kitchen in Leningrad.

"Got those bugs under control?" Katya asked.

"Not quite. But it's a little better, thank you." Every morning the girls still woke up weeping with welts down their legs.

The top button on Katya's blouse was missing. The material had been sewn together, torn and stitched up again. Sarah noticed Nadya, the rounder one, looking up and down at her long cotton skirt, at her loosely fitted white shirt.

"You wear such beautiful clothes," she said.

"These?" Sarah laughed. After all, she only owned two skirts, a couple of blouses, one sweater and an old winter coat. Surely, they couldn't see her as rich?

"Don't laugh at us. Compared to our rags, they're wonderful." Katya touched Sarah's cotton material.

"Here," Nadya said and took out a piece of brown soap from her apron pocket. "You'll need these for your girls. It's not easy keeping clean in this place."

Nadya was right. The seatless toilet down the hall had unspeakable filth in it. How do you live like this, she wanted to ask them, but their conversation was interrupted by more women coming into the kitchen to cook.

Sarah ventured out into the hallway and spotted Susan and Carol running down the narrow, long corridor with two boys. The girls shouted at the top of their lungs, "I'll catch you yet," and ran faster, trying to overtake the boys. Sarah was about to call them when she got distracted by two other boys, both about ten years old, leaning against the wall outside the kitchen, legs crossed, talking about Pavlik Morozov. Not him again. Sarah was so sick of him. Everywhere she turned she saw the headlines in *Pravda* or *Izvestia* claiming he was the new hero for denouncing his father for his Kulak ways. Over and over again, she had read how Pavlik's father did not want to give up his private farm and join the collective with the other peasants. So, putting the needs of the state first, Pavlik turned his father in and watched as he was arrested and taken away. Days later, Pavlik was murdered at night by his neighbors, the peasants who considered him a traitor to his people.

"Could you do the same?" one boy, bouncing a small

ball against the floor, asked the other.

"My teacher said he died a martyr. That we should all be brave like him."

Sarah didn't want to hear any more. "Carol, Susan, come right over here, this very minute," she yelled, but they only continued running around.

"In school, they say we must keep a watch on everyone. Even our parents."

"I'm so happy my mama and papa are good citizens."

"Yeah, mine too."

"Are you sure about that?" A third, older boy appeared out of nowhere. The younger ones looked up at him, laughed right in his face and ran away. They glanced back once to see if he'd join the chase.

"Susan and Carol," Sarah called again. She couldn't listen to this nonsense. Turning in your own parents for arrest. It was simply unimaginable. "Girls, come right now."

This time they heard. Carol and Susan ran right into her legs, clasped their arms around her thighs. "We were having so much fun, Mama." Their hair was sweaty, their arms warm. Their young pursuers scampered down the hall, entered a door, and shut it behind them.

"Why did you let the girls go running in the hallway?" she asked Leon, once they all returned to their room. "Can you help me here with these hot plates?"

"Why should they stay here all the time just with themselves?" Leon grabbed the steaming food and placed it all on the trunk. "They're children. They should go and play with others."

"They play plenty at the daycare." She glanced over at them. They had become so much thinner over the last few weeks.

"Can't we eat something else for a change?" Susan scowled at the carrots and potatoes, the cheese and the bread.

"I don't want to hear such talk again. We're eating much better than most," Leon said gruffly. "Your mother bought all this at the Torgsin shop with some dollars we were lucky enough to bring to Leningrad. Most people here can't do that."

They ate the rest of the meal in silence, and that was fine with Sarah. Later she delighted them all with her half a bar of soap. She took the girls together to the bathroom downstairs. She held them up, so no part of them touched the toilet, and then they washed up their faces and hands and returned the soap to her for safekeeping.

SOVIET STORIES

Cemeteries in the Morning

Bells drift into St. Petersburg
as winter disappears,
an abandoned palace
where thrones and crowns in glass cases rise.

There were days we walked the Moscow streets,
stepped into a quiet disappearing,
old women with kerchiefs round their necks
backs bent over, netted bags in hands.

I see him now by the window,
tall by curtains elegantly
darkening hair.

In his room Tolstoy's white beard
down the picture frame,
eyes of a prophet.
Can one land love a writer more?

It is what remains,
this and a Russian samovar tea set
on a flowered tray,
held by a Moscow Jew with an ancient name.

On a brisk October day, I spotted Volodya up the block from the *Institut Imeni Pushkina*. I wished it were Iosif there instead. But no luck on that one. Already that Rosh Hashanah afternoon, when Volodya took us all to the synagogue, then asked me to buy him books from poets who had disappeared from the Soviet bookstores, seemed far away. Time had slowed down since I came to Moscow.

I felt a chill in the October air as I stepped towards a woman in a white apron selling ice cream bars from a frozen cart by the Metro.

"Anna, can you get me those books now?" Volodya called to me in English.

"Can we do it another day? Today's not so good."

"Please, I really need these books. Please. It cannot wait." Volodya brushed his nose with the sleeve of his denim jacket. "We'll go to the Beriozka, and you'll buy me two volumes of Pasternak, Akhmatova, and Tsvetayava. All those writers of the 1930s have been banned here forever."

He seemed awfully pushy. I wondered if he planned on reselling them on the black market to someone desperate for this poetry, so desperate they might spend their last cent, risk getting into trouble with the Soviet state, just to own these sacred books. But I wasn't sure.

I understood that the Beriozka was a store where only foreigners could go—rubles would buy one nothing and only foreign currency was accepted.

"I can't get all that. I don't have enough dollars on me."

"But I'll pay you back in rubles."

Exchanging dollars for rubles sounded risky to me.

"You have to understand. I don't have enough dollars with me today. I can only buy what I can."

"All right," he said brusquely.

"Are you sure this is okay to do?"

"Of course. You're just giving me a present. There's nothing wrong with that. These poets are important to us. You must surely understand that."

We walked without speaking along the Moscow streets until we came to a small store; the word *Beriozka* glittered in golden letters across its windows. Across the road, Volodya waited.

Inside there were rows and rows of books: Dostoevsky, Tolstoy, Chekhov, Goncharov, and then I saw—among so many others—Bulgakov, Babel, Yevtushenko, all writers who had disappeared from a regular bookstore. I bought one volume instead of two of the poets Akhmatova, Tsvatayeva, and Pasternak in beautiful hardcover bound books.

Once outside, I crossed the wide street to Volodya and started to open up the white plastic bag with large swirling red and golden letters, *Beriozka*.

"No, not here," and he waved me away. "We'll take a taxi and there you'll give me the books. You'll tell me it's a present from you. Okay? Понимаете?"

"Да."

His eyes followed the outline of the plastic bag. "You only have three books here."

"I bought what I had money to buy."

"Okay. Okay. I'll pay you back for the books in rubles. But I don't have the money now. I'll give it to you the next time I see you."

I figured as much.

Volodya stood in the middle of the street and waved down a taxi. We sat together in the back seat.

"What's the name of the street you live on?" He spoke in tones barely above a whisper.

"Volgina."

"Take us to Ulitsa Volgina."

"Here, Volodya, is my present for you." I said my rehearsed lines.

Volodya took the books out of the Beriozka bag and placed them inside his briefcase before closing it shut. He then handed the empty Beriozka bag back to me.

"Oh, thank you," he said.

The cab driver sped along streets until we were outside the center of Moscow. Volodya told him to drop us off a few blocks from the dorm.

Once the cab had left, Volodya turned to me. "I want so much to read these books. Thank you, Anna. I hope I'll see you soon." He spoke as if he were reading lines from a script he had written the night before.

As we stood there, I saw five Vietnamese women, also foreign students at the Pushkin Institute, walk past us. One woman wore a flowered shirt and a long-oversized skirt covering her checkered pants. The Vietnamese women carried cabbage, apples, and potatoes in netted bags. They held hands with each other, laughing in a language I could not understand.

"Okay, you're welcome," I said and turned away from

Volodya, towards the dorm. I walked behind the Vietnamese women, most of them dressed in black coats several
sizes too big for them.

I knew I would never see Volodya again. And, fortunately, I never did.

The next evening the Vietnamese stood in the dorm
kitchen frying nuts, cabbage, onions, and carrots together.
Miloz sat on a chair chatting with three young women in
a language I figured was Polish. I wanted to somehow warn
them about him. But I looked away, pretended not to see
him, wished he could disappear though I knew it was
impossible. I had to push him out of my mind. When I
get home, I would deal with what had happened and all
my feelings that, for now, I had to stop feeling.

"We'll be finished here shortly," one woman said to
me in Russian. "Откуда Вы?" she asked.

When I said I came from the USA, she smiled. "Yes,
the American people are our friends. They helped us win
the war against your government. You must be our guest
after you finish your dinner."

"Sure, thank you."

The Vietnamese women carried their food from the
kitchen to their rooms down the hall.

"We will see you soon," they called to me.

"Да," I replied.

I placed five small potatoes, my dinner for the evening,
in the oven. The potatoes were sweet; their crusts would
burn. I bought them for dollars in the grocery store where
only foreigners were allowed to go. Otherwise I'd have to
wait in line for hours.

After the potatoes were finished cooking, I slowly ate

them without butter. They tasted like something sugary from the earth.

I came to the Vietnamese women without anything to bring them. I knocked lightly; the woman I spoke with in the kitchen peeked her head out and opened the door for me to enter.

"Наша молодая Американская подруга, заходите," she said and slipped her arm through mine. Together we stepped into the room. It was a room like my own: two single beds, a window, two dressers, and a bathroom. Three other women sat on the edges of the beds.

"Меня зовут Май," she told me. I thought of the month of May to help me remember her name.

"You must eat our Vietnamese nuts and tea," Quan, another woman, said. She gathered a plateful of raw nuts and left us for the kitchen. Bangs bordered her eyes; her black hair fell just below her shoulders.

A few minutes later Quan returned with the nuts darkened brown and a pot of tea. "This is tea from Vietnam," she announced.

Russian posters hung from the walls of their rooms— pictures of women athletes and the words *The Great Achievements in Soviet Sports* printed above.

"Tell me, what is life like in your country?" Quan asked.

I froze up and couldn't figure out what to say in Russian. "I don't know how to answer your question."

"Well, then sing us an American song," Mauy urged.

I went blank on that one too. Then I remembered the Peter, Paul and Mary song, "500 Miles."

"*Five hundred miles, five hundred miles,*" I sang off-key. "*I am so far away from home.*"

"We miss our home, too," Mauy said. "In Vietnam the

women drink green tea. Our fruits and vegetables grow on trees. Here, in Moscow, we're not used to the food."

I had five measly potatoes for dinner. I hated the food, too. In the dorm basement, where the dining room was, I might be able to buy some thick cheese and bread, but not much more.

"The green tea keeps us young. You must tell your American friends about us, about our green tea. You must tell the American people they are our friends," their voices echoed. "They protested the war against our country."

The women showed me their large woolen overcoats and black rubber boots. The Soviet government gave them these winter clothes once they came to Moscow, so they wouldn't be cold. "We've never worn this type of clothing before," they said. "We miss the warm Vietnam weather. We miss our families. But when we return to Vietnam, we will be teachers of Russian."

They spoke of their *rodina,* their homeland—of the bombs the Americans dropped on their country.

"So much is barren now. We have to build our *rodina.* But you must know how every year, on the anniversary marking the day when someone has died in the war, the family makes a dinner. The table is covered by a white cloth. Each place is set, including one for the dead. The family sits down to eat, opens the door for the lost one to enter and be with them.

"They eat and weep. Oh, how they weep. They wait for the spirit of the dead to sit by them. Every year they do this," Mauy said.

"Their tears fill the plates, stain the silverware. Наша молодая Американская подруга, we want you to understand us," Quan added. "You see, we won the war because we were not afraid of death."

"Not afraid of death." Another voice seemed to echo and fill the room as I first hugged each one of them, then got ready to leave, already half in love with these women in their checkered shirts, their flowered pants.

They made me feel I could leave all sorrows in this Russian land.

A week later, on a day in late October when most leaves had fallen to the ground, Iosif took me to the *zagorod*. The land rested in brown, golden and yellow colors, and the homes were the way I imagined them to be, with white paint embroidering the outside of delicately carved windows. A short distance from the train station, we found a cement path leading us into a darkening forest.

"These are real Russian woods," Iosif said and placed his arm through mine as we stepped through thickets of light layered trees; shadows receded and cobwebbed mists opened onto the path leading us to his grandfather's old apartment.

"Anichka, I have to say your Russian has gotten much better."

"It's still pretty bad." Dried mud clung to my brown leather boots. I gazed up at him, at his thin and lanky body, at his face that seemed young and old simultaneously.

"No, it's better." His praise meant more to me than I could say. Iosif was definitely the smartest person I had ever met.

"In Russian class, we're learning when to raise our voices higher, like at the end of a question. But when else do you do it?"

I didn't expect Iosif to start laughing. "I don't know.

I never thought about any of this."

"Depending on what you want to say, you're supposed to raise your voice a little or a lot."

"Really?" He stopped for just a moment, wrapped his arm around me. I leaned my head onto his shoulder.

"Now you tell me something. What do Americans talk about when they get together? Is it only about business?"

"No." I was the one laughing this time.

"Well, then, what is it?"

"I don't know. Movies, music, TV, maybe a book. The usual stuff, the election, the world."

"Do you ever tell any jokes?"

"Of course, we do."

"I see." We walked in silence for a while. As we got deeper into the forest, Iosif's mood changed.

"In the countryside, there's hardly any food. Only bread and grains. Some sausage maybe and cabbage." Iosif pushed away the strands of wind-blown hair from his face. "Tell me, do you know what a propiska is?"

I didn't have a clue.

"You must understand this if you're going to know anything about our country," he said, slightly impatient or impassioned. I wasn't sure.

"Propiska is a pass. We're actually supposed to carry it around with us at all times, but most don't. But if I want to go any great distance outside of Moscow, I must report where I'm going and get permission. Понимаешь?"

"Yes," I said, though I didn't really get it. I only knew there was a humming in my arm linked through his.

"Can you imagine? If I want to go to Leningrad, I can't just pick up and go. Do you see what I'm saying?"

"I understand," I said in my limited Russian, then

switched to English.

"Well, now I have a question for you." The rows of trees obscured my view of the sky, the afternoon light slipping away.

"Okay, then. Go ahead."

"When your parents separated, did they fight a lot about money?"

"Money?" Iosif paused. "Why money? They didn't have any to fight about. Why do you ask?"

"Because money was all my parents fought about."

"What can I say? America is a sick place," he said as he stepped into the moist dirt covered with yellow leaves. The soil smelled of rain from yesterday—the thin boughs of trees opened into a path of green and brown for us to follow. All of my life I had been waiting to be here. I leaned once more into Iosif's arm, felt his cotton jacket against my face.

He led us out of the woods, away from the scent of pine and nettle everywhere. We found another cement path taking us to a brown apartment building that stood all by itself, surrounded only by grass.

"Years ago, my grandfather used to come here a lot—to think, to work. But that was all before he lost his memory."

"When did that happen?"

"The last ten years, I would say. It was gradual. But it's probably better he forgets the past as far as I'm concerned." I remembered the soft and feathery feel of his grandfather's hand when I saw him at Iosif's apartment, his thick furry eyebrows, that dreamy, faraway look to his face.

We walked up several flights of dingy stairs until we came out into a dark corridor. I followed alongside Iosif, seeking the evening light. Inside the apartment, volumes and volumes of Tolstoy's books filled up most of the shelves lining the walls.

"How did your grandfather get all these books? I've never seen anything like this"

"I can't tell you that. But this is everything Tolstoy ever wrote."

More secrets. I was growing used to it, little by little. So much could not be said or shared. I wanted to know but would not ask again.

I stepped up to the blue-bound books, touched some with the tips of my fingers, as if it might be possible to hold the words inside them, to feel the spirit of the writer, the beloved prophet, through the printed marks, the black typeface etched there.

By the window, adjacent to the bookshelves, I saw a black stove used to heat the apartment in winter. Iosif went into the small kitchen at the other end of the room. He boiled water for tea, took several loaves of bread out of a netted bag, along with a chunk of cheese, and placed it all on the round table where I sat waiting for him.

"Пожалуйста ешь Аничка. Ты должен быть голодным."

The bread was sweet, its crust browned by butter. It started to snow as we ate. Every day, since the beginning of October, the snow would come for an hour or two and relieve some tension invisible in the air with its arrival.

Iosif poured brown, leafy tea into two plain glasses.

"There's hardly anything to buy in the stores out here," he said.

"Yes, I can see that." There were only a bunch of cans lining the empty shelves in the Moscow supermarkets.

"It's much worse in the countryside," Iosif said, as if

to read my thoughts. "This place, you must understand, is an absolute nightmare." He had repeated these words almost every time I had seen him. Кошмар, the word in Russian for nightmare sounded so ominous, I thought, as Iosif went over to a closet by the table and took down a rusted copper box and small key.

"Our family treasures," he said and smiled.

"What's in there?"

"Here are some pictures of my great-uncle Victor, my grandfather's brother." He handed me a photograph of a young man with a full beard; a fur hat covered his head, his left arm embraced a woman in a matching silver hat; the river, with icicles mixed with water, behind them. I saw a blur of gray in the background, an opaque tower, a sillhouette etched onto the fog of a winter day.

"That's the Peter and Paul fortress, a prison used in czarist times," Iosif said and pointed to the tower.

"Who's the beautiful girl?"

"That's Marina, his wife, the only one still alive."

"She must be very old now."

"She is." Iosif gulped down the last of the tea from his glass. "My favorite photograph is my great-uncle by the offices of *Izvestia*."

I held the pictures of their wedding day and their honeymoon along the Czar's overtaken palaces. Snow everywhere, on the branches of trees outside, over the dying grass, the slender bushes and plants covered by white flakes frozen into place.

"He was quite the Bolshevik star," Iosif said. "After the 1905 Revolution, he rotted for a while in the Czar's prison. But my uncle at nineteen was smart. He bribed his way out. Don't ask me how. I don't know. And he left the country for a long time but managed to sneak back in to fight for the October Revolution.

"So when did he meet Marina?"

"Shortly after he returned here. They were the same, like two selves that belonged to one soul."

"What do you mean?"

"They saw everything exactly the same way. Together they were building this new world."

There were letters in long and flowing Cyrillic characters on faded paper—love letters to Marina before their marriage; then later letters from the Lubyanka prison.

"I myself don't even know how we got this stuff. When there was an arrest, the police ransacked the apartment and took everything. All papers, documents, anything personal."

"But how can you not know where this came from?" Our fingers were lightly touching.

"It's just how it is. I'd really have to question my grandfather on this one, and as you can see from meeting him, that would be quite useless." He noticed the empty crumbs of bread on my plate. "Here, you must have some more." He cut a few more wedges of soft cheese for me.

"Thanks." I didn't realize how hungry I was. "But isn't there anyone else to ask?"

"My mother was just a baby when her uncle was arrested, so she doesn't remember anything. And now, it's the one thing she doesn't want to talk about." A small leaf of tea stuck to the side of his mouth until Iosif brushed it away.

"All I can say is that everything was going so well for my great-uncle. He became a major writer at *Izvestia*. He and Marina finally got out of that awful communal apartment. He was moving up in the party, so he managed to get a much better place—really decent for Soviet standards—a small apartment in the middle of town with their own bathroom and kitchen. Can you imagine? It seemed like a palace."

"What happened to that apartment?"

"After Stalin had him shot, Marina stayed on there alone. She's still there now." Iosif scratched a corner of his face until it reddened into a small circle.

"She is?" Everyone I met in this place had lost someone. Outside the snow had thickened until the countryside was a white stillness.

"Yes, but as I said, she's very old now and doesn't remember much. I do know, and it's hard to believe that a year before his arrest, my Uncle Victor actually became mayor of a small town outside of Leningrad. But I already told you all that. Right?"

I nodded as Iosif took another letter out of the box, stained with water, torn and taped together, dated October 1936.

Was I just a young dreamer or a fool, my love? We cannot give up on all we have fought for.

That's all I could make out from the curling Cyrillic letters.

"Those were his last words to her."

I put my hand over his; he moved closer to me and smiled. All the tautness in his face disappeared.

"Here, take a look at this one." He picked up a photograph of a young woman with a large furry *shapka* covering most of her head and face and a scarf wrapped around her mouth. She stood next to an older man dressed in a large hat as well.

"They're an odd-looking couple," I said.

"Why is that?"

"He looks like he might be her father."

I barely saw their faces beneath all they were wearing. But I did notice how the woman's eyes were brown, small, and sorrowful. The man had an altogether different look. He seemed full of confidence, even defiant, despite the many creases of lines around his mouth.

There was something familiar about the man in the picture, though I didn't know what it was. Then I felt everything in the room blur together. The table and the food on it, the empty tea glasses—I couldn't tell one object from another.

I had the strangest feeling that I was staring at my grandfather. I had only known him as an old man with just a few strands of gray hair; he liked to wear overalls with no shirt beneath. His face was only younger. And that must be my grandmother underneath all those winter clothes. But her eyes were the same, even if now one was closed, the other blind. Still I had to be sure before I said anything.

"Iosif, tell me. Who are these people exactly?" I could barely wait for his reply.

"I was told the couple came from America, though originally from here. They were foolish enough to leave their life behind there and move to Leningrad. Can you imagine?"

"I know this sounds crazy. But these are my grandparents. I see now it's true."

"It's simply not possible. How could that be?"

"My grandparents, like I told you, came here to Leningrad in 1931. With their children too, my mother and aunt. It was crazy. But they did it. I know it's them now. It just took me a few moments to recognize them." I took the picture from him.

"This is ridiculous. A lot of people here look the same, especially the women. They all have that same tired worn-out look. What probably happened to this couple is what happened to most people who returned in the 30s. They died here, unable to get out," he said.

"But my grandparents somehow were able to leave. It was a small window of possibility, and they took the boat all the way back to Boston. Let's see what else is in this box." I rummaged through it, searching for more photographs of my grandparents. Instead, I found an envelope from the USA.

"Is it okay to open it?"

"Yes, of course. Let's see what's here."

I took the faded paper out, filled with the delicate curves of Cyrillic script. I asked Iosif to read it to me since it was difficult to decipher the handwriting.

"*Vitya*," he began in a loud voice. "*I am returning finally to this land. I am arriving my dear comrade with my family, my wife Sarah and my two girls. Yes, even an old bachelor like me has actually gotten married . . .*"

> *. . . But enough of that for now. I can hardly believe that soon I will be on Russian soil. But it is true. I have the tickets for us all. I only hope this letter finds you.*
>
> *Life has been difficult in the faraway country of America. I ended up settling in Boston, Massachusetts. There is no work anywhere. Just some scraps of a job here and there. You knew long ago we would set up a worker's state. All those conversations we had in the Saloon. You remember then now? I didn't understand then but now I do. The workers of America are also beginning to understand.*

For years I have been longing to return to our homeland. But I didn't know how I could do it. Finally, I have gotten the tickets. I still can't believe that on September 10th, I will arrive into Leningrad. The ship will dock there, I think, in the afternoon. I can only hope this letter finds you and you will be there to meet us, my dear friend, my comrade, Vitya.

Yours,
Lenya

My right eye started to twitch open and shut a few times as I took the letter from Iosif, made out the one word, *rodina,* homeland. I imagined my grandfather bending down to kiss the Russian earth when he arrived from Boston to Leningrad almost fifty years ago.

Iosif gave me the red rusted box. I looked through the torn and pasted together photographs until I found one, folded in half, on the bottom of the box. There I saw my grandmother, a young woman who already looked old in her features and mannerisms. She wore a black dress that fell quite a few inches below her knees; her hips were wide. Her pale neck, partially covered by a black cardigan sweater, highlighted her face, so austere and mournful in the afternoon light. She sat on a bench next to my grandfather but already they seemed far apart. This time he wore the overalls I knew him by and a long, gray shirt underneath that did not hide his muscles, hardened into bone and flesh. Another man stood next to my grandfather. I figured it was Victor. He wore round spectacles and had a passionate, concentrated gaze to his eyes.

"Look, Iosif. Look here. Look."

"Представляешь? Представляешь," he repeated. "I remember now some story about a beloved friend, Lenya, from my uncle's childhood. I had completely forgotten until this moment."

"Childhood?"

"Yes, from Baronovitch, you know, part of Minsk. My grandfather told me some stories a while ago. Now he wouldn't even remember he had a brother Victor."

"Please, tell me everything you know." I wanted him to keep talking.

"I don't know much. Only when your grandfather's father died, my uncle would come over to the saloon the family owned. Supposedly he was helping them out. Maybe he was just there to get a drink or two. I don't know. Can you imagine seven children running a saloon?"

I longed for these tales. "What else? Please tell me."

"I know they did all try to run the saloon for a while. And then an aunt showed up and did what she could to put a stop to it. But it didn't work."

"But how do you know all this?"

"My great Aunt Marina. As I told you, she's still alive but very, very old. She told me Victor loved to speak about his friend, Lenya. He was heartsick when he left Leningrad and returned to Boston," Iosif said and paused so I could take in his words. "But now we know how lucky your grandparents were to get out of here."

All of my life it seemed I had been waiting to enter this room where the round thick pipes of the black stove spiraled up to the ceiling, where Iosif sat with me at a table sipping Russian tea with sweet yellow bread and creamy hunks of cheese on a plate. He took my hand and together we walked over to the beige couch with its stiff, rectangular pillows. He was just touching my hand, but I felt his touch down my legs and arms, some longing, as if I had been calling to him from far away and did not even know it until this moment.

"For now, please don't tell anyone about this, not just yet."

"Not even Tanya?"

"No, for now, no. At the right moment, I'll tell her, definitely, I will."

"Okay." Always secrets, a web of secrets. Now even my own life was caught up in it. I didn't, couldn't understand. I only knew I wanted to make love with him here in this room. It seemed I had known him a very long time ago, longer than I could ever remember, and had found him again here in Moscow.

"Let's open this," he said, throwing the two pillows from the couch to the floor, and pulling the handle out for the bed, a thin mattress on top of wire springs. He slipped off my snug-fitting sweater, my red corduroy pants. I unbuttoned his shirt, admired the two long black curls of hair on his belly and kissed him.

"Is anything the matter?" he whispered. His hands on my back eased away some sorrow I did not know was there.

"No." I didn't want to tell him I felt some fear in me. It was always there, waiting for me. Outside I heard the wind against the window.

He ran his fingers through my hair, said quietly, "Anichka." There were no similar endearments for my name in English.

I kissed his neck, took in the scent of his hair and arms. He pulled me to him, his mouth on my breasts, my belly, down my legs. I rested my body on top of him, guided him inside me. Together we went back to a place where there was no time, no beginning or end, only the silence of snow.

Lying in his arms, I wanted to tell him I had been waiting all of my life to meet him. But I didn't say it.

Instead, I drifted into my grandmother's song, Сижу и играю я на гитаре, я сижу и веселюсь . . . The next line went, *No one knows my grief.* No one had. I wanted to bury it all in this Russian land, to forget and leave it here, so I could start my life all over again. At least this much was clear.

The dorm room concierge at her desk by the elevator would spoil my plans to stay here with him. She was the last person I wanted to remember. But I had to be at the dorm by ten. Maybe I could stretch it to ten thirty. Otherwise, they'd notice I wasn't there.

Iosif knew what I was thinking. "I have to get you back to Moscow," he said. "I don't want to. But we better go."

"You're right. We have to go," I repeated. I got out of the bed and looked at Iosif, at his lean, long body.

He hugged me once more before we dressed quickly.

"You didn't forget anything?" He had already put the couch back together, so there was no trace of us anywhere.

"I think so." I gathered up my backpack, my blue down coat and brown Russian fur hat. I needed to know when I would see him again, needed to know that he wouldn't just disappear and become some mirage in my mind.

Outside the air was crisp, the wind on my face. The snow rested on my furry hat, blended into the strands of my hair.

There was an awkward silence between us as we walked back through the forest, past the white carved wood delicately bordering the windows of small houses, past the slender branches of trees covered by snow, past grass and soil, to a solitary bench outside, where the train would soon come.

We waited a few moments. There were a couple of other travelers bundled up in thick coats and large fur hats, their backs stooped over with fatigue. No one said a word.

On the train, I rested my head against his shoulder. He closed his eyes and fell asleep.

After thirty minutes, I tapped his arm. "Iosif, wake up."

"What is it?"

"We're almost there. There's so much I want to say. Can we speak now?"

He glanced up at the people on the train. "No, it's not the time to speak. Not now."

When we reached Ulitsa Volgina, Iosif did not walk me part way along the grass path leading me to the dorm entrance. He must have been wary someone might see him. He wanted to say good-bye to me on the corner.

"We'll see each other soon," he said. "I promise."

"When?"

"As soon as I can. But I can't tell you when that will be."

He wrapped his long arms around my shoulders, holding me for just a second, so no one could notice us. He lips grazed against my own.

"You better go," he said.

"Okay," I said, agreeing to let go of him, for now. I turned toward the gravelly path, made my way over stones and dirt; the light from the street created shadows on my face. Before I got to the entrance where the concierge would surely nod and note my arrival, I looked back once to catch another glimpse of Iosif, but he had already gone.

Weeks passed and I didn't see Iosif. He didn't come to the Friday night dinners Nadezhda prepared. He didn't appear down the block from the entrance to the *Institut Imeni Pushkina* when my classes were over for the day, and the phonetics teacher's words, "My Name is Maria Filipovna, and we will study melodia," continued to echo in my ears as I left the red brick building.

I didn't see him as I walked along the Kuznetsky Most Bridge, past the yellow buildings and winding streets where mainly women waited many hours in lines for fruits and vegetables, meat or cheese. I even went by the *bylochnaya* where only bread was sold. But he was not there either.

LIFE IS GETTING BETTER, THEY SAY

Folk Song

In the afternoon the deli man cut his salami, packed up
fish in a smelly paper folded up like star fish glittering;

there she heard her mother singing beyond the sawdust
scattered floors, her mother thrown in the sea years ago.

My great-grandmother in the *sishu igrayu* words
sung by a daughter old and blind but still seeking

her from behind curtains of nursing home windows leading
only to parking lots and highways, floors taking her higher,

closer to dying as alarm clocks ring, dictators fall,
someone will be king, *ya na gitarye,* the old woman sings.

Both Sarah and Leon wondered why Victor had never introduced them to his wife. It was all some strange sort of mystery until one Saturday morning Victor showed up unannounced with the most beautiful woman Sarah had ever seen.

"Everyone, this is Marina," he said and put his arm around her slender shoulder. "And we've come to take you on an outing to the Czar's Winter Palace. We've reclaimed it for the people, and now all citizens can come and view it any time of day."

"Приятно познакомиться." Sarah held out her hand. Marina, instead, kissed Sarah's left cheek. She had the faint scent of a flower that was familiar.

"Ah, you've been hiding your wife from us," Leon said and came closer to embrace her.

"I was just waiting for the right moment. Okay, maybe two months was too long to wait. But we've been busy, and I wanted Marina to come here when we could all take a little trip together."

Marina had thick, dark hair that fell to her shoulders and pale porcelain skin, green eyes. "We'll have some fun today," she smiled. Sarah kept looking at her. She wondered how every strand of Marina's hair managed to stay in place after she took off her large fur shapka.

"Uncle Victor!" Carol jumped up and down. Victor twirled her around one time in a full circle before placing her down on the floor. Marina bent down and kissed the top of Carol's curly hair.

"Come on, let's go." Susan gathered up the coats for the two of them.

Leon, who rarely showed much physical attention to anyone, took hold of Susan's hand. Carol had already claimed Victor's arm. Sarah bustled about, found an old lipstick she hadn't used since she got there and slipped on her black galoshes. "Get your boots on, girls," Sarah said, as she folded up her netted bag in case they came across some food to buy.

The bus was crowded, but today Sarah didn't mind being pushed and jostled in between all those people. She passed large squares with tapestries telling the story of the Revolution, how the Winter Palace was stormed and restored to the people; she even marveled at the city's panorama of stately buildings. But nothing could have prepared her for the vision of the palace bordered by the river on one side—turquoise stucco arching, gold columns.

"There are fifteen hundred rooms in there," Victor pointed with his longest finger.

"Yes, the czars lived well while they bled our country." Marina leaned her shoulders against Victor.

She seems to finish Victor's sentences as though their thoughts are one, Sarah noticed. It was such a stark contrast to her own marriage.

"These times are over forever, thank goodness," Leon said.

"Did the king and queen live there all by themselves, Papa?" Susan asked.

"We called them czars. They ruled while the rest of us

lived like dirt. And they had hundreds and hundreds of servants."

When Sarah was in Gornostyapol, it was hard for her to imagine Czar Nicholas in such a palace while they all lived in their little hovels. Nicholas was always some faraway, unreal idea. The learned men of Gornostaypol would often shake their heads when they spoke about him. Nicholas so hated the Jews. Life had gotten so much worse for them under his reign.

They passed a large poster with the words, *We are on Guard in Defense of Socialism,* and then a more colorful one read, *We will Keep Out Kulaks From the Collective Farms.* Below the letters, a young man in a red jacket stood behind a table, presiding over the crowd.

The bus left them by the palace's snow-covered rolling lawns, which led up to the baroque stucco buildings, painted greenish and blue. Outside cement fountains spewed water. Soviet citizens dressed in dark worn clothes walked up the path to the entranceway.

"See if you can catch me." Carol bounded away from Victor. Susan ran off behind her. The girls made snowballs, snuck up behind Victor, and hit him in the back with them.

"You got me!" He laughed, turned around, and picked up each one of them until they squealed to come down.

"The girls seem so happy," Marina said, walking ahead of the men.

"Well, yes, today, they are."

"So how do you like our city of Leningrad?"

"It's very beautiful here. But life, I'm sure you know, is difficult."

"Yes, I do know." Marina slowed down her steps. "One

day it will all be worth it. You'll see."

Sarah was about to ask Marina how she and Victor met, but then she decided against such a personal question. She glanced over at the girls lying down in the snow, their arms and legs spread out wide.

"Girls, you'll get too wet," she called to them. "Come out of the snow now."

"We're angels, Mama."

"You'll catch cold."

"Girls, I have something I want to tell everyone right away. You'll miss out if you don't come." Victor raised his voice but did not shout.

"Okay, wait for us." When they got up, the thick clumps of snow clung to their clothes; the cold made their cheeks red, their noses run.

"I guess this is as good a time as any." Victor drew Marina close to him. "I have an announcement, everyone. Today is our fifteenth wedding anniversary. We thought we'd celebrate by coming to the Winter Palace with all of you."

Leon ran up to them, hugged them both at the same time with his strong arms and repeated, "Прекрасно, Прекрасно!"

Sarah joined their little circle from the outside. The girls jumped up and down, their boots landing in the soft snow.

"We met in the summer of 1916 and married in late October." Victor kissed Marina's long neck. Even though Victor was the same age as Leon, he looked younger to Sarah, more boyish. He had a gentler edge to him.

"And every day since, we've fought together to create our Soviet Union," Marina said. The two of them seem so in love, Sarah thought. Glancing over at Leon, laughing like a young boy, she had to admit that nothing had worked out as she had hoped. But it would be different, she knew, for them.

"I want us to be like sisters now," Marina linked her arm through Sarah's and began to walk. The girls, in front of them, skipped towards the palace entrance.

"Yes. This is a wonderful day." Sarah felt calmer with Marina next to her.

Inside the palace, Sarah couldn't believe the marble floors, the gold, the walls with oval windows, balconies, jeweled chandeliers, tapestries from Egypt and Asia, statues of full-breasted women. The men grabbed the girls' hands. They all spoke in hushed whispers. Then Carol wanted to see what happened if she shouted, "Mama." Would the sound echo and repeat? It did.

Sarah overheard Leon telling Victor in a low voice, "Look how she smiles, how she works, now that we are here."

"Yes, Lenya, we are creating a new future for her, too."

Sarah ignored them. "Come, let's explore another room," she called to Marina.

"To think all these riches finally belong to the people," Marina said and walked over to her.

"Yes, it is really something," Sarah had to admit as she looked up at the swirling golden ceilings.

The drafty shoe factory created a chill in her bones that never went away. Even Sarah's old wool sweater didn't seem to help. To make matters worse, none of the other women spoke to her. She was what they called an "American Soviet," and while they were curious about why she had returned, they still kept their distance. Sarah entered the dark cave they called the factory, where hundreds of electric needles stitching coarse material created a hypnotic buzzing sound. She let herself drift off to it, daydreaming of the seagulls in Boston Harbor screeching as the ship left the port.

Sarah's reverie was interrupted by her supervisor, a man with a thick, bushy mustache overgrown into a flip at each side of his mouth. He stood in front of the women by their sewing machines, calling out names in a monotone voice. One by one her coworkers were removed. A hush fell over the factory floor.

Sarah watched as her fellow workers stepped behind a large man in baggy clothes. "Don't worry," he said to them. "Just some routine questions to help us keep our country safe."

In a couple of hours, the twenty workers returned to their places, cleared of any suspicious activity. "There are those who want to destroy what we are building," a woman in thick glasses, who worked alongside Sarah, said. "It's important to be vigilant. So, I didn't mind their questions."

"But what did they want to know?" Sarah whispered.

"Just some questions about family background. I had nothing to fear. It's those rich peasants, pretending now to be workers . . . we need to watch out for them," she said and continued her stitching.

Why make us all afraid, Sarah wondered. She certainly came from the poorest stock of Russian Jews if they asked about her background. But Leon . . . his family had owned a tavern. Would anyone take issue with that? She had never considered any of this before, and now this new question made her afraid. After all, a tavern was a business, even if who knew what meager profits they made from it. It was all so far in the past. Who could possibly care? Well, she couldn't think about it. She needed to finish up her time in this dungeon of a factory and go pick up her girls.

At two-thirty, Sarah rode the crowded bus into the center of Leningrad, past the cobblestoned square of the majestic bronzed horseman, Peter the Great, on his black stallion. The bus was inching along, and she was restless anyway, so she got off and walked the rest of the way. Outside the empty shop windows, Sarah saw, as she did every day, the peasant women, with their children, begging. *Pravda* insisted any talk of a famine in the countryside was just a rumor created by enemies. But when Sarah observed how thin the children were—their long faces, their protruding shoulder bones—she wished she had something to give them.

First Sarah waited in line for an hour for bread. The wind nipped at her face; her woolen coat did not keep her warm. She stood silently with the other women. Why bother speaking? What would they say to each other anyway? When she finally bought her one loaf, her back already aching, she decided not to queue up again somewhere else for cabbage or potatoes. Who had the energy for all this, she asked herself, turning around, and heading for the Torgsin store. She still had a few dollars left of the money they'd borrowed from Leon's brother, so she might as well spend it and enjoy that little luxury. She could get carrots, onions, beets, and milk for the girls there. Thank goodness for those dollars.

The store was filled with people from other countries using their foreign currency or Soviet citizens bringing in their jewelry to trade for food. Just as Sarah was about to purchase her goods, she spotted Nadya, talking to a tall, smartly dressed man, at the back of the large store. It seemed odd that she was here, too. She wanted to say hello, but Nadya didn't see her, and besides Sarah was hurrying to get to the daycare center to pick up the girls. But then she changed her mind. Maybe Leon was right and she should be a little more social and at least greet her neighbor. People in some strange way were actually friendlier here than in Roxbury. After Sarah bought her food, she made her way to the other end of the store where Nadya still stood, very engrossed in some conversation. Sarah didn't want to interrupt anything. Fortunately, Nadya looked up when Sarah got closer to her.

"Sarochka!" Nadya walked over, very animated and smiling. She kissed Sarah's cheek. "What a great surprise to see you."

The man in the dark suit nodded to Nadya. In another moment he seemed to blend into the crowded store and disappear.

"I still had some dollars left. There's hardly anything to buy in the other stores," Sarah said.

"I turned in my necklace for some food coupons to shop here."

"Why is there so much more food here?" Sarah asked. "What about all the people who can't shop in this store?" She wondered why Nadya's blue-netted bag was still empty.

"Life here is not perfect. But little by little our Soviet state is striving to take care of all our citizens. You must forgive us our faults." Nadya stepped closer to Sarah. "But I better go now and find what we need for our dinner.

And you also must get those darling girls," she said and kissed Sarah once more. The faint scent of Nadya's perfume still lingered after she stepped away. Despite Nadya's warmth, it was clear to Sarah that she did not want to talk anymore.

It was already four o'clock. She had no more time to wonder about Nadya. Outside Sarah trudged along the cobblestone streets to the daycare center, her eyes turned downwards; her netted bag hung from her shoulder, swaying back and forth. Even the weight of the meager food she had bought made her feel lopsided, slightly tilted, and when she arrived at the daycare, she still had to climb up five flights of a winding staircase. All that dust tickled her nose, made her sneeze uncontrollably. Just when Sarah didn't think she could tackle another step, she entered a large room filled with what seemed like a hundred children, though there were probably only forty. Some ran to and fro, others cried; coats were thrown into piles. Instead of using a whistle, two older women clapped their hands.

"Mama." Carol saw her first and ran towards her. "You're always so late."

"I got here as soon as I could. Come, let's go." Sarah ran her fingers through their greasy hair. She only washed it once a week. She had to do better, Sarah resolved. Why should her girls walk around with dirty hair just because soap was scarce?

"I'm hungry." Carol wiped her nose on her mother's skirt.

"Me too," Susan chimed in.

It was always the same greeting and the same reply. "I have some bread for you. The rest needs to be cooked so let's get home now." Sarah watched her girls gobble down the sweet bread. At least they didn't complain but ate what she gave them, Sarah thought. She should be grateful today for that.

The daycare director, a rather severe type, narrowed her gaze; Sarah could feel her eyes on the netted bag filled with goods from the Torgsin store. As they began their descent down the stairs, she heard the older woman call to her, "I see Leningrad is treating you well."

"Mama, I don't feel good," Susan said as they stepped into the entranceway where the old woman sat at the desk all day long, looking at everyone who entered and left. She was small and shriveled, her hair in a tightly wound bun on top of her little head. She stared at the cabbage and beets, the potatoes and cheese in Sarah's netted bag.

"Me too. My throat hurts. And my head." Carol pulled at Sarah's coat.

"You always say everything I say," Susan said.

"But it's true."

The old woman nodded, like she always did, as they walked by.

The world would be better off without that woman, Sarah decided, gathering her girls closer to her. She was some busybody with nothing to do. "You'll rest together while I get the dinner ready," she told them, opening up the door to their one-room apartment. Her head was also starting to pound.

Sarah tucked the girls into the double bed they shared. They felt warm. But she had no medicine.

"Mama, don't leave," they begged her.

"When you wake up, I'll have more food for you."

Sarah stroked their thin hair until they fell asleep. A little rest will do them good, she told herself. They'll be better then.

Just as Sarah was about to step out of the room and start in the kitchen, she heard the familiar sound of a woman crying, then shouting, "How can this be? You tell me, how can this be?" More muffled sounds—it was Katya.

"How can they accuse us of this?" Katya cried through the thin walls of the apartment. "How can it be possible?" she repeated over and over again.

"Katya, stop making a scene." A man's voice—must be her husband's. They lived next door, so even though they spoke in low tones, Sarah heard everything.

"Who could have done this to us?" Katya asked. "Accused you of having past links to those enemy Kulaks."

"It doesn't matter now who spoke ill of me. We'll find another place."

Sarah heard the shuffling of furniture, a suitcase dragged along the floor, a small child whimpering. Must be their son. Who had caused this to happen? The old woman by the door? At first, that seemed the only plausible answer to this riddle. But no, it wasn't her. That old woman was just an annoying busybody. But who? Who could it have been?

She left her sleeping girls and tiptoed into the kitchen, eerily empty for five o'clock, and began chopping her carrots and onions. The monotonous sounds of the knife hitting the cutting board made her head pound even more. What would become of Katya and her family? Where would they go?

"Sarochka," Sonia said. She was another American from California. Sonia, like her, was once a Russian Jew in czarist Russia. She too had left for America before the revolution and had returned to the Soviet Union, with her husband and daughter, just a year ago.

A few days before, Sonia had told Sarah her story—how they had heard about Birobidzhan from the Yiddish newspapers in California. Stalin had created a Jewish homeland, here in the Soviet Union, near the border of China where Jews could work the land, grow their own food, and live in socialist collectives. Sick of the Depression and joblessness in the United States, they packed their bags, pulled their daughter Leah out of school in Santa Monica and set sail with great hopes to the Soviet Union.

Sarah kissed Sonia's cheek; the skin sagged around her mouth. Sarah wanted to wrap her arms around this woman who was old enough to be her mother. "You sit now for a while." Sarah placed her hand on Sonia's arms.

"No sitting for me." Sonia let the water from the sink run onto the dirty potatoes. She switched from speaking in Russian to English so no one would understand what they were saying.

"Yes, I know about Katya," Sonia whispered. "Two official-looking men came earlier and spoke to them behind the closed doors of their room."

"Who could have done this to them?"

"I don't know. I really don't."

"You sit. Let me do this for you." Sarah took Sonia's dirty potatoes and began to rub off the dirt with the fleshy part of her thumb. "You talk to me and I'll clean."

Sarah found some old tea left over in a samovar. It was lukewarm, good enough for drinking, she figured, and poured some for Sonia. She took nothing for herself. She just wanted to be near Sonia for as long as she could. All her worries quieted down when she was around this woman. They had met in the kitchen a couple of months ago, and just like today, they were preparing their family's dinner from whatever food they could find, which was always much better than what most Soviet citizens had.

"They'll be okay," Sonia said. "They'll find another place. Bad people who do not mean us well are in every country."

"I just wish I knew who it was." Sarah watched Sonia take a sip of the tea. "Tell me more about Birobidzhan." Sonia's tales of the region made her feel her life in Leningrad could be a whole lot worse.

"Ah, Birobidzhan," Sonia sighed. "It seems crazy to me now that we went just north of Siberia to the new Jewish homeland. Do you know what we saw when we arrived? A wooden plank in a sea of mud, mud shacks, and yes, thatched roofs. The Yiddish papers in California never told us there would be no running water. They never said the land was so wet it couldn't grow anything."

Sonia took out a crumpled cloth handkerchief and wiped her brow. "They told us in time, life will get better. So, we said okay. We believed, and we still believe in this great country."

"You need to eat more than potatoes to get your strength back. You're too thin, you know," Sarah said.

"Ach, the April rain soaked the land. You can't imagine. Then Leah says she doesn't want to stay in Birobidzhan anymore. She's young. She should be in a city. So we understand. We let her go. After all, she's seventeen years old. It takes a week by train to get to Leningrad. Can you imagine? It's five thousand miles away."

"Five thousand?"

"Yes, five thousand, exactly. We didn't know that two months later, we'd come here, too. I know now you have to be young for Birobidzhan. It's true. But for Leah, she gets a job in a factory in Leningrad. She joins a choir, goes to school a couple of evenings a week, takes excursions with other young people around the city. She's having a wonderful time."

"I never see her," Sarah said. "She must be busy running from here to there." Sarah ran cold water over the potatoes until her fingers stung.

"Leah is so much happier in Leningrad. At first, we thought we'd be better off in Birobidzhan. It took some getting used to. The outhouse was a good long walk in the mud from our little hut. But we thought that once April ended and the weather dried out, the mud would go, too.

"We ate all our meals in the dining room with the other settlers. It was coarse black bread and soup. I understand now that hunger is the hardest part. But then we noticed the managers always seemed to have more food than everyone else. The rest of us just got scraps.

"But we know this wonderful new state would correct any corruption. We wrote letters to the town council. We told them there are people taking more than their share of food while the rest of us are almost starving."

"What did they do?" Sarah looked around to make sure no one was listening to their conversation.

"At first, the letters came back marked 'returned.' All of a sudden no one wanted to be our friend. No one wanted to speak to us. We were considered western and bourgeois. Others said we were spoiled. But we knew the town council would do right if they knew. So, we wrote more letters. They also came back returned. Then just when we were about to lose all hope, the corruption was fixed. The managers were removed. New ones were appointed. We knew this country would make good. Socialism, I tell you, is not some pipe dream."

Could it really be true, Sarah wondered. Maybe Sonia, Marina, Lenya, and Victor were right. Maybe life would eventually get a lot better for them all. She peeled the skin off ten potatoes, sliced them into quarters and dropped them into the gray pot.

"But we still had a problem," Sonia said. "We had no energy to work the land, to live with no running water, to lie awake all night bitten by bugs. And people all around us were getting sick, very sick.

"So, we came to Leningrad, to Leah. It's hard here, of course, but it's much easier than the life we had in Birobidzhan. You must understand," and Sonia wiped her thick hair away from her face. "We love this country."

"You do?"

"Yes, of course, we do." Sonia placed her hand on Sarah's arm.

Sarah realized at that moment that she loved Russia too, loved it in a way she had never before understood, even though she did not want to remain here.

Sarah wanted to tell Leon Sonia's story about Birobidzhan, about all those promises broken. And then about Katya and her family being forced out of their communal apartment. She had better somehow warn him. He would refuse to listen, but just maybe, if she were forceful enough, he might.

Sarah divided the potatoes up in two bowls and handed

one to Sonia. As she got closer to Sonia, Sarah smelled something dank in her clothes.

"You're an angel, Sarochka. That's what you are," Sonia said and kissed her on the cheek.

BREZHNEV DAYS

New York Times, December 9, 1980
John Lennon of Beatles Is Killed; Suspect Held in Shooting at Dakota: Wife Reported Unhurt; John Lennon Shot to Death; Suspect Is Seized at Dakota, Obtained Autograph Earlier "Crouching in Archway"; Continued to Write Songs; Emblem of the 60's

New York Times, December 11, 1980
To Deter Invasion of Poland
WASHINGTON, Dec. 10—The last time anybody invaded Poland, a World War began. This time, the West is direly warning the Soviet Union that any movement of Soviet forces across the Polish border would be met with coordinated cries of anguish and nicely orchestrated hand-wringing.

I looked for Iosif everywhere. I hoped he would be near the man selling his znachki at Station Barricadnaya. One week passed, then two. Without a phone, he seemed to exist in some other world, inaccessible and silent. Since I could at least reach Tanya, I decided to call her from the payphone across the street from the dorm. We had all been warned over and over again by the group leaders, do not under any circumstances call your Soviet friends from the dorm phone.

I had to know what happened to Iosif.

Thick snowflakes covered the soil and the telephone booth glass. But at least the daily snow had arrived. For an hour, while the snow fell, all worries vanished.

"Да," Tanya answered the phone.

"Привет, Мы можем встретиться?" We had to make this conversation quick. Outside a man in a black fur hat and large boots paced back and forth.

"Tomorrow by the Statue of Pushkin at three."

"Хорошо." I hung up and slid out of the booth so the man could take his turn.

I arrived early the next day. Bouquets of fresh red, white, green, and yellow flowers surrounded the majestic statue and rested at Pushkin's feet. At exactly three o'clock, Tanya came down the cement path bordered by trees on both sides, their boughs meeting in midair to create an arc above the people walking by.

"Iosif has been very sick." She motioned for me to sit with her on a bench. "He got better for a little bit but now he's back in bed with a horrible cough."

"Has he been to a doctor?"

"No, he needs to rest. A doctor won't help him. We'll see him soon, I hope. When I spoke with him, he said he was very sorry he could not come to meet us."

"You spoke to him?" I wondered if she knew about my grandparents and his great-uncle. But Iosif had asked me not to speak of it, and so I didn't.

"Yes, I went to see him several days ago." I wished I could have gone with her, could have had just one short conversation with him.

"Come November, half of this city is sick," Tanya said. "And not much can be done for anyone." It seemed there was so much she wasn't telling me. But to ask her more questions would be useless.

"Anyway, for today," Tanya forced a smile, "I want to take you somewhere different. There's a monastery outside of Moscow. We can get there by bus. The stop is just a few blocks away."

I had never been to a monastery before. The bus took us to the edge of the city; we passed posters of Misha the Bear and signs of *Victory to the Revolution*. When we got off, we entered a quiet place where the cupolas on the rooftops of churches were sun-bleached by winter light. We walked arm linked through arm inside the white stone buildings, passing the paintings of Madonna and child in every room.

I still did not understand exactly why Tanya had taken me here. The few people I saw wore long, brown robes, their heads bowed as they stepped.

Tanya's short, cropped hair had no strands out of place. Her blouse was tucked neatly into her skirt beneath a dark green coat. "Come, let's sit outside." She led me to a gray bench.

"The monks live in the mountains you see in the distance. They have to walk down here in order to pray." Tanya's voice became faint as I strained to hear her. "Iosif is having some problems. He got called down to the KGB building and they told him if he doesn't get a job within a couple of months, they're going to ship him off to fight in Afghanistan."

I didn't know what to say. I felt so afraid for him. "But I thought he had a job teaching English."

"He just has a few students he works with. They mean a real job. They'll accuse him of being a parasite and let him be a soldier instead."

"What's he going to do?" The wind and her news made my fingers feel numb.

"He has a further problem. He never joined the Komsomols, the Communist Party's youth organization. He just flat out refused. When he was admitted to the University, it was expected he'd join."

"So, what does that mean?"

"It's going to be a lot harder for him. He's got friends he says will help him. He's got a couple of months to come up with something."

"But I don't understand one thing. It seems to me that hardly anyone works all that much here. So why are they coming down on him?" As we spoke, a pigeon came close to my boots. I kicked the bird away.

"Most people have something they can call a job even if they don't work very hard at it."

I didn't say anything, just waited for Tanya to keep speaking.

"Last week, once he got a little better, someone from the police caught up with him when he was outside the apartment on the way to the bus and reminded him he better come up with the job. And after that, he got a lot worse," Tanya said.

"Is he going to be okay?"

"Yes, of course, he will. We are used to this. Iosif will find a way. He always does."

I wasn't sure I could believe her. I looked at Tanya's furrowed brow and decided she was also trying hard to believe her words.

"It's not like the thirties with Stalin and his murderous purges. But you must understand, we're still quite scared here. In 1936 my grandparents were arrested and sent to a labor camp. They died there when my mother was just a baby, and so my mother was raised by my grandmother's sister." Tanya folded one arm over the other above her chest to keep warm.

All this time and I never knew Tanya's grandparents perished just four years after my grandparents returned to Boston.

"My great-aunt died many years ago. It's just my mother and me now. My father left us years ago."

"So she never knew her parents?"

"No, they were arrested together. Her aunt took her, hoping it was all some mistake. Then when they were sentenced to Beregovol, she hoped over time, they'd get released and come back here. But they never did."

I had no words to respond to such a story. I just sat there listening as a monk walked by us with his prayer beads, chanting under his breath.

"Now the Soviet government tells us we have equal rights here as women. Yes, equal rights to work all day, wait in lines for food for three hours a day, cook, clean, and take care of the men."

"Believe me, you don't have equal rights here." The afternoon light made it difficult to see Tanya's face.

"Well, that's what the government tells us. And what we have here, you don't want," Tanya said.

I nodded, distracted by five or six black birds sitting rigidly on the monastery roof.

This unending sorrow everywhere—so much terror passed down from one generation to the next, etched into the faces of my friends. Everyone, every single person I met here was afraid. Tanya and I sat for a while on the bench and then made our way back to the center of Moscow without speaking much. When I got to Ulitsa Volgina, dom shest, the diggers in the soil with their large metal teeth looked unyielding to me.

Once in my dorm room, I took out my journal. I wrote, never referring to any specific circumstance or story:

> *I'm awfully tired and run down and need some time to just rest and take everything in. I've been running around like crazy.*
>
> *And the other day I had a large realization about silence and already it is hard for me to put into words what I felt, only that there is so much silence here and the silence of people's lives form lines, deep wrinkles on their faces, makes them grow old. But the silence is what I fear in myself, is what I've been afraid of here.*
>
> *And I need to face this silence. Yes, I need to trust the fabric, the looms of silence, where an old woman sits patiently pedaling threads into textures of sound, and I need to trust this*

silence in order to love, and it is in the silences, in the exchange of glances, of eyes that love takes place, and I have not been able to rest in the fabric woven underneath the daily conversations.

More on Silence

How the people keep their stories, their grief in their bodies, in their faces, and they grow old with it, and I, I speak so much but I am afraid of silence, and finally I understand my grandmother's silence, her distrust of words, how everything is communicated in the music of her language and not in her choice of words, how everything is condensed. It is not necessary to speak so much.

And today with Tanya, I felt so much sadness. How I loved her, her life, her silence. I will never forget the seriousness of her face and her beauty; and sitting there I felt so stupid as though I couldn't express anything when I tried to explain my feelings. It all comes out as глупость; and I felt the sadness of the time, in my friends' faces, in their long history. Today coming back home to the dorm, I thought that maybe only when I return to America will I be able to release the tears. But they are not really tears. They take the form of melodies, of songs that live inside me and make images out of silence.

Six days after I met Tanya, I saw Iosif at Station Barricadnaya. He stood waiting for me, by the woman selling ice cream next to the Metro sign, after I finished all my lessons at the *Institut Imeni Pushkina* at three o'clock. His lips were dry and chapped, his thin face thinner. The cold wind wrapped around our shoulders and arms on this late November day.

"Iosif?" I had thought I might never see him again. It seemed as if a ghost had somehow appeared out of the air. He looked so pale. "Are you all right?"

"Yes. Now I am." He smiled for a moment. "You must know I've been very sick."

"Tanya told me. Are you all better now?"

"Yes, I think so," he said and coughed a dry but raspy cough.

"You don't sound completely better." I followed beside him as we passed by the familiar yellow faded buildings. From a distance, I saw the Hotel Ukraine and its grand Stalinist architecture from across the river.

"It's been over three weeks. If I only could have heard your voice on the phone."

"Yes, but you know I don't have a phone."

"But what about through Tanya—just some word from you, so I wouldn't think you'd totally forgotten me."

"There was no way. You have to understand that. Sometimes you Americans are too quick to jump to conclusions," he said and I heard the faintest tinge of severity in his voice. But then he trailed his long finger down the arm of my thick down coat. "We're going to start all over again today. Okay?"

I nodded. At least I was near him again.

"Did Tanya tell you if I don't have a job—that is, a real job, I've been informed I'll be drafted into the army and sent to Afghanistan?"

"She did." I looked up at him. He did not look well. I couldn't imagine him as a soldier in Afghanistan. If he went there, I knew he would die. I just knew it. And I would lose him forever. "What are you going to do? Did you find something?"

"Yes, for now. My friend helped me out. But I'm not sure how long it will last." Iosif wiped away a droplet of snow that had fallen onto my face. "I don't want to burden you with my troubles. It will come out all right in the end. It's just our way of life here." He wrapped his scarf tightly around his neck.

Around us old women carried bread, cheese, beets and potatoes in their netted bags. Their bags were sturdy, their legs wide.

"I have some other news for you." Iosif took hold of my hand buried in a large mitten. "I started asking my mother if there were more letters from Uncle Victor. I didn't tell her why, all of a sudden, I wanted them. She's too burdened as it is. But to my shock, she said quite reluctantly that she has my Uncle Victor's papers—mainly his journal, all these years hidden in a space beneath the floor. Victor must have given it to my grandfather for safekeeping before his arrest."

"How could that be possible?"

"I didn't know my grandfather had hidden it so well. I must have walked over it a million times." Iosif let go of my hand and slid his arm through mine, pulling me a little closer to him.

"So, what have you found?" I leaned easily into him.

"It's difficult to make out my uncle's handwriting. The dates are blurred, the pages water-stained."

"But what about my grandparents? Are they mentioned?" I couldn't ask my questions fast enough.

"I'm not sure yet. I'm trying my hardest to decipher what I can."

We came to a circular cement mound; on top of a large platform stood a statue of an imperial-looking man, his hand in his long coat draped down to his legs, his beard coming to a rectangular point a couple of inches down from his chin.

"Do you know who this is?" Iosif asked.

I didn't say anything. I felt the cold wind on my face

once we stopped walking. My shoulders, arms, and legs were freezing.

"Dzerzhinsky, the first head of the Cheka. That's what the KGB was called back then. A brutal man, a real bastard ... he killed and executed countless people. Now he's considered a hero."

Pigeons surrounded the statue—their gray blended with the disappearance of light and the onset of evening.

"Let me go through the papers. Then I'll share with you all I know," Iosif said as we stepped away from Dzerzhinsky and moved onto the widening Moscow streets. Snow partially covered the billboards of men holding red torches above the slogan, *Be your Best.*

The following week, on Friday evening, I took the train to the outskirts of Moscow to Lev's apartment. I came by myself since Barry was back in the dorm, sick, like just about everyone else in Moscow.

Lev, Nadezhda's boyfriend, liked to direct the Sabbath dinners she made from the entranceway, asking, "Is it ready yet, can we start?" while he held a glass of vodka in his left hand. He bought the food Nadezhda cooked. He definitely seemed better off than most of them. I didn't have a clue what he did. Lev never entered the kitchen but stopped just short of the partition separating it from the only other room in the apartment.

"So, tell me. Who have you met in Moscow? Are they Russians or Jews?" Nadezhda asked and took the clean peels of carrots from the counter, carefully placing them in a bowl; then she mixed in raisins, a little mayonnaise.

"I've met both. But I don't get the distinction. Only everywhere I go I'm asked this same question. Why is that?" I leaned against the counter in this tiny kitchen of just a few square feet.

"Ah, you'll see."

No one ever explained anything in this place. People always spoke in cryptic words and phrases.

"Yesterday, Maria Filipovna, our phonetics teacher, stood in front of the American students in her class and wanted to know how we could choose a former actor for a President. 'Can't you do any better?' she asked."

"So how did you answer her?" Nadezhda offered me a taste of the peeled carrots mixed with raisins, but I shook my head no, I'll wait.

"What can we say? We shrugged and pretended we didn't hear her."

"We're hoping your new president will help us get out of this place," Nadezhda said. "You have to understand, we can't become Refuseniks. I don't know how we'll survive that."

"I wouldn't get your hopes up on our president intervening for you." When I looked at her face, her eyes tearing up with my words, I wished I could take them back. I had been to her apartment just once a few weeks ago and couldn't believe how eerily empty it was—a little table, a few chairs and some beds to sleep on, and that was it.

"How are you managing?"

"How are we living?" Nadezhda laughed and bent down to pull her nylon stockings up. A few strands of her thick black hair brushed against my face for a moment. "Yes, that is the question. I don't know. Our friends help out when they can. We take it day by day. If you see some guy cleaning the public toilets, maybe that's my father, the engineer, who lost his job once he filed his papers."

The front door opened, interrupting our conversation. Iosif, even thinner than when we met a week ago, entered Lev's apartment. I wanted to run up to him and hug him. But instead, I kissed him on the cheek.

"Are you all right?" I asked.

"Finally, I seem to be. I had another relapse and got sick all over again."

I wondered if they were still threatening to draft him to Afghanistan. Did he still have his job, the one some nameless friend helped him find? I knew I better not ask him here.

The doorbell rang again. "Ah, it's Elijah." Nadezhda called out to the tall lanky man with a guitar on his back. "Ilya, come in, come in."

Elijah moved among the guests to say his hellos and settled into a corner of the room. He sat on a chair, legs crossed, his guitar in his arms, and began to sing.

"Понимаете?" Elijah turned to me.

"No," I shook my head. "I can't make out the words."

"I'll sing more slowly then. How about now?"

"It's still difficult," I said. "But it doesn't matter. I get some of it."

Elijah put down his guitar. "Well, tell me, what do you want to do with your life? What do you live for? What would you die for?"

The cold I had been fighting made my nose run, my eyes water. I took out a tissue from my bag. I wanted him to leave me alone with his deep questions.

"How can you not know this?"

My mind was blank. I thought for a few moments. "I would die for freedom." I blew my nose, dabbed the water from my eye.

"That's quite the pat answer. You must figure this out. Or you'll sit like this your whole life with your tissues, wondering what to do," Elijah said and turned his back to me.

"Oh, just ignore him," Nadezhda said. "He does this to everyone. He thinks he's being clever."

"Yes, Nadya's right. Let's get away from him." Iosif took my hand and led me over to Lev's glass bookcase, where Goncharov's *Oblomov* glistened from behind the glass.

"I've found out a little more," Iosif whispered. "But later, I'll tell you."

Just at that moment, Nadezhda walked over to us, looked Iosif up and down and then did the same to me.

"Looks like you two have some secrets."

"Yes, family secrets," Iosif teased.

"Anichka, will you come with me for a few moments to help me out, please," Nadezhda said. I trailed after her to the kitchen. I didn't want to move away from Iosif, but I had no choice.

"Soon you'll leave," Nadezhda sighed. "I thought I would travel back home with you. For nineteen months we've waited and still, we've received nothing." She took the pancakes out of a pan and transferred them to a large plate. "And yesterday I heard several Jews were beaten up in front of the synagogue. Just last week a stranger showed up at the home where Adelanda teaches Hebrew."

"Who was he?"

"KGB most certainly."

"What did she do?"

"Nothing. Everyone ignored him," she said and put

the limp dishtowel on the counter.

The men took shot after shot of vodka, dancing with the women to their favorite song, "A Hard Day's Night." How ironic, since no one I knew seemed to work all that hard. I said my good-byes to Nadezhda and Lev and made my way with Iosif down the block to the bus stop.

"I've missed you," I said. His fingers brushed against my hand.

"Me too." He stopped for a moment, put his arms around my small frame. "Let's meet tomorrow in front of the Tretyakov Gallery after your school is finished."

"I'll be there. But tell me please, do you still have your job?"

"Yes, for now, I'm all right."

His words did not assure me. He bent down to kiss me just as the bus arrived. His breath was warm from the vodka he had been drinking.

"До завтра," he said.

I repeated the same words, "Until tomorrow," and stepped away from him onto the bus; and when I looked out the window, Iosif was barely visible beneath the street lamps that made his face appear older than his twenty-five years.

The next day, after Maria Filopovna had taught us all about melodia and the Russian language, and our history teacher delivered his lecture making excuses for the Stalin-Hitler pact, and Barry raised his hand to question Stalin's motives and the ease with which it was broken, finally three o'clock arrived, and I left the building without speaking to anyone and headed over to the Tretyakov

Gallery.

I saw Iosif from a distance. His wrists stuck out of a jacket that looked just a bit too small for him. Coming closer to him, I admired his furry shapka and his black strands of hair blown all over by the wind.

"Привет," he said. I liked how he always greeted me hello in the same way. "Are you warm enough?"

"Yes, in this coat, I'm good." I stuck out with my blue down coat. My own soft brown shapka was a discordant match.

"Пошли." He kissed me on the side of my face and placed his hand on my shoulder, guiding me to the bus stop that would take us to his home.

"How are your classes going?" he asked after we pushed ourselves onto the bus.

"Not bad."

We stood without speaking until we piled off the bus with hordes of people arriving at their homes on the outskirts of Moscow.

Once inside Iosif's apartment, I knew the routine. I placed my boots on a shelf and sunk my feet into the slippers left at the entranceway.

"Let me check on my grandfather." Iosif knocked on a door down the hall, and when there was no answer he poked his head inside the room.

"He's sleeping," he said, coming back over to me. "That's good. He needs his rest." Iosif hung my coat in the closet and grabbed hold of my hand as we moved into his room.

We fell easily onto Iosif's makeshift bed. "We have to hurry," he laughed. "My grandfather, you know . . . "

"Some days I didn't even know if I'd ever see you again," I said.

"I felt I disappeared even from myself." We slipped off each other's clothes; my blue jeans, pink sweater, and boots fell into a pile on the floor, next to his buttoned-down shirt and cotton black pants. We condensed hours into minutes—our bodies wrapped easily round each other.

"I don't want to get up from here, ever. But who knows who might come looking for me." Iosif kissed me once more and slid back into his pants and shirt. "Everything has felt so difficult."

"I understand," I said, though I knew I really didn't. I wished somehow we had more time.

Iosif was already in the closet, rummaging around, his hands behind some books on a shelf.

"Is that the journal?"

"Yes, just a minute. I almost have it here," he said and tugged and pulled at a lot of stuff in there. "It's hard to believe it was here all this time and I never knew it. My mother wanted to keep it all away from me. But my grandfather must have taken it out from the space beneath the floor at some point and put it up here. I don't know."

I put my clothes back on, straightened out the coverlet, and waited for Iosif to come back over to me. I could see the book was brown with curling Cyrillic letters.

"I didn't even offer you anything. Some tea or something?"

"No. I'm fine." We leaned against the wall, our legs stretched out touching, our shoulders pressed against one another, the book in his lap. I was able to make out some words, but for the most part, I couldn't comprehend much.

"Are you all right?" Iosif took my hand in his—the

journal now straddled along both of our laps.

"Please Iosif, tell me what's in here." The pages were lined; there were stars and checks and whole paragraphs circled. "Did you make these notations?"

"No, it's my Uncle Victor. He wrote all of this and then before his arrest, he must have known it was coming, he went back and made all these notes in the journal. You can see it's written in so many fragments. Here and there I found parts related to your grandparents, interspersed with a whole lot of other notations," Iosif said and began reading.

December 15, 1931

Lenya's incredibly upset. I have never seen him like this. His hand is shaking—Lenya the strong man—the man practically without emotion, a kind of machine that man is, and I repeat, the word shaking. He tells me Katya and her family have been ordered to leave the communal apartment.

"Okay, Vitya," he says to me and I know what's coming is not good. He wants to know why something like this has happened. We walk on Pionerskaya Ulitsa in the evening—the snow falls everywhere—as we pass the statues of our great leaders. How I love this city and my friend who has appeared from my past like a ghost, except he is no ghost. He is real and now so agitated. I don't know what to do.

Now a week has gone by since Katya and her family have left, and as it turns out, I have found out some truth about them. First of all, I now know that Katya's husband was raised on a large farm outside Kiev. His father was a well-to-do kulak, and this husband hid his background from everyone, even Katya. Well, what does he expect keeping such secrets, even from his wife? Our state is not perfect, but there are too many out there plotting to destroy everything we have been working for with the sweat of our hands to build.

Lenya must understand that, and I tell him so.

I could have predicted what he would say. I know him so

*well. "Katya's husband is not the same person as his father,"
he insists. Yes, I do know, my dearest friend.*

*"Okay," I explain. "So Katya and her husband will get a
different apartment, farther away, outside of our beautiful
city. And yes, it will be more difficult for them. But they'll
manage. It's not so bad. And perhaps it's only right that sons
atone for the excesses of their fathers."*

*I tell him he must understand that the kulaks have opposed
this revolution from the start. They'll survive—Katya and her
husband.*

*But I'm simply not prepared for his response. This time he
has caught me completely by surprise when he turns to me and
says, "But Vitya, what about me?"*

*What could he possibly be talking about? Has he lost his
mind altogether? Lenya is the true patriot, the revolutionary
returned to build this new socialist society, the very first in all
the world. We will be the model for every country to emulate.
We are the real pioneers.*

*Yet, he tells me, "Vitya, you know as well as I do that my
father owned a tavern. We made a living. I never thought of
it before as a small business. But others might. We were eight
children—orphans, so no, we were not rich," he says. "But
still, you must understand what I am saying."*

*His words completely surprise me. I mean, who could take
issue with Lenya's devotion to the Revolution? He gave up
everything in America to return here with a sick wife and two
little children who will be the future of our socialist country.*

I repeat to him everything that is in my heart.

But that night after I leave him, I am restless. I sleep poorly.

"I never in a million years could have imagined that
my grandfather was ever afraid. You have to understand
that he was strong, stronger than anyone—physically and
mentally. My mother used to tell me stories that he'd be
repairing their house and rested it on his shoulders. Yes,
I mean the house on his shoulders," I said and gazed at

251

the photograph of Tolstoy that hung over Iosif's desk. His long white beard, his glittering eyes, gave me comfort.

"Everyone was afraid in this country. Even my Uncle Victor became afraid and died for his innocence."

"I'm finally beginning to understand," I said, the book leaning into my thigh. "But what does he mean that sons should atone for the excesses of their fathers?"

"You see the kulaks, or rich peasants, were considered the enemy of the people. Anyone with this background was suspect. My uncle then would defend his beloved Soviet Union and feel Katya and her husband's punishment was somehow justified. He didn't see the nightmare that was about to unfold until it was too late."

"I have to admit that it's hard for me to imagine that my grandfather, of all people, was worried about himself."

"Yes, I'm sure he was. You seem to know so little of history."

Iosif was right. His words stung. But then he changed his tone with me.

"Are you sure I can't get you a little something to eat. I'm not much of a host to you." I kissed Iosif's long neck, and he drew me closer to him, our knees folded into one another.

I put my hand through his, felt his fingers press against my own. "I wish I could make out the handwriting here."

"It's all interspersed with odds and ends, and a lot of fragments." Iosif turned several pages of the book, the ink faint, black on worn paper, dried and cracked in places. "Here, let me read you this."

March 1, 1932
Lenya's girls have had a fever and a sore throat for ten days and now a cough. They are so sick. They bend down doubled

over, coughing so hard they pee all over themselves and then gasp for breath. Sometimes they vomit from all this coughing. I could weep just looking at them. Sarah stays home all day with them. Yesterday, I met Lenya in the evening and he told me Sarah took them to the doctor, a specialist, in the hospital. His office is a couple of small rooms with so many people. Lenya couldn't believe how they waited and waited, the girls so sick and desperate for some medicine.

I simply must interrupt his long descriptions and ask him, "For goodness sake, what did the doctor say?" There's no reason to wallow in such details.

"It's whooping cough, Vitya. Whooping cough," he repeats in case I didn't hear it the first time. "Who knows where they caught such a thing—the doctor gave Sarah medicine for them, but so far they seem no better," he says, and I can hear the worry in his voice.

I try my best to reassure him but fail. I fail miserably. I tell him, "Children get sick, Lenya. And yes, of course, this is serious. But this can happen anywhere. They'll get better. They're young. They're strong." I try hard to calm him down.

"I know, I know," he says. "But you have to understand, Sarah's out of her mind with worry. You simply can't imagine it. Every night she sobs when the girls are asleep. She insists we must get out of here, get the girls home where there's better care for them. 'I lost my mother,' she weeps. 'I won't allow you to take my girls from me now.' That's what she tells me, Vitya. That's what she says. What am I to do? What can I possibly do?"

I let him rant. It will be good for him. Finally, he says, "She's broken me down. If we stay here longer than a year, we'll lose our American citizenship and then perhaps we'll never be able to leave."

How can this be? I know even before I say anything that he will leave me soon, just as I had gotten used to the idea that we would all share our lives together. For so long, I knew he lived in America, a place so far away. And then all these years later, he appeared, like in a dream, getting off a steamer with his family. And now I know he will descend back into that dream, and I will never see him again.

I try and convince him even though I'm sure my words are wasted on him. Still, I must try.

So I plead with him.

"Please, Lenya," I say. "You have to give this place a little more time. It's only been six months. The girls will get better. You'll see. Believe me, I know it. They will. You've wanted to return here ever since you left so long ago, and now after this short time you're going to leave us again forever."

I speak, one thought piled on another, and wonder if I can figure out in time what to say to him, to get him to reverse his mind. Outside it is freezing cold. I can see his face chapped, reddened by the wind. But Leningrad is always beautiful to me. I point out to him the Neva River in front of us, its icicles mixed into the freezing water.

"I don't want to leave. But I don't know what else to do," he says. "Sarah is out of her mind with worry, with grief, with that damn melancholy." Then he tells me another story about that older couple, Sonia and Morris, fellow Russians and Jews, who left before our Revolution to America and returned, like Lenya and Sarah and their little girls, to their beloved homeland.

"Yes, I remember them. They settled in Birobidzhan for a couple of months, with their daughter Leah . . . at least I think that's her name," I say.

"The daughter Leah can't get a visa to leave and go back to America with them." Leon is very agitated. He speaks quickly, and I'm having trouble following everything he is saying.

"But I don't understand why Sonia and Morris are leaving the Soviet Union in the first place," I tell him.

Leon's tone is sharp. He walks hunched over. "They say they're leaving because they're too tired, too old, to be pioneers here and build the revolution in their beloved country. That's what they say." He pauses a moment. "But didn't you hear what I'm saying, Vitya," he yells at me. He has never before raised his voice with me. "They cannot leave with their daughter, their daughter, I repeat."

I've got to calm him down. He tells me when Leah started her job at the factory in Leningrad, some apparatchik gave her some papers to sign and said something to her about needing to become a Soviet citizen. "So," Leon says, "Leah thought nothing of it and signed. Now she can't get out, and as a Soviet citizen, the Soviet government can deny her the exit papers."

I have to convince him this will all get straightened out in a short time. And I know it will. I'm certain of this.

"Our government would never keep American citizens here against their will," I tell him. "I'm sure, quite soon, Leah will join her parents in America. Yes, I know this."

But our conversation doesn't go well.

"Okay, you are probably right here. I'll believe Leah will soon follow her parents back to America."

At least Leon admits my words must be true.

"But the problem is my very sick girls, my sad and angry wife. You have to understand how hard this is on me."

There's nothing more I can tell him. It's just that I'm already starting to miss his absence.

"This section ends so abruptly," Iosif said, closing the journal.

"In mid-sentence, it seems. All of these years I believed they left the Soviet Union because of my grandmother. I didn't think my grandfather would ever admit so many doubts or fears to anyone." I stared at the black notebook, its cover and binding in remarkably good shape.

"I'm sure he only spoke his words to Victor. But you have to understand that your grandparents got out right before it became impossible." I placed my hand on top of his. I too understood what it feels like to miss someone before they are gone.

"A lot of American passports went missing. When

foreigners came into the country, passports were often seized in customs and never given back to them. They were told the passports were lost. Or if they worked there, just like Leah, they were encouraged, as they said, but really forced, to become Soviet citizens. She must have never even understood what she was doing when she signed the papers presented to her," Iosif said.

"I never knew how sick my mother and aunt were here. My grandmother must have been terrified they might die in Leningrad." I wanted to bring the conversation back to my grandparents, to rest for a moment in my grandmother's anguish.

"This was not a good place to get so seriously ill. Medicines were scarce then and the doctors overworked," he said. "Death, you must understand, was a real possibility for them. Especially since they were so young."

I looked up at Iosif's drawn but beautiful face. "I can see those little girls wrapped up in blankets on the ship taking them back to Boston. Their illness must have broken my grandmother."

"I'm sure your grandfather was scared, too, even if he could not express it. Men feel things too, Anichka, even beneath their gruffness." Iosif placed his pen and its cover on the table next to the couch. "Do you know what happened to Leah? Did she ever get out of here?"

"My grandmother once mentioned something to me in the nursing home about a friend's daughter who had finally gotten out of Leningrad after forty years. I didn't know until now what she was talking about. Forty years," I repeated to myself. "Forty years. That's a long time to wait to leave and meet your parents."

"This place closed up like a prison right after your

grandparents left. Did you ever ask her about them, this family, I mean?"

"Yes, but she just became silent. My grandmother was like that when she didn't want to speak about something."

"Forty years," Iosif sighed. Our arms rested around each other. I knew we had met before, in a time and place I could no longer remember, and our meeting here in Moscow was a reunion I had been waiting for all of my life.

"Let's keep reading," I said.

"Yes, but first let me get you something to eat." Iosif smiled for the first time since we had been looking at his uncle's words. I heard the sounds of his slippers against the floor as he left for the kitchen.

I picked up the journal. Victor's elegant and often-hurried script eluded me, but I was able to make out something from the beginning of the book.

> *October 3, 1931*
>
> *Electrolytic—how I delight in such a word. And to think Leon will enable the All-Union Scientific Research Institute of the Aluminum, Magnesium and Electrode Industry to do its important work—to show the world how this workers' state will reverse centuries of backwardness in a mere decade— accomplish one hundred years of industrialization in ten. To think Leon is working in the Krasnyi Vyborzhets plant, where aluminum is produced, no longer from Tikhvin bauxites, but from domestic materials through electrolysis. Yes, electrolytic, I will repeat it over and over again. We no longer need to use soda and limestone and electro-smelting to create slags of calcium aluminate. Our new means of production will make our Soviet Union a world power, no doubt. And Lenya, my dearest friend and comrade, will be a part of it.*

All those technical words made it easier to read. And

there was my grandfather's name in Victor's journal. I circled the word, Lenya, with my fingers, understanding for the first time their great love for this country, their hopes and their dreams for the Soviet Union. Try as he might, my grandfather never would forget this country, his *rodina,* his homeland.

I turned to another part of the book and recognized some fragments from Mayakovsky.

> *"I'll join you*
> > *In the far communist future."*

"My uncle was devastated by Mayakovsky's suicide," Iosif said. He put down on a table a tray of butter cookies and the steaming hot tea I had grown so used to whenever I was with him. "These are the best lines," he said and began to recite for me:

> *"My most respected*
> > *comrades of posterity!*
> *Rummaging among*
> > *these days'*
> > > *petrified crap*
> *exploring the twilight of our times,*
> *you,*
> > *possibly,*
> > > *will inquire about me too."*

"I also love 'At the Top of My Voice.'"

"You know the poem?"

I nodded. "I've struggled to read it."

"That's excellent, really excellent." I wanted him to keep praising me.

I turned to the end of the journal and saw something about a poet S. It was hard for me to understand. The script became even more obscure.

"What's this?" I asked.

"Won't you have a cookie?" He took the tray and held it for me.

I didn't understand why Iosif wasn't answering my question.

"But what about the poet?" I took a bite of the butter cookie he handed me.

"It was my uncle's undoing. I don't even want to talk about it."

"Why can't you trust me just a little bit?"

"It's not that. It's too painful to revisit." The journal was in my hand, our legs stretched out, parallel and touching. "Okay, okay, I'll read it," he said and took the book from me.

March 20, 1932

Today the poet S arrested for treasonous behavior. I know it must be some mistake. And all will work out. He's too great a poet. I'm sure he'll get released quite soon. And yes, it was stupid, that's what it was of him, to invite his friends to his apartment and announce he will read some of his newest poems. The man has too much ego, if you ask me. But he goes ahead and reads a long poem denouncing Comrade Stalin in front of everyone there, right there in his home. I'd like to know what he was thinking to take such an action. He trusts they are all his friends. After all, he personally invited each one of them. Today, three days later, he's arrested. I know he'll be released soon. Our Soviet government is just. It too can make a mistake. But it will be corrected. I know this for sure. I just hope it will be soon.

But I need to explain all this to Lenya. And it will be even harder to make sense of this for Sarah. I probably should not even burden them with this when they're consumed in the evenings with taking care of their sick little girls. But I'm afraid they will hear about this from someone else.

I know I must go to them right away.

And I do.

They're eating in silence when I enter the room. The girls sit up in their beds, two bowls of soup on a tray across their laps, and Sarah beside them, while Lenya kneels on the floor, the cabbage soup in a gray pot on top of a cloth that covers their black trunk. Thank goodness Lenya eats by himself—Sarah and the girls are separated in another corner. The tension between them could cut down a door.

At least the girls seem a little better, even if it's only a little bit, from this whooping cough. But not Sarah. I can't believe how haggard she is, how old-looking she's become. The girls look up and smile at me. My little dear ones, I like to call them. But then they start coughing, and I'm scared out of my mind that they're gasping just to breathe. Lenya runs over to them. But he can't do much to help them. He rubs their backs with his large hands. In a few minutes, they're breathing normally again, but it takes a little longer for all of us to calm down.

Lenya kisses their foreheads, one then the other, and nods to Sarah, since he knows she will put them to sleep.

They don't talk, Sarah and Lenya—absolutely not one single word. What has gone wrong? I can't bear to think this is somehow my fault.

So, I won't. At least not for now.

Lenya hands me a bowl of the cabbage soup Sarah prepared, but I tell him I've already eaten. I don't want their food. They will need every bit of it.

I whisper to him, sitting cross-legged on the floor, that I want him to hear this from me and no one else. His brow turns into a thousand creases. What could you possibly want to tell me, his face says to me.

So, I relay everything to Lenya, try my best to give him all the details I know . . . the gathering in the poet S's house of his so-called friends, his public denunciation of Comrade Stalin, and now his arrest. Leon listens and asks very faintly, "But who do you think informed on him?"

"It doesn't matter," I say, even though I've been wracking

my brain, wondering about the very same thing. "I need you to understand that in this first socialist country, at this very moment in history, we must support how socialism is developing even if we don't always agree with it." *I hope he understands my words.*

I assure Lenya our poet will be released shortly. "Though, if you ask me," *I say,* "I don't know why S had to make such a spectacle. The whole thing was childish."

"Yes, you're right," *he says, and I'm simply overjoyed he sees it the same way I do.*

We don't think Sarah has heard us, but we're wrong. The girls are asleep. She walks over to us, her hair matted down with sweat even though the weather is cold. She takes a piece of the black bread lying on the trunk.

I shoot Lenya a glance, and he understands that it's better if I speak. There's too much anger between them, which, as I write this, I feel is partially my fault. Maybe I needed to take more time with Sarah to help her get used to this country and its difficulties. I know I waited too long for her to meet Marina. Sarah needed her friendship sooner, before all this misery set in. But I can't dwell on this. Not now.

"I simply do not understand either one of you," *she says.* "How can you possibly support a state that would arrest such a poet?" *She is practically spitting at us. I have never seen her so angry.*

"Listen," *I tell her.* "I know this is not a perfect place. But we are the first country in the world to build a socialist state. We cannot lose sight of this."

She doesn't hear me. "You said the exact same thing when Katya and her family were thrown out of their apartment."

"Okay, maybe I did."

"So Vitya," *she asks,* "How can even you defend this loss of rights?"

Iosif stopped reading. Everything else on the page was crossed out, illegible.

"What happened here?" I asked.

"My uncle must have come back to this page later and got scared of what he wrote when he began to fear for his own arrest. That's all I can think."

"But you still haven't explained why this was his undoing. I don't get it."

"You have to understand. Everyone at *Izvestia* publicly denounced the poet. That is, except my uncle. He was confident that this poet S, as he called him, would be released soon and all would go back to normal. But, as you know, it didn't."

Iosif's hand felt cold. I understood now that beneath the snow on the thin branches of trees, beneath the night covering the city and its drab apartment buildings, beneath all the whisperings, the vodka-soaked Sabbath celebrations—fear invaded every moment, defined all conversations.

"Do you really think Victor believed all that stuff about supporting socialism even if he didn't agree with everything that was going on?"

"Absolutely. It was the only way he could justify himself what he saw happening around him." Iosif scratched the back of his left leg. "This was how everyone working so hard to build a new future for the country thought."

"It seems my grandfather only admitted his doubts to Victor."

"I don't think my uncle could ever acknowledge the brutality of this state, even to himself, until he was facing his own death. But your grandfather knew."

"You think so?"

"Yes, he got out of here, didn't he? And it wasn't just because of your grandmother. Here, let me read you one of my uncle's very last entries." Iosif skipped to the end of the journal.

> *Now that Kamenev and Zinoviev are convicted of treason, I fear what will happen next. But it is hope I hold onto, the life we, I mean Marina and I, have fought to create. The dream, I know now, is all that matters.*

"Maybe this place is cursed," I said.

"No, just tragic." Iosif laughed and closed the notebook. "I better get you back to your dorm. It could take a while."

Did he want me to leave, I wondered. But then he kissed me, which confused me more. "I've told you before that I'll never be able to get out of this place."

"You've also said that you probably wouldn't want to, even if you could."

"That may be true," he said quietly as he put on his torn socks.

"I'm going to Leningrad with the other students next week." I straightened out my bulky pink sweater.

"You are? How long are you staying?"

"Just a week."

"You must call Marina. I'll give you her number. But you have to put it somewhere very, very safe."

"Do you think it's okay to call? I don't want to put her in any danger."

"We can't reach her here without a phone. At least you can tell her how much we miss her. My grandfather never stops talking about her." Iosif went to a dresser, opened a drawer and found another notebook. After reading some writing there, he ripped out a page and scribbled down her number.

"Here. Just be careful with this."

"Are you sure?"

"What else can they do to her? They already broke her spirit long ago."

I placed the number in a small zippered compartment in my backpack.

We tiptoed out of his room, past his sleeping grandfather and down many flights in the elevator. We traveled together but alone on the empty bus back to my dorm. Neither one of us spoke more than a few words the entire way to Ulitsa Volgina, dom shest—the night filled with a misty fog drizzled downwards to cover all sorrows.

"Hey, Anna. Wait for me," Paula shouted and ran to catch up with me. I was already a block away from the *Institut Imeni Pushkina* on an early December afternoon, hoping Iosif might appear as I turned a corner by Station Barricadnaya. But he didn't. As the weather got colder, and he recovered from being sick and relapsed again, I saw him less and less. I didn't know if he was in grave danger. I only knew I hardly slept most nights.

"Will you come with me to get my visa extended? I don't want to do this alone." Paula's fur hat slid over one eye. She pushed it back on her head. "I got myself a job for a diplomat's family as a governess for the next few months. It's the only possible way to remain here."

"You're going to be a governess?"

"Well, I can't stay here otherwise. I can teach some little American kids five hours a day. And then I'll have the rest of the day free. It's not a bad deal."

"I thought you hated Moscow." I also wished I could stay in this city just a little longer. I didn't want to leave Iosif, and Tanya and Nadezhda, behind. America seemed so soulless compared to the people in this country. And yet life here was impossible.

"I'm just beginning to understand this place. I'm not ready to go home yet. Besides, who knows if I'll ever get back to Moscow." In a few blocks, we entered a nondescript building with a Soviet flag hanging outside.

"Thanks for coming with me," Paula said in English. We sat on two chairs in a small, bare room with several desks, where a bunch of middle-aged men sat, scribbling onto notepads. One of them, a bald, clean-shaven man, called the two of us over.

"Where are you from?" he asked in Russian.

"Соединенные Штаты," Paula replied.

"Yes, I know. But what city?"

"Нью-Йорк."

"Ah, New York." He took a long puff from his cigarette. "What a terrible city. It's so dirty, and there are so many Jews there. More Jews live in that city than Americans."

I didn't know how to respond to him, so I didn't say anything. I finally understood a Jew could never be a Russian. That's what Nadezhda was trying to tell me the last time I saw her.

The bald guy behind the desk said little else to us. He stamped Paula's documents, giving her the permission to stay in this city a few months longer.

Paula linked her arm through mine as she steered me out onto the Moscow streets.

"That bureaucrat is quite the piece of work," I said.

"Yeah, well, what do you expect?"

"I guess."

"Don't be surprised if last minute you're offered ten

thousand dollars to marry a Soviet guy and get him out of here," Paula said. The air held the scent of snow soon to arrive.

"I don't think that's happening."

We were about to pass by a small art gallery. "Let's check this out," Paula said. We climbed over a little fence and entered the building. Inside we saw the word октября in bold letters, celebrating photographers from the 1920s, Alexander Rodchenko and Boris Ignatovich among them. The blurb below their names explained that they were using experiments with photomontage to create new images to express the revolutionary spirit of the twenties.

We gazed at a large photo called *Mother* by Rodchenko. An older woman, her head covered in a black headscarf, squinted through one half of an eyeglass held by her left hand. Her sagging face took up the entire portrait.

"I like this one," I said to Paula in English. It seemed to celebrate all the nameless women and their countless working hours.

"It's really amazing," Paula said. All around us we heard Russian words.

"Rodchenko liked to photograph his mother Olga Paltusova," a man behind us said in English. He had a thin beard and small eyes. Behind him stood a well-dressed woman in a brown fur shapka. "She was a washerwoman who had been illiterate and then a few years before this photograph was taken, she learned to read."

"How old do you think she was here?" Paula asked him.

"Fifty-nine. It's quite famous," he replied.

"She looks much older," I said.

"You have to understand our life here has not been

easy." He and the woman in a large hat moved, and we followed them to the next photo—a man in aviator gear connected to a parachute, fully opened in mid-air. Clouds were above and below him.

"This is cool," Paula said.

"Rodchenko wanted to capture the achievements of the young Soviet state," he explained. "He sought to create the sense of great movement in air, a sense of velocity. He wanted to celebrate a man suspended and moving at the same time."

"You know so much," I said.

"These are the great photographers of our nation. It's my pleasure to help you understand them."

At the other end of the gallery, I saw a photo of black limousines lined up one after the other in the foreground, and then behind them and much smaller, the Kremlin and St. Basil's Cathedral.

"Here you can see how Ignatovich liked to experiment with perspective."

"We're lucky to have you explain everything to us," I said.

"Yes," Paula chimed in.

"I'm happy to do so."

I wondered why the woman beside him never said a word, but my thought was interrupted when I saw a photo of a scary-looking guy with a military cap and scruffy goatee, his long face angular and thin. Beneath were the words *Felix Dzerzhinsky.* I remembered Iosif's bitter words about him. He did look evil. It had to do with his eyes, the way he stared out and beyond the frame of the photo.

"By the way, I'm Yuri," the man said. "And this is my wife, Masha." He nodded to the petite woman following along behind us. "How do you like the exhibition here?"

"It's interesting," Paula said. The four of us formed a natural circle.

"You must be Americans. What do you do in Moscow? And how long will you stay?"

We gave them our standard answers, told him about the *Institut Imeni Pushkina,* and how we'd leave in mid-December, a date fast approaching.

"Let's talk outside," Yuri said.

We followed them out onto the windy Moscow streets.

"Will you be our guests? We live only several blocks away from here."

He seemed so friendly, and we were used to being invited to people's houses. Besides, we were freezing. "Sure," I said and turned to Paula.

"That's fine with me," she replied.

We walked with them until we came to a brick building with three steps leading to a door. After several flights of stairs, we entered a light and airy room with a couch, two chairs, and a Persian-looking floor rug. Prints of factories, wind turbines, tractors, and men and women bending in fields, planting some kind of grain, hung from the walls. This place was fancy compared to all of the other apartments I had seen in Moscow.

"Masha will make tea. Please sit down." Yuri pulled over a wooden chair. Paula and I went to the couch covered with a quilt embroidered in delicate flowers.

Masha got right up. I started to follow her, but she insisted, "No, please sit down. I'll be right back."

"You must tell us all about yourselves," Yuri said. "You see, I'm studying to be a psychologist, who will treat the mentally ill. Of course, you know, there are many in our institutions for political reasons, but we have sick people there, too."

Masha returned with a tray holding a kettle of tea and black fudge cake. She poured the tea into cups before cutting the cake into four pieces.

"Americans and Russians are very similar, I believe," Yuri said.

"Yes, this is true," Masha agreed. She ate without getting a single crumb on her face.

"What do you mean?" Paula asked.

"Well, we're both a friendly people, a warm people. If it weren't for our governments, I'm sure we'd be great friends. Don't you think we're so much the same?" Yuri shifted in his seat, so he could turn directly to face Paula and me.

"I don't know about that," Paula said and laughed.

"Well, tell me then, what kind of people have you met here in Moscow?" Yuri asked.

"Mainly Jews," I said.

"How often do you get together?"

"At least once a week."

"Ah, this is good," Yuri paused for a moment. "The Jews have suffered a great deal in this country. They have a lot to teach you. The government here can be cruel. You've probably noticed that for yourself."

"We certainly have," Paula said and got up from the couch. "But it's time for us to go. We've got to get up early for school tomorrow."

"Yes, of course. You must understand things have improved in this country since the czars. Economically we're all better off. But we have no freedom," Yuri said and stood. Masha took the cue from him and rose as well.

"Tell me," Yuri spoke more quickly. "Have you heard of Eastern religion existing in the Soviet Union?"

"No." I was surprised by his question. It seemed out of the blue.

"You have not met anyone who practices this religion? You see, I am very interested in all of this."

"No, not a one." Paula put on her sheepskin coat and matching hat.

"You'll call us, please, won't you? We want you to come back and be our guests again," Masha said, moving closer to kiss Paula and me on our cheeks.

"Yes, will you promise to call us and come back again?" Yuri repeated.

"Definitely," Paula said, as we stepped up to the door. "You have been so good to us."

"Excellent."

On the street, the wind blew my Russian fur hat off my head. I caught it in mid-air. "What great people," I said. "That's one thing I do love about this place. You can meet people and become close right away."

"Yeah, they really are."

A week later, I called, but the phone just rang and rang. Then Paula tried. The same. We began to call every day. No one ever answered.

"They're probably KGB," Paula said, after our second week of calling.

"You really think so. I find that hard to believe. They were so nice."

"Yes, definitely. We're not going to see them again." Paula plopped down on her small, narrow bed.

"You always conclude the worst. Maybe they're just busy." I sat opposite her on my bed.

"You're so naïve. Come on. They act real nice and charming so we like them. And then they invite us over. Just when we're really comfortable, they start grilling us about who we've met. I didn't think much of it either, I was so busy having a nice time, but now it's starting to make some sense to me."

I knew Paula was right. And I had told them about the Russian Jews. "Do you think my friends will get in trouble now?"

"You didn't say much about them. You weren't, thank God, very specific."

"I'll call them every day next week." I threw my blankets over me.

"Go ahead, but we're not going to see them again."

And we never did.

A few days later, I took a train with the other American students from Moscow to Leningrad. I slept all night on a single pullout bed, the train rocking, chugging, making its way to Leningrad, the city where my grandparents lived for nine months almost fifty years ago. Trees whisked by my window, their branches gnarled, lit dimly by a faraway moon.

On our first afternoon in Leningrad, we visited the Piskarevsky Cemetery. Half a million dead in World War Two were buried beneath rows and rows of tombstones covered by snow, surrounded by sorrowful music pumped in from an unknown place. Each gravestone had an engraved star and a date. By thin branches of trees and crystals of ice, I stood before a statue of a woman with a wreath of flowers in her hands and the words etched into Cyrillic letters on the walls behind her, *We Will Never Forget the Dead.*

"For nine hundred days no food came into this city, and slowly a million citizens of Leningrad died of starvation," our guide told us. A flock of birds flew, undulating downwards, before rising higher in the sky above us. "In all there were twenty million dead in the war. You must understand," she said, and looked directly at us. "We do not want another war. You must go home and tell the American people this. We know the loss of war."

Paula and Barry, busy taking photographs, walked on ahead. I rushed to catch up to them. Together we reached another statue of a young woman, her arms extended outward. Behind her, engraved into the walls, were more figures of women bending.

"In Leningrad the ballet still performed. Frail and starving, they danced." I still heard the guide. "If an air raid came, the dancers would go to the basement and then afterwards, when it was safe again, they'd come back to perform, their bodies thin and trembling."

We stepped away from the Memorial wall, from all those anonymous stones lined up in neat rows, where thousands of people were buried silently beneath snow.

In my hotel room, I took out my journal and wrote this down—

> All day I felt such intense rage here in Leningrad, as I saw the places I had always dreamt about, and I feel strangely lost in America.
>
> Leningrad reminds me of raindrops, of trees covered with snow. I feel Pushkin's magic everywhere. The muses own the streets of Leningrad.
>
> In America people don't want to look at suffering, and here, people in this country have known horrible grief. How can I explain what it was like to be in a cemetery where half a million people were buried? How do I begin to find words?

I think of my mother and long for her to hold me. I long to tell her of my journey here—my journey to the city where she lived when she was just five years old. When I return, I want to spend days and days with her, just speaking of all I have seen here, learned here, speaking beyond so many silences between us.

In Leningrad, caps of ice form crests on the water. If my grandparents had stayed, they would have died. I look out the window, following the movement of water, the mystery of light.

How I miss my grandmother—

"A mother is a precious thing, Anushka. You need her when you are very young and very old," she once told me, long before she tripped over her bedspread and had to leave her little apartment for the Hebrew Home for the Aged, another type of prison.

On another day, after we ate, the butter cookies that my grandmother saved for guests still lying on a plate in the center of the table, she began to sing me the songs of her girlhood. "Ах, зачем эта ночь . . . " Oh what a night . . .

"Do you mind, Anushka, if we sleep a little bit. Sometimes I get so tired," she said to me.

I walked behind her as she grabbed hold of her cane and made her way into the bedroom. I crawled beneath my grandmother's blankets and rested with the feel of her body breathing next to me. I turned to see her face. She did not wear her glasses, those pointed rims with a brown border. Her eyes closed and then opened. "Anushka, do you need more blankets? Are you warm enough?"

"Yes, I'm fine."

We took a nap together and I breathed in her life, Russian sounds that curled up inside of me.

I came to Russia, now the Soviet Union, seeking the life of my great-grandmother. If I stand very still, I can feel her tears beyond the quiet of this majestic city.

The truth is I'm scared to return home, but I can't stay

here either.

Two days later, I walked past Dostoevsky's home, past the orange faded building on the way to Marina's apartment. At three o'clock night descended on the Leningrad streets. The day before, a tour guide had taken us upstairs where Dostoevsky once lived, into the stark, eerily empty room where his wide, black desk remained. I had wanted to kneel down and bow my head to it. She had shown us the streets where Raskolnikov had feverishly stumbled. Now I took the same route as yesterday, past streets with paint peeling off of buildings, darkening into narrow sidewalks as I stepped.

I had come to Leningrad to discover some secret only partially revealed to me. Marina's phone number, etched into a torn white paper, clung to the bottom of my coat pocket. That morning when I called her, I heard the usual *Da* at the other end.

"I am Anna," I shouted into the payphone across the street from the hotel. "Iosif is my friend. He gave me your number," I said, using the simplest Russian words.

"Iosif?" she paused. And then her voice, animated, replied, "Прекрасно! You must come to me this afternoon."

"Да, Уа приеду," I replied.

She didn't need to tell me the way to her. Iosif had given me careful directions on the paper with her number. My hands, stuffed into my coat pockets, were shaking. While it was bitter cold outside, damper, more frigid than Moscow, drops of sweat formed on my forehead. I felt warm, cold, then hot. I crossed a footbridge and stared at the water winding its way through the city. Marina had known my grandparents almost fifty years ago—half a century, a period of time inconceivable to me.

In the darkness, street lamps made a path for me.

I came to a worn white building and pressed the first buzzer in the vestibule. "Заходите девушка," she answered through the intercom and poked her head outside her door to greet me.

She was so much smaller than I had imagined, her hair tied back in a bun, her face filled with elegantly formed wrinkles. Nothing seemed real to me—not this wizened but beautiful woman who took my hands and led me inside her two-room apartment, or the window in the corner where ice made a damp and foggy imprint on the glass. I saw myself in the reflection, my thick down coat, and brown Russian shapka, a clash of styles no Russian would ever commit.

A black round table with chairs took up most of the main room—a small kitchen in the corner and dressers with photographs of the wide Leningrad Squares, where enormous silk-screened posters of Lenin hung from buildings. Marina stood in one photo, a striking young woman with dark curly hair, holding hands with an equally good-looking man that I assumed must be Victor.

"Your husband was handsome," I said, standing in front of the picture.

"Yes. He was." Her back was stooped though she moved without a cane. "Some say he looked a bit like Trotsky, with those round spectacles he wore. But you know, I never saw it." She held my hand and led me over to the table. Her fingertips felt chapped.

"Заходите девушка. Let's sit down." Every meal was the same—the teapot on the table, the bowls of carrot salad and potatoes.

"Так, расскажуте мне немного о себе," she said. *So,*

tell me about yourself.

I didn't know where to start. "Я Американка."

"Yes, I know you're an American," she smiled.

"Я студентка института имени Пушкина в москве."

"I'm sorry, I forgot the bread." Marina stepped over to the kitchen counter and carried a loaf of white bread, browned on top by the sweet butter melted into it. She wore a wool black skirt falling down below her knees, nylon stockings and flat lace-up shoes.

"Here, let me get this for you." I rushed out of my chair. I wished she had not gotten dressed up to meet me.

"No, you must sit down. I have it fine." She had several white hairs growing out of her chin. "Here, you must eat." She filled up a plate for me. "Help yourself to some bread, please."

The soft bread crumbled as I cut into it.

I told Marina how my Russian teacher in America had sent me with a children's book for Iosif's father, but it was Iosif I met in front of the synagogue on Rosh Hashanah eve, and then I explained how we had discovered that my grandparents knew her and Victor.

"They knew us?" The shards of light coming into the room gave Marina's white hair a silvery hue.

"Iosif found a photograph of all of you together, and a letter from my grandfather to Victor. He even has some of Victor's journals."

"Really? I am trying to remember." Marina's hands were blue-veined and spotted brown. "Tell me, what was your grandmother's name again?"

"Sarah." I took a spoonful of boiled potatoes, cut up and seasoned with green herbs.

"No, I don't remember her, sweetheart. But your

grandfather . . . I think I do. He was a carpenter by trade, I believe. Is that right?"

"Yes." The sweet-tasting potatoes dissolved in my mouth.

"He was a carpenter at the aluminum factory. Yes, I think so." Marina's right hand rested on her chin. "He was a strong man, very strong, not tall but wide, very broad," Marina laughed unexpectedly. "He didn't speak much. Very quiet man the times I saw him. But I do remember now how Victor wept when your grandfather left. Yes, I remember that."

"I think my grandmother was miserable here. And my aunt and mother, just little girls, hated it here too."

"They were all here? I have forgotten." Marina seemed smaller, more petite and thinner than when I first saw her opening the door for me to enter. "Well, now we know," she shook her head. Her apartment smelled of dusty papers, unswept soot on windows.

"They knocked hard when they came to our door. We woke up, lay in bed in each other's arms for a moment. They were here and would not go away, we knew. And yes, they took my husband away in the middle of the night. So quiet it was.

"I waited in line for a long time with so many others outside the prison. Day became night. Night . . . morning. But here I am darling, talking on and on and not even giving you some dessert."

"Please, I want you to sit." I walked over and scooped up the plate filled with the crumbling crepe-like pastry. Chocolate sauce dripped out of its center.

"Sit, sit, devushka," she argued with me. "Okay, what can I do? You move quicker than me. Here, let me at least pour you some tea." As she spoke, I noticed her side tooth was slightly chipped.

"It was the same for almost everyone. If he didn't confess, they would come after me. That's what did it. So he signed the papers declaring he had betrayed the state, become its enemy. Two months later he was shot. They let me be here. They couldn't do anything more to me really."

"But why? What could they possibly blame him for?" I breathed in the smell of wood.

"Why?" She scratched her chin. "Why not, is the only answer I can give you. Nothing made any sense and still doesn't," she said. She paused for a moment and then asked, "Do you know about the poet Semyatin?"

"Iosif told me the story about a poet S. How he wrote a poem denouncing Stalin."

"So, I don't have to tell you. I can barely remember anyway. Only that Vitya was silly enough to print some of Semyatin's early poems in *Izvestia* long before he was arrested. What a boy he was. Then later, of course, he wrote Semyatin was wrong. But he also wrote his other poems had artistic merit. That's all. He felt it was a shame the poet was so shortsighted. We forgot it. Years went by. We forgot everything until the men came."

Marina's apartment became darker as three o'clock arrived and the sun set.

"What do you think happened to my grandparents when they were here?"

"Your grandparents?"

"Yes."

"I don't know. It was so long ago. Tell me, again, what was your grandfather's name."

"Leon."

Marina took another sip of tea. "Leon. Yes, of course. Tell me. How is he?"

"He died when I was nine years old. He was hit by a car one evening when he was walking."

"When he was walking?"

"Yes, near the beach in Oak Island, in Massachusetts. He bought some houses near the end of his life, fixed them up, rented a couple of them out." I didn't know why I was giving Marina all these details.

"Is that right? Your grandfather became a bit of a capitalist, after all," and she smiled suddenly. "And your grandmother?"

"She's in a nursing home near Boston."

"Nursing home? Ach . . . what a terrible place for her. We had no children, you know. But still I have some friends who look in on me. You know, she came to me one afternoon."

"Who did?"

"Your grandmother, of course."

"She did?"

"Yes, I remember now. The picture in my mind is clear. She sat on the couch with me, with her black pocketbook. Its clasp snapped into place. Yes, I can hear it now. She wore red lipstick. Your grandmother liked to wear very red lipstick.

"We didn't know each other very well, so I was surprised when she knocked on this door. She was thin like a ghost, I tell you."

"So what happened?" I hoped she could stay with her story.

"She came right here, sat on the couch with me."

"Yes, then what?"

"Well, at the time, it was very strange. Of course, I made her some tea, just like now. It was all I had to offer her then, but at least it was something hot for her." Marina finished her brown leafy tea.

"What did she say?"

"You see, I was quite surprised. She leaned back on this very couch, then looked me straight in the eyes and said so faintly, 'We have to get out of here. I'm afraid, I'm afraid.' She repeated, 'I'm afraid, my sick girls will die here if we don't leave.'"

"She said that to you?"

"Yes, she did. I was surprised myself, that she trusted me enough." Marina lowered her voice as she spoke.

"What did you say to her?"

"What did I say? What could I say? Everywhere on the streets were posters of Stalin and the words beneath his smiling face, *Life is Getting Better. Life is Getting Merrier.* And we believed it, too. But it seems your grandmother knew. She knew what was coming."

A pigeon flew over and landed on the dark ledge outside Marina's window.

"You must understand, I am a woman and not a machine. So I leaned over to her and spoke quietly to her, so no one else could ever hear, 'You must take care of your family.'"

"You said that?"

"I did. And I never told anyone until today. Now you know. You are the first. Now eat up. Here, have another pastry." She slid the dessert from the serving platter onto my plate.

"No, I'm fine. Really I am."

"Eat some more, please. I got these especially for you."

I had no choice. From the sugar and the caffeine, and from our conversation, the room swirled around me in combinations of gray and blue. The fourth cup of tea made my heart race.

"What did my grandmother say back to you?"

"Oh, yes. I almost forgot to tell you. She said Lenya would never agree to leave. She was in a very bad way then. She didn't know what to do." Marina pushed away some strands of hair that had fallen from her bun onto the corner of her face.

"What could I say? 'He will go,' I told her. And the minute I uttered those words, I knew it was true. I never even let Vitya know about our talk. I had to keep her secret. It was between women, you know. A month later they were gone." Marina dabbed her lips dry with a handkerchief.

It was hard to know what was true and what was not. I scratched the space in between my second and third fingers until my skin there became red with splotchy little bumps.

"So, tell me. How is your grandmother? Is she well?" I didn't know how to answer her question for the second time, so I said, "Yes, she's fine."

Marina walked over to her closet, her hand on the wall every few steps so she would not lose her balance. I followed alongside her.

"Marina, what can I get for you?"

"Here, it's up on the shelf," and she pointed to a tin box, similar to the one Iosif had in the *zagorod*. Beside it were piles of loose papers.

I couldn't believe how heavy it was.

"Just put it down on the coffee table here by the couch." Marina pulled open its clasp. Papers were shoved in there haphazardly. Some fell on the table; others stayed put. Marina searched and rummaged, sorted and put back, until she came up with letters rubber-banded together from the bottom of the box.

"Yes," she said, seeming to read my thoughts. "Some are from your grandfather. Sit, darling. I will show you."

This time I could make out the Cyrillic writing of the letter she held in her hand.

July 1, 1932
My dearest Vitya!

I am already missing you and Marina more than any words could ever say. We are finally back after two long weeks crowded into a single room on the ship. We could barely breathe downstairs in that berth. Sarochka was seasick the last few days. I had no such problems. But wait. Problems would find me soon. There's no work in this country. Finally, I found a position as a janitor, and I'm lucky to have that.

"Happy Days are Here Again" is the motto of Roosevelt's presidential campaign. Can you believe it? Capitalism still continues to unravel our lives. How I wish I were back with you.

But at least, I must tell you, the girls are getting better and better from their whooping cough. They gave us quite a scare.

I have no words to say how I miss you.

Yours Always,
Lenya

The white paper had turned yellow, but the ink still remained.

"Did Victor write him back?"

"He did, at first, but I'm sure his letters didn't go through. Then as time went on, we became afraid as the arrests came, so Vitya didn't answer."

"Do you think my grandfather's letters were . . . you know, read by others?" I asked, stammering and stumbling over Russian words.

"Yes, of course. Our letters are still being read." Marina leaned closer to me and said, "Yes, they were used against Vitya. They were . . ." She stopped in mid-sentence and appeared more mournful than anyone I had ever met before.

"Read before Victor ever got them," I finished the sentence for her.

"Yes," she said and lowered her voice. "It's a good thing your grandfather is dead. So he'll never know. How long ago did you say he died?"

"Thirteen years."

"Yes, that's good," she said. "That's good."

"But tell me," I said and stopped, not knowing how to ask the question I had been wondering about since I saw the photos and letters in the *zagorod* with Iosif. "Do you think my grandfather knew what happened to Victor? I mean, how he died?"

"Yes, I know he did." Marina shifted her weight and leaned one shoulder into a torn pillow on the couch.

"How? He definitely never spoke of it."

"In 1951, after Stalin died, I wrote to him and told him everything. I'm sure he figured it out before in the nearly twenty years of silence between us."

So this was the unknown story my mother referred to at the train station before I left for Moscow. I remembered her words, "Something happened when your grandfather was in Leningrad, but he would never speak about it."

"My grandfather never got over it."

"Yes, I'm sure he didn't." Her voice seemed far away. "None of us did, my darling."

I didn't want to leave her, but this afternoon too would come to an end. I glanced up at a photograph of Marina and Victor, his arms squeezed round her shoulder. She wore a black woolen coat with a matching black fur hat.

"You look so beautiful here. And so elegant," I said.

"That was all a long time ago. Vitya saved up every penny he had to get me this coat." She picked up the photograph before placing it down once again on the table.

"I wish I didn't have to go." Before I knew what I was doing, I flung my arms around Marina's small frame.

"You must go back to New York now." She took hold of my hand.

"Yes, soon I will fly home."

"I hope you know such love," she said and handed me my blue down coat and shapka from the front closet.

"I wish you could come with me."

"Come where?" she laughed.

"Come back with me. To New York."

"Oh, no. I've grown fond of my little room here. And they leave me alone now. No one bothers me anymore. But please, you must remember me to your grandmother. Tell me once more, what is her name?"

"Sarah."

"Sarochka, of course. She sat right here in this couch. Yes, she did. I can still see her."

Marina adjusted my hat so it didn't cover my eyes. "A lovely woman she was," Marina said. "Come darling," and she kissed me on the cheek. "Hug me good-bye once more." With my bulky clothes on, Marina seemed even smaller.

"Your grandmother always stayed by herself," she said, her face right next to mine. "I still miss her." Marina called to me as I walked out the door onto the dark Leningrad streets, "Tell her that please, Anichka."

A few days after I got back to Moscow, Tanya and I walked arm linked through arm along the cement path leading to Iosif's apartment. We took the elevator up several flights. Tanya's knocking on Iosif's door—one two, then again one two—announced the onset of evening.

"Заходите, Заходите." Iosif opened the door and ushered us into the hallway. He first kissed Tanya on her cheek, and when he came to me, his lips felt wet against my cold skin.

"Come, let's sit in the kitchen," he said and handed us the *tapochki* to wear on our feet. "My mother's still at work." We sat on stiff wooden chairs, their backs slightly broken. Iosif took out of the refrigerator the customary salad of potatoes mixed with mayonnaise, carrots, and raisins.

"The government's still threatening to draft me to Afghanistan," he said, his face paler than the last time we met.

"What are you going to do?" I wanted to go over to him. But I just stayed there and felt afraid for him.

"I'm all right for now." I knew that was all Iosif would ever tell me.

"He always finds a way," Tanya said. But I didn't know if I could believe her.

"Enough of all this. You've been to Leningrad. And I've been waiting for you to return. You must tell us everything."

I hesitated, unsure how to proceed. Iosif sensed my mood. "I've told Tanya the whole story of our families."

"You did?"

"Just the other day." Tanya placed her hand on my arm. "We are practically the same now," she said.

I looked up at her somber face.

"So now it's just the three of us who know," Iosif said.

"You didn't tell your mother?" I asked.

"No, not just yet. I don't want to burden her with the past. It's still too painful. But I will." Iosif cut up a tomato, his knife making quick, sharp movements. "I will." His voice trailed away for a moment. "Well, tell me at least, how is my Aunt Marina?"

I described for them how we sat in her two-room apartment and ate sweet pastries. "Marina told me my grandmother came to her one afternoon. She sat on her couch and confessed her wish to leave Leningrad."

"Confessed?" Tanya asked.

"Yes, I think that's what she did. The way Marina told the story, it seemed as if my grandmother were asking for her permission to go."

"Marina would never believe back then that returning to America could be the right choice," Iosif said as Tanya began to clear away our dishes.

"It's not true. She understood my grandmother. Maybe she was even the only one who did."

"But Marina was an ardent believer," Iosif said. "That's before Victor got arrested. I think you must have misunderstood her."

"Okay, maybe I did." There was no point talking more about it. I couldn't sort the truth out. Marina did seem a bit confused.

"It was all a long time ago," Iosif said. "And yet we've never stopped living it." Iosif turned his head towards the kitchen, where Tanya stood washing some dishes. "Please come back and join us. We're missing you too much."

"But is my aunt all right?" Iosif asked. He turned back to me and laughed. "As all right as can be, is what I mean."

"Yes. Her mind drifts a bit. But otherwise she seems okay."

"I'm finally done cleaning up in here," Tanya called to us and sat down at the table next to me.

"That's to be expected, I guess. At eighty years old, she's lived with too much already. But she's a survivor."

"She is." I decided not to tell them about my grandfather's letters to Victor. Or even Marina's letter to my grandfather. I needed time to take it all in. Now I had my own secrets.

The three of us sat drinking our tea out of small glasses.

"Here, take some more. You're not eating enough." Tanya spooned many helpings of carrot salad onto my plate before I had time even to answer her.

"You give me too much."

"No, you must eat. Please eat," she repeated.

"Perhaps one day I can come for a short visit to New York and see you there," Iosif said and placed his fork by the side of his plate.

"But, how can you? How would you ever get the permission to leave? I will write and invite you. I will file all the documents needed. But won't you get in trouble for asking for this?"

"They'll never let you out," Tanya said. "Anna's right. It will only mean problems for you. And you'll have to fill out so many papers. And in the end, you won't get out."

"Okay, okay. I know you're right. I guess I'll never see the United States. Never see New York. But perhaps the two of us can meet at another place. Maybe in Bulgaria, or somewhere near there."

"But how?" I asked sharply. And then I regretted my tone. I looked up at Iosif and saw him wince for just a fraction of a second.

"Well, at least we'll see each other one more time before you leave. On Thursday, stand by the Station Kalyshskaya, and I'll find you there."

"Okay." That was two long days away.

"Have you got that journal hidden away?" Tanya whispered.

Iosif nodded.

"My grandparents died in those camps. They left no records." Tanya rested her cheek in the palm of her hand. "And then we're all wondering, after Brezhnev, what will be here."

"It will only get worse," Iosif said. For a moment his eyes met mine, and in his glance, I saw reams and reams of sorrow. "But you probably have to get back now."

"You're right. I have to go."

Iosif got up and led us to the hallway. His grandfather stood by the row of slippers and shoes near the door. He smiled without recognizing us.

"Dedulya, this is Anna. Remember, she's from New York."

He pulled his pajama bottoms up to his waist and held on to them. "I can't find my passport."

"I have it for you. You must not worry. It's safe with me."

After I put on my brown boots, Iosif bent down to hug me good-bye. I rested in his arms before he shifted his embrace to his cousin.

"Station Kalyshskaya. До четверга," Iosif said to me. Then he turned to his grandfather. "Let me help you back to your room."

"No, I can make it alone," he said and stepped away from us down the hallway.

"Until Thursday," I repeated back to Iosif in Russian. I placed my arm through Tanya's as we left his home together. Once outside we chatted about the snow, how it had come finally today, and yes, the air is colder now than before.

We rode the bus to the metro station. Tanya was going eastward and I west, so we separated to take our different trains.

Once I got back to the dorm, I walked into the kitchen for a small apple I had left in the common refrigerator. On blue-cushioned chairs, Miloz sat with several young women from Poland. I wanted to warn them about him, but there was nothing I could do but take a deep breath and pretend not to see him. So much had happened inside of me since my second night in Moscow when I was stupid enough to follow him into his room. I was no longer the same. Would anyone notice when I returned home, I wondered.

I saw his bulky presence out of the corner of my eye even when he shifted to turn his back to me.

"Martial law has been declared in Poland. We had to come here to study Russian, so we could teach in our country. And now who knows if the Soviets will invade.

Besides, we are more watched than you," a woman with long blond hair said to me in Russian.

"Да, я знаю," I said and moved away from her, walking back to my dorm room to get away, far away from Miloz.

"Of course, you must know that," she called out to me.

The next day Tanya stood in a small kitchen, peeling a carrot. Liver coated with flour sizzled in the pan. I sat across from her at the table, staring at the reflection of myself in the window. A few hours earlier, I had my first haircut in Moscow. Now I was sorry. I hated how it hung bluntly above my ears.

Tanya placed the food on a plate for me to eat. She took only a tiny portion for herself.

"But why aren't you eating? Here, please take more."

"No, I'm not hungry. I can't eat now."

The door of the main room, where Tanya's mother lay sleeping, was closed. I could hear the sound of coughing, hacking, rasping through the apartment.

I had never met Tanya's mother, could only hear her behind the closed door of the only other room in the apartment. I wondered if she looked like the large women I often saw on the subway, their backs bent over with the weight of their netted bags.

"I don't want to be like my mother," Tanya said. "But I don't see how my life will be any different from hers. You see, I want to marry, but I could never be with someone who wants to stay in this country, and I couldn't be with someone who wants to leave either." She moved her face closer to me.

"My mother has a secret job. She'd never get permission to leave. So we're sentenced here forever."

Just like Iosif's mother, I thought and wished I had a napkin to wipe the brown breaded crumbs from the side of my mouth.

"We must speak more softly. I don't want my mother to hear what we are saying. I tell you, I don't think it's so great in your country, either. It's only a matter of time, and there will be anti-Semitism there, too. If I could leave, I'd go to Israel. But I'll never get out of here."

We sat for a while, listening to the long, prolonged bout of coughing that filled the apartment, until I opened up my knapsack and took out the poems of Akhmatova that I bought from the Beriozka.

"Какой подарок! On the black market I can't even tell you how much this book would cost. Do you know what we do when we get such a book? We type over each page and give them to friends, so they too can read these great poems. You can't find these books anywhere."

Tanya ran over to a pile of newspapers. From underneath, she pulled out two record albums, so she could surprise me with more Russian folk songs to take home—winding melodies that spoke of journeys in search of a home.

Then the phone rang. It was Iosif. Tanya's words unfolded too quickly for me to understand them. "Here, take it," she said and handed me the receiver. Iosif told me his friend's mother had just died unexpectedly, so he would not be able to meet me at Station Kalyshskaya tomorrow. "But at least I can say good-bye to you on the phone now before you fly back," he said. We spoke briefly since conversations did not take place on telephones.

I knew this would be the last time we would ever speak. Our dialogue was abruptly interrupted in mid-sentence.

I hung up the phone, surprised by the tears on my face.

"I don't want to go away. I wish I could stay in this kitchen and speak with you more."

"I will write, but I don't know if the letters will go through. You may not receive them," Tanya said quietly.

So you will all drift into some place not accessible by phone or letter. And I will leave wondering if I have ever known you.

"Come, I'll walk you to the train. You better get back on time."

"Should you check on your mother?" Another round of coughing, a moment of silence so she could catch her breath, and then more short, staccato rasping.

"No, I'll let her rest for now."

Downstairs the lobby was strangely empty. Once outside we took the cement path. I welcomed the cold air on my face.

"It must be hard for someone like you to return to America," Tanya said. "You're too sensitive to live in that country."

It was strange that Tanya was comforting me for leaving—Tanya, who would always remain in Moscow, even though she longed to go away.

We walked a few blocks to Station Bukovskaya. The streetlights were shimmering. Together we descended the steps into the Metro.

"Не забывай обо мне. And do not forget any of us," she said. We hugged each other once before my coin slid into the turnstile.

I looked back at Tanya, wanting to hold her in my mind forever, as she began to step away. But then she called once more to me, "Do not forget."

EPILOGUE

I did write to Tanya, Nadezhda, and Iosif, but the letters must not have gone through because I never received a reply from them. They remained faraway, unreachable. When my grandmother died a year after I returned home from Moscow, I knew I had to write down everything I could about my journey to Moscow—all the incredible stories Iosif shared with me and the tales I learned from my grandmother.

Twenty years disappear before I know it. And the book is still unfinished.

Then, in 2005, I have the chance to travel to Russia with the language department at the university where I teach, and the reality of my unexpected journey makes me long to find my friends. Could Tanya and Iosif still be in Moscow? The Soviet Union has fallen. Did they leave? I'm sure Nadezhda is somewhere here, so I put her name into Google, and find her so quickly. I don't even know what made me wait all these years to search for her.

I call Nadezhda and discover she lives in Boston, is married with four children.

Nadezhda tells me everything. How she came first to Israel in 1985, and then to Boston—how Tanya and Iosif got permission in 1990 to leave for Israel. I still see them in a kitchen in Moscow; we are drinking hot chai in a glass, the tea leaves rising to the top.

Nadezhda tells me Tanya works for a Jewish relief agency in Israel. She lives there with her one daughter and husband.

Nadezhda tells me Iosif became a professor in Israel, married, and had four daughters before dying in a jeep accident there. His life ended at age thirty-seven. Her words stun me. Somehow, I always hoped I'd see him again.

How can Iosif be gone? I start to write again, wanting to recreate his life, those months in Moscow so long ago. But no matter how hard I try, I can't seem to finish the book. Perhaps I don't even want to.

Then there are Nadezhda's words on the telephone, just several weeks before I leave once more for a six-day trip to Russia.

"Oh, Anna, forget Russia. You're in America now. Forget Russia."

I never did forget any of them—that autumn of 1980 remains in my memory. It invisibly defines the way light falls on pavement, or how the wind wraps round streets at night, making a mournful sound as I wander easily back into the past.

ACKNOWLEDGMENTS

"Folk Song" was published in *The Mom Egg*, 2013, Vol. 11. The first section of "Get Ready, We're Going Back to the USSR, 1925-1931" was published as an earlier version, "1925," in *The Mom Egg* (online), Fall 2009, Vol. 7 (66).

Without the support of many, many people and institutions, this book would not have been possible. I want to thank Ramapo College of New Jersey for its continuous support of *Forget Russia*, as well as The NYU Faculty Resource Network, The New York Society Library, The Writer's Room, La Muse International Writer's Retreat, and The Virginia Center for the Creative Arts. My students at Ramapo are always a tremendous source of inspiration. Their brilliance, creativity, insights, and incredible spirit never ceases to move and encourage me.

The NYU Faculty Resource Network's seminar on *Uprooted and Displaced: Refugees, (Im)Migrants, and Exiles in World Literature,* led by Hariclea Zengos and Adrianne Kalfopoulou in Athens, Greece, enabled me to rethink the novel within the larger framework of immigrants and exiles. Workshops with Alice Mattison and Carolyn

Forché at the Provincetown Fine Arts Center were essential. Fiction workshops at the Writers' Institute at the Graduate Center were life-changing. I received invaluable feedback from editors and writers Jonathan Galassi, Matt Weiland, John Freeman, Leo Carey, and Patrick Ryan as well as fellow writers.

I can't thank enough, Julia Royzrakh, my dear sister-in-law, for consulting with me about all of the Russian in the novel. Lieber Katz, Susan and Irwin Oreskes, and Rosalyn and Bernard Saltzman all offered tremendous insight into the experiences of those Jews who went back to the Soviet Union in the 1930s. Chella Courington, Lisa Jarnot, Nick Westfall, Karen Stephens, Jon Durbin, Sheila Miller, Anne Dycus, Mary-beth Hughes, Susan Katz, Karen O'brien, and Lisa Low generously read earlier and later drafts of the novel. Elizabeth Merrick also read and gave me feedback on a chapter. My uncle Al Servi and my late, beloved Aunt Caroline, helped me in countless ways throughout the writing of this novel.

There are others who are no longer with us, who made the writing of this novel possible. *Forget Russia* began in a workshop in Esther Broner's home many years ago. Julius Lester told me I must write. And I have the deepest gratitude for the towering life of Toni Morrison, for the example she set, for her wisdom, and her kind and encouraging words to me.

Nothing would have been possible without the constant love and support of my husband Rich, and our son, Sam. Rich read every draft of this novel, and there were many. Special thanks to Daisaku Ikeda—poet, author, philosopher, educator, peace and human rights activist and mentor.

FURTHER READING

Mary Leder's memoir, *My Life in Stalinist Russia, An American Woman Looks Back,* edited by Laurie Bernstein (Indiana UP), deeply influenced my understanding of the plight of Russian Jewish immigrants who returned to the Soviet Union in the 1930s, and then could not leave. I am also indebted to Orlando Figes' *The Whisperers: Private Life in Stalin's Russia* (Henry, Holt, and Co.,), Sheila Fitzpatrick's *Everyday Stalinism, Ordinary Life in Extraordinary Times: Soviet Russia in the 1930's* (Oxford UP), Freda Utley's *The Dream We Lost: Soviet Russia, Then and Now* (The John Day Company), and Elie Wiesel's *The Jews of Silence: A Personal Report on Soviet Jewry* (Schocken Books), as well as John Reed's iconic *Ten Days That Shook the World,* Vasily Grossman's *Life and Fate,* and Ludmila Ulitskaya's *The Big Green Tent.* Special thanks to the wonderful *Dear Mendel, Dear Reyzl. Yiddish Manuals From Russia and America,* edited by Alice Nakhimovsky & Roberta Newman (Indiana UP), for giving me permission to reprint a quote from Ayzenshtayn Dov Yitskhok. Nora Levin's *The Jews in the Soviet Union since 1917* (NYU Press) led me to the 1917 *Razsvet* journal.

FURTHER READING

ABOUT THE AUTHOR

L. BORDETSKY-WILLIAMS is the author of the memoir, *Letters to Virginia Woolf* (Hamilton Books, 2005, http://www.letterstovirginiawoolf.com); *The Artist as Outsider in the Novels of Toni Morrison and Virginia Woolf* (Greenwood Press, 2000); and three poetry chapbooks (*The Eighth Phrase* (Porkbelly Press 2014), *Sky Studies* (Finishing Line Press 2014), and *In the Early Morning Calling* (Finishing Line Press, 2018)). She is a Professor of Literature at Ramapo College of New Jersey and lives in New York City.

CPSIA information can be obtained
at www.ICGtesting.com
Printed in the USA
JSHW040817100621
15606JS00002B/29